Praise for Josh Lanyon's
All She Wrote

"...there are few novelists in any genre whose work I find more satisfying to read."

~ *Dear Author*

"Mystery check, witty sarcastic dialog check, and sexual tension that practically sizzles off the page check check check. If you've read *Somebody Killed His Editor* YOU CANNOT MISS OUT ON THS ONE, I mean it."

~ *Smokin' Hot Books*

"The perfect balance of mystery, romance, and eroticism. I particularly enjoyed the sexual and romantic aspects because of its significance sexually and emotionally for Christopher and J.X. (And because it's hot as hell.)"

~ *Joyfully Reviewed*

"I am a big fan of Josh Lanyon. He writes some of the smartest, funniest romance/mystery/capers out there. This one was no exception. I really love the way the author pokes fun at the book world with this series. Even the tongue-in-cheek Arthur Conan Doyle character names add to general atmosphere of 'not taking oneself and one's book too seriously.'"

~ *Buried by Books*

Look for these titles by
Josh Lanyon

Now Available:

The Dickens with Love

The Dark Farewell
Strange Fortune
Come Unto These Yellow Sands

Crimes & Cocktails
Mexican Heat
(Writing with Laura Baumbach)

Holmes & Moriarity
Somebody Killed His Editor
All She Wrote

The XOXO Files
Mummy Dearest

Print Anthology
To All a (Very Sexy) Good Night

All She Wrote

Josh Lanyon

Samhain Publishing, Ltd.
11821 Mason Montgomery Rd.. 4B
Cincinnati, OH 45249
www.samhainpublishing.com

All She Wrote
Print ISBN: 978-1-60928-206-6
Digital ISBN: 978-1-60928-200-4

Editing by Sasha Knight
Cover by Scott Carpenter

First Samhain Publishing, Ltd. electronic publication: December 2010
First Samhain Publishing, Ltd. print publication: October 2011

Dedication

To Wave, who always did enjoy a mystery. Thank you.

Chapter One

"I knew it," J.X. said. "I knew you'd do this."

I held onto my temper, although that's a comment guaranteed to fry anyone's fuse—and mine isn't the longest to start with. My fuse, I mean.

"No, you didn't. *I* didn't know I'd do this. How could I have known this would happen? Anna didn't know this would happen. If Anna *had* known this would happen, I'm sure she'd have done her best to avoid falling down those twenty-two flagstone steps in her garden."

"And if your old former mentor hadn't taken a tumble down the garden path and needed you to fill in for her with this writing seminar in the Berkshires, you'd have come up with some other excuse for why we couldn't get together this weekend."

I think it was more annoying because J.X. was using that vastly reasonable tone of voice on me. Like my predictability was *almost* amusing. But the main reason it was annoying was because deep down inside I knew he was right. I had been thinking of possible reasons for canceling before Anna's phone call.

I said vehemently, "Bullshit."

"No, it's not." No trace of amusement now. "I wish it was."

"Anna needs my help. She's got a broken ankle and busted ribs. What was I supposed to tell her? No can do. I've got a hot date?"

"Kit…"

"What?"

"In three months we've seen each other three times—two of which times you had to cut the weekend short. It's pretty obvious that this…relationship isn't something you want to pursue."

My heart sank like a stone. I could almost hear the lonely little plop.

"That's not true," I protested. "You're not being fair. I'm just out of one relationship. Of course I'm proceeding cautiously."

"*That* I could understand. The problem is, you're *not* proceeding. Three times in three months is not proceeding. Your brakes are locked and your transmission is stuck in park. I think it's bad timing, Kit. Again."

J.X. didn't sound angry. He didn't sound hurt. He sounded resigned. A little wry. And I knew he'd been thinking about this—as he waited for me to cancel yet again—and that his mind was already made up.

And that was probably for the best, right? Because it *was* bad timing. It was too soon after David. I wasn't ready to start up again—let alone with a guy five years my junior. It was doubtless a good thing that one of us had the presence of mind to see that it was not going to work between us. We'd had our shot and it hadn't taken. That was that.

So why did my heart keep foundering in that arctic bath, trying vainly to gain some kind of purchase on the icy walls?

"What are you saying?" I asked. "I'm off your Christmas card list?"

"I'm saying..." J.X. took a deep breath and I understood that it wasn't as easy for him as I'd thought. "I'm saying that if you ever...change your mind, give me a call."

I opened my mouth, but the words didn't come. Not because I didn't want to say them, but I wasn't sure I would be saying them for the right reason—and whatever J.X. thought, I cared too much for him to say them for the wrong reason. I was trying to make my mind up when he disconnected.

Like fine wine, I do not travel well. Sure, when I was young, fresh, low in acidity and not so tannic, I was a more adventurous spirit. But at forty, divorced—or as good as—and my career having been through the shredder and back, well, let's say I had developed a taste for home and hearth. My own home and hearth.

Especially after being involved in a homicide investigation three months earlier. Of course every cloud has its silver lining, and the bright side of my being suspected of murder was that my books, featuring intrepid spinster sleuth Miss Butterwith and her ingenious cat Mr. Pinkerton, were once again hitting the bestseller lists. Well, some of the bestseller lists. As my agent Rachel kept reminding me, platform is everything in publishing these days, and my wobbly new platform was apparently that of amateur sleuth. Which was still an improvement over my previous platform of crotchety reclusive has-been. *That* platform had more closely resembled a scaffold.

Anna Hitchcock was one of the few people in the world I would break my no-travel rule for. Way back when I was a student in the MFA program at UC Irvine, Anna, already touted as the American Agatha Christie, had been my professor and my advisor. She had been more. She had been a mentor and a friend. I owed my writing career—and it had been a highly successful career until recently—to Anna. So when she had called to say she desperately needed my help, even I—famous for my lack of, er, helpfulness—could hardly refuse.

Even if I'd wanted to. And I hadn't—not least because it gave me an excellent excuse to avoid another awkward weekend with J.X.

Which was something I didn't want to think about as I staggered off the plane at Bradley International Airport in Windsor Locks, Connecticut. Anna's estate was in the Berkshires. Nitchfield, to be exact.

From what I remembered, Nitchfield was a historic small town right there at the intersection of Routes 202 and 63. It was in the heart of a region that referred to itself as "America's Premier Cultural Resort". The Berkshires were popular for hiking, biking, skiing, fishing, white-water rafting, antiquing, wine tasting...you-name-iting. In the fall the area was famous for its gorgeous autumn foliage.

But this wasn't the fall. This was dead winter. February. And Nitchfield was buried under a scenic blanket of snow. Did I mention I hate driving in snow? It should go without saying. I picked up a car at Budget Rent-A-Car and proceeded north to the Asquith Estate.

I'd been there once before, more than ten years earlier. The house, designed in 1908 by noted architect Wilson Eyre, was a registered historic place. Ten thousand square feet of hand-carved chestnut wood paneling, marble staircases, limestone fireplaces, hardwood floors, and French doors opening onto fifty acres of garden and landscaped woodland. It was an authentic classic English country estate complete with tennis court, pool, garden house and a guest cottage where the writing seminars were held.

In short, the Asquith Estate was proof that some people did

still earn a nice living from writing fiction. All that it lacked was someone named Bunty and a corpse in the drawing room.

I felt qualified to apply for the part of corpse after I arrived shortly before dinner. What the idea is behind combining the serving of salty packets of dry snacks and overpriced alcohol might be, other than trying to turn airline customers into desiccated fossils, I can't imagine.

"We haven't met." A tall, serious-looking young blonde woman greeted me as I stood studying the stately life-sized portrait of Anna which hung over the enormous fireplace in the entry hall. She offered a cool hand. "I'm Sara Mason. Anna's PA."

"Lucky Anna."

I meant lucky Anna to be able to afford a PA, but Sara gave a weary smile as though she was getting rather tired of predatory men hitting on her day in and day out. "How was your trip, Mr. Holmes?"

My trips are always horrible. That's why I strenuously avoid traveling. I spared Sara the gruesome details, restraining myself to a mild, "I don't think any of the passengers will actually sue. And they did eventually find my luggage."

Sara gave me another of those polite and automatic smiles. She was taller than me, and probably about my age—it's hard to tell with women who take care of themselves. She looked younger than I felt at the moment. Her eyes were a steely gray and her hair was that shade of blonde that is closer to white. A snow princess. I half expected to hear the tinkling sound effects for ice crystals as she beckoned me to follow her.

"Anna is upstairs. She's anxious to see you."

"How is she?"

"Lucky."

"What exactly happened?"

Sara's direct gaze faltered. "An accident. She was on her way back from the guest cottage and she slipped on the garden steps. They're icy this time of year." She added huskily, "It was a miracle she wasn't killed."

My luggage had already been whisked upstairs by well-trained minions, but I wished I had time to splash water on my face, freshen up before I faced Anna. Not that I would dare demur once the chilly Sara had given me my marching orders.

I followed her across shining parquet floors and up a marble staircase past a gallery of oil-painted nobles who I happened to know for a fact were not related to Anna. We came at last to a walnut door in the private wing of the house.

Sara tapped politely, and I recognized Anna's rich, cultured tones bidding us enter.

The room was furnished in soft grays and muted creams. At the far end were three banks of diamond-paned bay windows half veiled by gold and cream brocade shades and valences. The windows looked out over a frozen ornamental lake. There was a seating arrangement of chairs and loveseats in front of the windows. Against another wall was a large fireplace and across from that was a king-sized bed. Anna was ensconced in the bed. She was wearing some kind of lacy, sage-green peignoir, and she reclined against a mountain of satiny pearl-gray pillows. There was a tea tray on one side of her and a computer table on the other. But she wasn't drinking tea and she wasn't working at her laptop. In fact, she was staring moodily up at the delicate vines and flowers of the plaster ceiling overhead.

As Sara and I walked in, she turned to face us and a bright smile lit her tired face.

"Christopher, *darling*. Look at you, all grown up and sophisticated. I always thought they'd bury you in jeans and a flannel shirt." She held out a hand in greeting. Of course I'd have had to climb on top of the giant bed to take it, so I settled for circling around and bending to kiss her cheek.

"Anna. It's been too long."

"And it would have been longer if I hadn't played the guilt card." She was chuckling, and I felt the old irresistible tug of her charm. Anna would be in her sixties by now, but you'd never guess it. Her hair was still that incredible shade of fiery copper, her eyes—always her best feature—were still wide and green and striking. Her hands and face and feet were meticulously cared for—I could tell because I could see her perfectly polished toes sticking out of the cast on her left ankle.

"How did it happen?" I asked, nodding at the cast—it had several signatures scrawled on its hard shell.

"*So* fucking ridiculous," Anna murmured. I'd forgotten about her potty mouth. Anna always did swear like a sailor. The rumor was the irate student reports used to send shivers through the UCI administration. It takes a lot to offend the sensibilities of your average college English major. "But never mind that. How was your trip? Did the plane have to make an emergency landing? Was your luggage lost again?"

"They found it. And our takeoff was only delayed about an hour."

Anna said to Sara, "Christopher has the most horrendous luck traveling of anyone I know. The only way it could be worse is if the plane actually crashed." She gave that delightful chuckle again. "Do you still have to get plastered before boarding, darling?"

"I'm much more disciplined. I wait for in-flight service now."

"Did you need anything, Anna?" Sara inquired.

"No, darling." Anna waved her away. As the door closed behind Sara, Anna said, "That girl is a fucking *jewel*. My ciggies are on the table, darling. Would you?"

I retrieved her cigarettes from the low table in front of the gray velvet loveseat by the window. There were white roses on the table and more of them in a crystal vase next to the bed. I handed Anna her gold cigarette case.

"Lighter." She nodded to the gilt table beside the bed.

I opened the drawer and blinked at the sight of a pistol nestled beside a couple of paperbacks—all Anna's own—an enamel pill box and a tube of AHAVA hand lotion. The pistol was a Browning Hi-Power, which I recognized from my research for *Open Season on Miss Butterwith.*

"Is that thing real?" I asked.

"Absolutely. Guaranteed or your money back. Straight from the laboratories by the Dead Sea in Israel. The bath salts are amazing. My skin is as soft as a baby's behind."

"I mean the gun."

"Oh. Yes. It's real. Don't worry. I have a permit."

I handed Anna her lighter. "I don't remember you packing heat before."

"Things change. How's David?"

"We're not together."

She raised her eyebrows, lit her cigarette and flicked shut the lighter. "Don't tell me you finally left him? No. Of course not. Well, I can't say I'm surprised." She took a long drag on her cigarette and expelled a blue stream of smoke. "Let me guess. He ran off with your neighbor."

"My PA."

She laughed. I laughed too, although I didn't really find it funny. I doubted if I would ever find it really funny.

"Seeing anyone new?"

I thought of J.X. "No."

"Poor you. But you've still got Miss Butterwith. Although I'm surprised, frankly. I'd heard through the grapevine you'd been dropped by Wheaton & Woodhouse." Her green eyes studied me shrewdly. It was the look that used to make it impossible to come up with a good excuse for handing papers in late.

"We took the series to Millbrook House's Crime Time line."

"Oh, they'll do a lovely job. Such adorable covers. What kind of advertising budget are you getting?"

I shrugged. "It's not extravagant, but it's better than we were getting at Wheaton & Woodhouse."

A sudden silence fell between us. I could feel something was wrong, but I couldn't put my finger on what or why. Anna was still smiling through the veil of cigarette smoke, still watching me.

"What's wrong?" I asked.

"Wrong?" She gestured with her cigarette for me to pull one of the white velvet side chairs over to the bed.

I slid the chair across the glossy floor and sat down. "Not that I'm not flattered by your faith in me, but I don't have any teaching experience, and you know plenty of mystery writers a lot more successful and well-known than me. Why did you call me?"

Anna smiled. "Perhaps I thought it would be good for you."

"That's flattering, but I can't imagine you've given me more than the occasional passing thought in the last decade."

"You don't make it easy, Christopher. You've cut yourself off from everyone. You don't do signings, you don't do conferences, you don't do book tours. You were the best and brightest of my students, and you've lived up to that promise to some degree—"

I snorted.

Anna shrugged, then winced in pain at the unwise move. "Do you deny it? Do you deny cutting yourself off from the old crowd?"

"No. I've been focused on building my career."

"Haven't we all." Anna's voice was bitter. "Listen, Christopher, I know what I'm talking about. My own ambition cost me my first two marriages."

"Third time's the charm?"

"There is someone again, yes."

"Congratulations," I said, surprised, although I guess there was no real reason for surprise. It's not like Anna was in her dotage. Sixty is the new fifty, right? And fifty is the new forty, and forty is the new thirty. By the way, how come I didn't *feel* thirty?

"Thank you." She seemed preoccupied.

"I'm still not sure what I'm doing here."

Anna sighed. "All right. The truth is, I read an article in *People* magazine about what happened to you at that writing conference in Northern California. How you solved that murder."

"Wait a minute. You're not saying—"

She gave a funny laugh. "I think I am, actually. That is, I'm not absolutely positive, but I think someone might be trying to kill me."

Chapter Two

"You think—"

"Yes. Don't laugh."

"As side-splitting as the idea of violent death is..." I stared at her doubtfully. "Are you serious? You are, aren't you?"

Anna had an expression I'd never seen before—not that I really remembered all her expressions. In fact, *exasperated* and *much tried* were the only two that really rang a bell.

"I'm not sure. After all these years of writing about murders I'm afraid I'm letting my imagination run away with me. There have been one or two incidents...odd occurrences."

"Like what?"

"To start with, my fall down the garden stairs. I can't swear to it, but I've been up and down those stairs a million times in winter, spring, summer and fall."

"No pun intended? Listen," I said, "because you never slipped before doesn't mean you couldn't slip this time."

"There was ice on the step. Solid ice. Not snow, not frost, not the usual thin glaze of ice. Thick ice as though someone had poured water on the stones and let them freeze over."

"That's it? That's pretty thin, Anna. It's not impossible that there could be some...some ice anomaly." Mr. Wizard I am not.

"There have been other things. Nothing conclusive. Nothing

in itself conclusive, but when you put it all together…"

She put it all together. The case of violent food poisoning that affected her but no one else in the house, the stone urn that fell off a balcony and narrowly missed crushing her, the brakes failing in her car. I heard her out in silence. Well, for me it was silence. Close to silence. I hardly interrupted at all. For me.

"Christopher, would you kindly shut up?" Anna requested at last. "This is my story. I'm trying to tell it my own way. I do know about maintaining proper levels of brake fluid. I have an excellent mechanic."

"The thing I don't understand is what you imagine I could do about it if someone *is* trying to harm you? If this is true, you need to go to the police."

"That is what I absolutely can*not* do."

"Why?"

"What if I'm wrong?"

"That would be a relief, right? Personally, I wouldn't mind looking a little paranoid in order to be wrong about people trying to kill me."

"I'd be ruined. There would be no way to keep something like that quiet. This is a small town and I'm a big name."

Modesty was never Anna's weak point.

"Surely five minutes of embarrassment is worth—"

"It would either look like a publicity stunt or it would look like I'm losing it. Either would be intolerable."

Not as intolerable as being dead, in my opinion, but I'm very fond of me. I would miss me a lot.

Anna said, "Keep in mind that the pool of suspects is small. I would be accusing a friend or a student or one of my long-time trusted employees of wishing to do me ill."

"Seriously ill. Which is still better than terminally ill. I mean, you do suspect one of them of wanting you dead, right? Who is it you suspect? Everyone? Or no one? Or all of the above?"

She looked pained. "I've told you I'm not sure about any of this."

"Yeah, yeah. I get that. It's not nice to blame the friends and family of wanting to do away with you, but you must have some inkling. Some gut feeling about who it might be—assuming it's anyone."

"But that's it. I don't. And that's why I want your help. You're very observant, Christopher."

"I never noticed."

"For being almost totally self-absorbed, yes. You're also surprisingly perceptive about people so long as they're not connected to you. As glib as the Miss Butterworth novels are, you're very good at ascribing believable motives to your characters. Especially the killers."

"That's fiction."

"The best fiction captures the truth of real life."

Was there an echo in here? I remembered that mantra from way back when. Way back when I used to cut the majority of my non-writing classes or spend them scribbling stories in the back row with the stoners and sleepers.

"So you're thinking that I can snoop around and figure out if one of your merry band is planning to knock you off? I knew you didn't drag me out here for my teaching skills because I don't have any."

"You don't mind, do you?" She gave me the closest thing I'd ever seen to a beseeching look. I didn't trust it for a minute. One thing Anna was not was the beseeching brand of damsel.

"Do you want me to be honest or polite?"

"I want you to help me."

"You must truly be desperate."

"I am."

"Well," I said slowly, "it's your life. I'll do what I can."

She looked relieved. That made one of us.

My room might have been the same room I'd had the last time I visited, a decade or so ago. My memories were vague. These days I was no longer impressed by genuine antiques or opulent furnishings or prints that didn't come from Art.com— which is to say that I didn't take my shoes off before walking on the handwoven blue and green Persian rugs, and I avoided sitting on the gold-threaded emerald brocade bedcover merely because I wasn't that tired, *not* because I was intimidated by a few bed linens.

The bed itself looked like it had been modified from a sacrificial altar on some obscure Grecian isle. There were four dark wood Corinthian columns, leather panel inserts with brass studs on the head and footboards, and a canopy frame of wrought-iron ivy and grapes. Green velvet draperies dusted the glass-slick floor.

There was companion furniture, of course, but it seemed to exist merely to keep the bed from brooding over its change of fortune. Stephen King could have written a book about that bed. If I hadn't been crazy before, I surely would be after a couple of nights beneath those curling grapevines. It was moot, since I obviously *was* crazy. How else to explain agreeing to go along with this loony plan of Anna's?

I shivered thinking about it and started looking for a warm change of clothing. I'd forgotten how cold it got in states that had actual winters. Invisible hands had unpacked my suitcase and stowed my things where I'd be least likely to find them. I finally located a change of clothes in the Louis XV black lacquered commode. I pulled out a clean pair of Levis—relaxed fit because even if forty *is* the new thirty, this time around I'd rather be comfortable—and a tan Ralph Lauren lambswool pullover with a shawl collar. The sweater was not the kind of thing I would have ordinarily bought for myself, but part of my career rebirth was a new look. That apparently meant fancy haircuts, grooming products you needed a science degree to figure out how to use, and a lot of overpriced clothes someone else had picked for me.

It still gave me a start of surprise every time I caught sight of myself in a mirror or a window. Apparently clothes did maketh the man, and my clothes makethed me look less like a curmudgeonly recluse and more like a hip writer guy. The kind of guy I'd have loved to be when I was twenty—or even thirty. The kind of guy J.X. belonged with. The only problem being that I wasn't that guy. Inside I was still a forty-year-old schlub writing cozy mysteries starring a spinster sleuth nobody wanted to read about, dumped by both my publisher and lover in the same year.

Make that two lovers. Because J.X. was past tense now too, and encouraging that was about the first thoughtful thing I'd done for anyone in a long time. Maybe his feelings were a little hurt, but J.X. deserved more than I could give him. He deserved better. Which he'd have been bound to figure out on his own before long.

I nodded in approval to the brown-eyed man with the expensive blond highlights in the oval mirror over the dresser. He nodded back. Hey, come to think of it, he'd lost some weight over the past months. Terror, no doubt, that he was going to have to get naked with a gorgeous young stud one weekend.

Heading downstairs, I ran into the snow princess. Sara was carrying one of those white DHL parcels publishers usually send galleys in. She bore it before her like she was delivering a glass slipper on a silken pillow to Cinderella.

Good to know Anna was writing again. It had been a while since her last book as I recalled.

"Hi," I said. "I wanted to walk down to the garden and take a look around the guest cottage before tomorrow's session."

Sara gave me a wintry smile. "There's really nothing to see. I'll handle all the details for you. All you have to do is conduct tomorrow's seminar." She didn't add *and for God's sake don't break anything*, but I could read the subtext loud and clear.

"That's nice of you, but I'll be more comfortable if I can size up the room first." That sounded appropriately neurotic. Sara preserved an exquisitely blank expression.

"If you insist. The guest cottage isn't locked. You can look around to your heart's content. But if you're walking down to the garden, there are snow boots in the downstairs closet beneath the stairs. I'd suggest you borrow a pair. I'd be *very* careful on those steps going down to the garden."

It wasn't gracious, but it was what I needed to know. I thanked her, continued downstairs where I grabbed the snow boots as directed, pulled them on and stepped outside.

We don't get a lot of snow in Southern California. Not where I live. We have swimming pools and palm trees and skateboarders. I walked out of Anna's mansion into a winter wonderland.

It took my breath away—and not merely because it was so cold the oxygen seemed to freeze in my lungs.

Everything, every flat surface, was covered in lovely, sparkling snow. Those surfaces too slanted or irregular were glazed in ice, glittering in the petrified sunlight like a jeweled crust, tiny flashing prisms of red and blue catching light like frozen fire. Ice garlands seemed to twine through the trees and I guessed that there were strands of lights beneath the frost. The tree limbs were spindly and attenuated where the ice had started to melt and then refroze. It added to the otherworldly appearance.

I crossed the snowy courtyard, crunched over the lawns and went down the crooked flagstone steps to the bottom garden. It was like traveling through a snow globe. Dryer, I suppose. And easier to breathe, although it did occur to me I really did need to start working out more regularly.

The cottage looked like a scaled-down version of the house. Same quaint gothic door and multi-paned windows, same exact everything, only in miniature.

As Sara promised, the cottage was unlocked. I opened the door and went inside. The heat was not on though the electricity worked. Again, it was a diminutive version of the main house. No marble staircase, but gleaming parquet floors, chestnut wood paneling and a limestone fireplace. French doors opened onto a snow-blanketed patio. A carved stairway led upstairs.

Everything was spic-and-span. There was nothing out of the ordinary, but I wasn't expecting anything out of the ordinary. My reason for coming down here was mostly to have an excuse for going up and down the garden stairs. And my reason for that was I had to start my investigation, to use the term loosely, somewhere. The scene of the crime seemed the obvious choice.

A large, rustic-looking round table sat in the alcove with its diamond-paned windows. I had a sudden rush of memory of the first time I'd taken part in the Asquith Circle.

It seemed like a lifetime ago.

Not so long ago that I couldn't remember the feeling of having been handed the keys to the kingdom—and the conviction that it had to be a mistake. I'd expected everyone else to be much more learned, confident and advanced in their career. The reality had been different. Yes, everyone taking part in the seminar that year had been further along in their career, but they had seemed nearly as confused about our industry as me—and certainly no more confident. The first and foremost lesson I had taken away from that year's seminar was that writing was an insecure business. That underlying sense of precariousness had driven me ever since—at some cost to my personal life.

I poked around, opened the fridge which was stocked with snacks for the following day—nobly refraining from snitching a brownie—and went upstairs to check out the two rooms there: a bedroom and an office space. The office window offered a view of the flagstone steps leading up to the house and its surrounding grounds. The bedroom was an ordinary, impersonal guest bedroom—with a wrinkled bedspread on the queen-sized bed.

Maybe the gardening staff liked to take a nap in the afternoon. There couldn't be a lot to do in the winter, could there?

I returned downstairs and stepped outside—and nearly jumped out of my skin.

An elderly man stood on the flagstone step.

"Did I startle you? I'm sorry." He offered a leather-gloved hand and a quizzical smile.

"No, no. Not at all," I assured him, as though my normal means of locomotion was to bound like a startled deer through every doorway. "Hi." We shook hands.

He was tall and willowy, with wavy hair as smooth and white as the snow, and handsome, even youthful, patrician features. He looked like someone famous, but I couldn't quite place him.

As though he read my thoughts, he said, "You don't remember me, do you? I'm Rudolph Dunst. It's nice to see you again, Christopher."

"I knew I recognized you. I'm still jetlagged. It's good to see you again, Mr. Dunst."

"It's been a few years back," Dunst said easily. "And please. Call me Rudolph."

Rudolph Dunst was Anna's longtime editor. She'd introduced me to him back when he was a Senior Editor at Theodore Mansfield and I was first starting out. Dunst had the incredible bad taste to pass on the first Miss Butterwith. Granted, he'd done it with great kindness and diplomacy. He was one of those old-school gentlemen editors that the new breed use as dipping sauce for their lunchtime sushi. In any case, Miss B. had the last laugh by going on to become an award-winning national bestseller.

Now, ironically, both Dunst and I were fighting to stay afloat in the new publishing environment. Environment being a polite word for acid bath.

Rudolph smiled, displaying impressive dental work. "So you're going to run the AC for Anna, I understand?"

"The AC?"

I was thinking he meant air conditioner, which Mother Nature seemed to have well in hand, but he explained, "The Asquith Circle. Anna's writing seminar has produced some marvelous talent over the years. Yourself included."

It would have been silly to quibble with that. Anna had certainly been instrumental in helping me get published, but I'd sold my first book my final semester of college. Anna had invited me to take part in the Asquith Circle two summers later, so the AC had zero to do with my success. It would have been ungracious, though, to make that point.

Instead, I said, "Are you scouting for new talent?"

Rudolph raised his brows. "Are you working on something new?"

"Me? No." I was nonplussed at the idea. Give up Miss Butterwith? For what? Another kickass, foul-mouth, bad-mannered female cop/secret agent/bounty hunter? Another kickass, foul-mouth, bad-mannered vampire/demon/witch slayer? Another kickass, foul-mouth, bad-mannered chef? Hmmm...maybe that last wasn't a totally terrible idea. The research might be fun...

"Still enjoying the Miss Butterwith books?" Rudolph seemed gently amused. Why, I couldn't for the life of me imagine.

"Yes," I said staunchly. "I am. Very much so. Totally."

"Ah."

"Were you going inside?" I started to move from the doorway to allow him entrance, but he stepped back.

"No, no," Rudolph said. "I noticed the light was on in the cottage and..."

He looked faintly self-conscious. I wondered if Anna had confided her fears to him. She had said not, but I've found that people tend to talk a lot more than they think they do.

"I was trying to get comfortable with the setup before tomorrow."

He patted me on the shoulder as we started back across the snowy garden, trudging past the black iron bones of obelisks and trellises.

"You'll do fine, Christopher. Besides, I'd be very surprised if Anna didn't drag herself down here at some point during the weekend."

With that cast on her leg? Down those stairs? In the dead of winter? If that were the case, why wouldn't Anna run the damned seminar herself? But Rudolph probably knew her better than I did. For years the persistent rumor had been Anna and Rudolph were involved in a decades-old on-and-off romance. The only time I ever saw them together was at conferences, and they seemed to be behaving themselves as much as anyone does at those things. Which is to say that they weren't actually jumping each other during panels.

But I didn't want to think about J.X. now. I was finding it surprisingly painful to contemplate the fact that I might never see him again outside a professional context. And why the hell that phrase should instantly remind me of how beautiful he was stark naked, I do not know. Except that I thought of J.X. naked a lot. But I'm sure he'd look equally nice in professional context. It would go nicely with that honey brown skin of his.

"Is something wrong?" Rudolph asked, glancing at me.

"Wrong? No."

"You were scowling so ferociously, I wondered."

"No, no. I was hoping we wouldn't be late for dinner."

"We're in plenty of time," he reassured. "Anna does have a wonderful chef."

He was telling me all about the potatoes au gratin they'd had for lunch the day before as we started up the stairs. I listened with half an ear, while I wondered if Anna had been going up or coming down when she fell. I assumed coming down, but I should probably verify. Did it make a difference? Hard to know. Miss Butterwith would certainly think so.

How many other people used these steps on a regular basis?

Did Anna even use them on a regular basis? I couldn't imagine she had a lot of cause to be tromping around her snow-covered bottom garden at this time of year. In a mansion the size of hers it was hard to believe she couldn't find a quiet corner to write, so what had she been doing down here?

Meeting someone away from the house?

I made a mental note to remind myself to find out.

The steps *were* slippery, but there was a low, rustic wooden railing, and I hung on to that. Anna, of course, being familiar with the staircase, might forgo clinging cravenly to the support.

"Were you here when Anna had her accident?" I asked Rudolph who was a couple of steps ahead of me.

He was moving briskly, but I noticed he watched where he put his feet. I didn't see ice—a dusting of snow, as though the steps had been cleared earlier in the day, but no ice. Weather was a changeable thing. Because there wasn't ice today, didn't mean there hadn't been ice the day Anna fell.

"Yes," Rudolph answered. "I'd arrived the night before and was sleeping late. I heard her scream." He spared me a grim look. "From the sound, I thought she'd been killed."

"It's surprising she wasn't. This would be one hell of a fall. How far up was she?"

"About halfway up."

We were about halfway up ourselves.

I paused—it had nothing to do with being short of breath—and looked down.

The snowy bottom of the garden seemed a long way away. Foreshortened, dark evergreens, a tiny, snowy sundial, courtly statues blanketed in white. The snow-globe effect again.

"Seriously? Halfway up?"

Rudolph read my tone correctly. "Anna might be

exaggerating. Or confused. She's always been a tad high-strung. However high up she was, I'm sure it was terrifying. If things had gone differently..."

I was nodding agreement. "It would have been all she wrote."

Chapter Three

What's that quote by Woody Allen? Why does man kill? He kills for food. And not only food: frequently there must be a beverage.

I was thinking of both murder and beverages as I sat at dinner that night in the elegant dining room at Asquith House, gingerly sipping my merlot (red wine always gives me a headache) and studying my fellow guests for signs of incipient homicidal mania. In addition to Sara, who was presiding in Anna's absence, and Rudolph, there were five writing students staying at the house that weekend.

I politely listened to their names as they were introduced, promptly forgot them all except for Poppy C. Clark which I heard as Poppy Seed Clark. She set me straight fast.

"Poppy C. C as in *Catholic*."

Trust a writer to drag her religious hang-ups into it. "Sorry," I mumbled.

Poppy wrinkled her nose in disapproval.

She was a small, birdlike woman around my age. She had very short black hair and slanted eyes of a unique turquoise color. She wore men's style chinos, a white tailored man's shirt, loafers and a man's watch. I didn't pick up *lesbian*, though, so much as affected. Like those non-Francoise non-painters who wear berets.

The soup was served as we were still untangling the introductions. Rudolph was right. Anna's cook was superb. The creamed pumpkin was almost worth the entire trip.

I do like my food. And it was sort of a relief to know that I could eat my dinner without fear that I was going to have to get naked in the near future. I could get as fat as I liked and no one would care. Heck, no one would *see*. Sheer bliss.

It was funny the way bliss took your appetite away.

"Christopher Holmes. You write the books about the Scottish police constable, don't you?" That was Victoria Sherwell, a tall and pleasantly plain forty-something. She wore spectacles and no makeup. An I'm-comfortable-being-comfortable vibe.

"No. I write about Miss Butterwith. She's an English botanist."

It was a bit lowering that Anna hadn't apparently even told her precious writer's circle who would be taking over for her in her hour of need, but I supposed she was preoccupied with people trying to kill her and whatnot.

Victoria smiled, displaying a cute little gap between the two front teeth. "That's sweet."

I tried not to bristle. *Sweet?* Miss Butterwith was not sweet. She was not some sweet old lady in a pink woolly cardigan with Life Savers in her pocket and grandchildren and a weekly bridge club. She was Justice personified. She had a mind like a steel trap and a resolve of iron, and she used scientific methods for solving crime. Okay, she was aided in her investigations by her intrepid cat Mr. Pinkerton—and the dashing Inspector Appleby, who was *not* gay no matter what anyone said—but other than *that*, she was as hardboiled as they come.

Poppy Seed said, "Are you sure she's not a librarian? I've read that series with the English librarian. It wasn't too bad considering all the typos."

Librarian? My hand froze on my glass. Someone was writing a series about an English librarian? Why didn't I know this series? Who was publishing it? Was it doing better than Miss Butterwith?

Naturally, I didn't let a flicker of that show. "I'm sure," I said pleasantly, as though a competitive thought had never passed behind my eyes.

"I only ask because I haven't heard of your series. Is it new?"

I was still smiling—through my teeth—as I said, "It's been around for over fifteen years."

"Has it? I find it offensive that any female sleuth would be referred to as a spinster." Poppy Seed turned to Victoria. "Don't you?"

Victoria smiled noncommittally and dipped her spoon in her soup.

I finished my wine, defiant of the inevitable headache. I was still brooding as the soup dishes were whisked away and replaced with plates laden with juicy prime rib, buttery whipped potatoes and tender asparagus drizzled with creamy tarragon sauce. I began to perk up.

Besides, some people think fullness in the face makes you look younger.

"Who's your agent, Christopher?" one of the male students asked.

It was going to be one of *those* weekends, I could tell already. "Rachel Ving."

Ving the Merciless they called her in publishing circles, though so far she hadn't killed anyone. That I knew of.

"How did you happen to land her?"

"I let my fingers do the walking."

"Eh?"

What was his name? Something unusual. Rowland...Bride. That was it. Rowland Bride looked like he was in his late forties. He was a short, roly-poly man with bright dark eyes and tight dark curls. He looked hot. Not like J.X. looked hot. Hot as in permanently perspiring.

Hot and perplexed. Maybe he was thinking of the Neil Young song.

"Just kidding," I said. "I sent the manuscript to several agents who indicated they were willing to look at a new author and were interested in handling mysteries."

Rowland looked unconvinced. Perhaps he thought Anna had written a letter of recommendation or something, but that wasn't the case. She would have, of course, but her own agent hadn't been taking new clients when I went looking. I had found Rachel all on my own.

Poor Rachel.

"How long have you known Anna?" I asked generally of the table.

"Nearly nine years," Rowland said.

"Have you been part of the AC for nine years?"

"No. I was only invited to join the circle last year." He pursed his mouth. I couldn't tell if the expression indicated discretion or annoyance that it had taken so long for Anna to include him in the festivities. As I recalled, invites to the AC were exclusive and much sought after by aspiring scribblers.

"Two years." Poppy Seed sounded curt. She was hacking away at her prime rib as though she had a score to settle.

"Two years," Victoria concurred. She was the only person at the table still on her soup. She had a half bowl to go and was serenely dipping her spoon as though she'd never heard of such a thing as a main course.

"Were you members of the writing group last year?"

"No."

"No." Poppy's portion of the table jiggled as she sawed.

At the far end, Sara and Rudolph were ignoring my efforts at sociability. They spoke quietly together, much like weary teachers supervising a sock hop. Do they still have sock hops? Do they still have socks?

I'd have liked to sit at the adult table too, but I'd been placed smack-dab in the center of the playing field to be more accessible to the students. It's true what they say about no good deed going unpunished. Granted, I was conveniently located for sleuthing, but it irked me nonetheless.

I called down, "I know how far back you and Anna go, Rudolph, but what about you, Sara?"

She fastened her cool gaze on me. "I've worked for Anna for five years." She turned back to Rudolph.

And clearly had a ball every minute. Jesus. Maybe Anna found her a jewel beyond price, but I thought she was a whey-faced bitch. As Miss Butterwith would have said.

Well, okay, Miss Butterwith wouldn't have said that, but it was my opinion and I was sticking to it.

"I met Anna this year." That chirpy voice belonged to the youngest member of the enclave. I'd managed to remember Nella House's name because of a not-very-kind name association. She was a big girl. A very, very big girl. One of those very big girls who you fear won't live to see forty if they don't take action now. She was perhaps in her early twenties, bright blue eyes, glossy brown hair and rosy cheeks.

"How did you meet her?"

"When I found out she actually lived *here*, in Nitchfield, I drove out to tell her how much I loved her, and we..." She pressed her fists together which I guess was supposed to signify what we grownups call rapprochement. Or maybe it was a gang sign. The Crips. The Bloods. The Quills.

Of course they'd hit it off. What's not to love about unconditional admiration? Nella's baby blues were sparkling even now with the remembered thrill of that first meeting with her idol. The shock and the joy of discovering Anna breathed the same air that Nella did.

For which I really had to hand it to Anna. I can't say I'd have been as gracious, let alone taken under my wing an admiring aspirant. Not that aspirants ever showed up at my front door to admire me. Frankly, no one showed up at my front door with the exception of the mailman, UPS and the pool guy. No, come to think of it, the pool guy used the side gate.

"How long have you been writing?" Perhaps I don't always do the right thing, but I do generally know what the right thing is.

"Since I was fourteen. I wrote my first novel when I was sixteen."

I swallowed the lump of prime rib that seemed to have wedged in my throat. "Are you published?"

"I've had sixty-three poems published. No novels yet."

"Your novel will be published," Rowland told her. He nodded at her with an assurance I'd have thought only Rudolph Dunst was in a position to offer. Nella blushed.

"You were both in the writing group last year?"

"Yes," Rowland said. "Me, Nella and Arthur."

Arthur Gohring was the other male student. Arthur struck me as more of a biker type than a writer type. Not that he couldn't be both, of course. He reminded me of Ving Rhames: brawny, bald and black. He looked like he'd have interesting things to write about—after he finished stabbing his pen through your neck.

"How long have you been writing, Arthur?"

It's my experience that aspiring writers and the newly published aren't nearly as tired of such questions as veterans of the writing wars. Arthur, however, said in his deep, deep voice, "A long time. How did you get an agent, Chris?"

Chris. No one calls me Chris. It's Christopher or Mr. Holmes. I don't even let my parents call me Chris—though they did draw the line at Mr. Holmes. True, J.X. called me *Kit,* but that was J.X. He got special dispensation for being...J.X.

"I got mine from the pound," I said. "I always think it's nice if you can rescue one of the older agents. They're usually housebroken and—"

"No, really," Poppy Seed cut in, no nonsense.

Hadn't I explained this to Rowland? Was this how the writing seminar was going to go too? Was I trapped in some annoying version of *Groundhog Day* 101?

I said, "I'd completed the first Miss Butterwith manuscript so I mailed it to several—"

Poppy Seed gaped. "*Mailed* it?"

"Right."

"Through the post office?"

"Yeah."

"You couldn't just email it?"

"No. This was back in the day when some of us still used paper and typewriters. Electric typewriters, of course, and later on word processors, but still antediluvian, I agree."

Nella, boldly reaching for seconds of those buttery whipped

potatoes, asked, "But how did that work? The agents would receive a package in the mail and then what? Did they mail you a letter to tell you they were accepting your work?"

"Usually it was to tell you they weren't accepting your work, but yes. Or they'd call."

"How long ago *was* this?"

"About sixteen years ago."

"Oh. So there weren't so many writers back then." She smiled knowingly.

I started to object, but in a way she was correct. Technology had changed publishing, and was continuing to change it in ways we'd never dreamed back when I was carving out shelf space in my comfortable niche. But it's not like hard work and, hopefully, some talent hadn't played a role in my success. At least, I wanted—needed—to believe so.

"How convenient. For the agents." Poppy's plate was now cleared of any prime rib. Had she already eaten it or had she cut it into such infinitesimal pieces it was no longer visible to the naked eye?

"Well, yeah. Basically they hold the keys to the citadel. At least in those days. And these days too if you still want a contract with mainstream publishing."

"Mainstream publishing," scoffed Arthur.

"That's where the money is."

"Money."

I gave that up for a lost cause. I happen to like money, so sue me—but not for all my money, please.

"I'd like a mainstream contract," Nella put in. I smiled benignly at her. I like common sense in a beginner.

Arthur said, "Mainstream publishing is obsolete. There's nothing mainstream publishing can do for you that you can't do yourself."

Nella said, "There's more prestige."

"Prestige."

I'd already noticed that Arthur and Nella seemed to disagree with each other every time the other opened his—or her—trap. They were both violently opinionated in the way only aspiring writers can be.

"I read in *Publisher's Weekly*—"

"That's not what I read in *Writer's Digest*—"

"Have you been with the same agent your whole career?" Rowland spoke loudly over their raised voices. He seemed preoccupied with my agented status, but that's not unusual when you're standing outside the hallowed gates of first-time publication.

I nodded in answer. By then I'd have had to shout to be heard over Arthur and Nella.

"Mainstream publishing is *dead*. Put a fork in it!"

"Only egomaniacs would consider publishing their own work!"

The others, including Sara and Rudolph, politely ignored the exchange.

Ever the ambassador of goodwill, I said, "Were you all staying at the house when Anna had her accident?"

Chapter Four

You'd have thought I stood up and sloshed a bucket of ice water over them. The silence that followed my words could only be described as *ringing*.

I'd been looking at Rowland, and he was the first to break that pregnant pause.

"No. I only arrived yesterday."

"I was here," Nella said. "I spend the weekend lots of times."

The others all said they hadn't been present at the time of Anna's fall. They answered so conscientiously, one by one, so that I felt like I was channeling Professor Plum in the Dining Room with the Candlestick.

"Why?" Sara asked in her cool way at last.

"Merely making conversation," I replied.

There was another funny lull and then Victoria mentioned finishing Caleb Carr's *The Alienist* and everything seemed to snap back to normal. A lively discussion began as to whether the book was a mystery, a historical, or—in Arthur's view—a total rip-off.

My attention wandered. Only Rudolph, Sara and Nella had been staying at the house when Anna took her tumble down the stairs, which surely limited the cast of suspects.

No, it didn't.

Nothing said a member of the estate staff couldn't hold some grudge against Anna. She could be pretty hard to please as I well recalled.

Still, if Anna had any disgruntled employees, they could simply leave her service. It's not like these days anyone was trapped in indentured servitude. Well, unless you believed everything you read in *Mother Jones* magazine.

The idea of Rudolph, Sara or Nella wanting to injure Anna seemed pretty unlikely. Maybe Anna *was* stringing together a coincidental series of close calls and coming up with a murder plot where none existed.

One thing I had noticed during the earlier introductions— though I didn't see how it could be significant—was that every member of this year's AC was local. The year I'd taken part, there had been writers from all over the country. There had even been a girl from Peru, an exchange student from one of Anna's college classes. My understanding was Anna chose each year's participants based on workshops and seminars she held all across the States—as well as recommendations from her publisher. This year's gathering seemed much less formal; it had a certain homegrown feel to it. If these students were all locally based, it was possible that one of them could have arranged for a fall in the garden—maybe even tampered with the brake fluid in Anna's car.

Arranging a bout of food poisoning would be trickier, but there was always the chance that the food poisoning really *had* been an accident and was unconnected to these other events.

Frankly, there was a chance—more than a chance—that all of these events were unconnected and Anna was imagining things.

All the same, that had been a very odd silence when I asked about who had been staying in the house. Almost as though I'd brought up something that was on everyone's mind, but that no one wanted to mention.

After dinner the others adjourned to the large, fully equipped home theater to watch *The Birds*.

Though Anna was no relation to *The* Hitchcock, in the early years of her career she had coyly implied a connection. I don't know if it had helped her career or not, but one of the traditions of the Asquith Circle weekends was viewing classic Hitchcock films each evening.

I wasn't sure if I was expected to sit in for Anna and play Siskel to Sara's Ebert, but I was short on sleep and I had a stack of manuscripts to read through—not to mention the fact that *The Birds* has always creeped me out.

Leaving my fellow scribes to enjoy an evening watching human Barbie Tippi Hedren trying to keep her fine feathered friends from permanently rearranging her hair and makeup, I retreated to my quarters.

I'd no sooner settled—cautiously—on the tomb-sized bed with an unnervingly tall stack of manuscripts then I heard a soft tapping at the door.

I took my reading glasses off, climbed down from the bed and went to answer the summons. Sara stood in the elegantly wide hallway.

"Anna was hoping she could see you for a few minutes before you turn in for the evening."

"Sure."

I followed her down the hallway. I was thinking how really awkward it felt to try and talk to her when she said abruptly, "Are you settled in all right?"

"Yes. Fine, thanks."

"Good."

It occurred to me that what I was interpreting as icy reserve might in fact be something more like awkwardness. Because Sara was eerily efficient didn't mean that she wasn't shy. I sometimes forgot that even though I too was on the introverted side.

Okay, a lot on the introverted side.

Feeling my gaze, Sara gave me a polite, cool smile.

Or maybe she was a cold, unfriendly android in woman's clothing. But I suspected that she was a shy person who had learned to compensate with a cool, all-but-uncrackable professional demeanor.

"Do you enjoy these writing weekends?" I asked.

"Of course." Was it my imagination or did she sound defensive?

"They must make a change from your usual duties."

"Yes."

"And you're the one who does all the running around and organizing everything?"

She hesitated. "Anna and I have it pretty much down to a science now."

No doubt, but one thing I remembered about Anna. She was never the one saddled with doing the dogsbody work. Even when she had been teaching full-time way back at good old UCI, she had plenty of TAs to do the grunt work.

"Do you write as well?"

She said dryly, "Doesn't everyone?"

These days it did seem that way.

We reached Anna's suite. Sara tapped on the door, pushed it open and stood aside.

I walked past her and Sara closed the door after me.

"Christopher." Anna held her hand out to me. "It occurred to me a short while ago that I never even thanked you for rushing to my rescue."

I walked around the bed, took her hand. "That's okay. My pleasure."

"Liar."

"Nah. When duty calls..."

She was still holding my hand. It was a little uncomfortable. Not that I minded holding hands with her, but it wasn't our usual style.

"It means so goddamned much. It really does. That you would drop everything for me. Especially after all these years."

She appeared to be quite serious. I said awkwardly, "I don't mind. I was glad to. I know I don't keep in touch, but I haven't forgotten how encouraging you were to me when I started out. How kind you were. I'm glad to do something in return."

"It's..." She stopped. Her expression twisted and she said, "It's just that for the first time in a long, long while things are going *right* for me."

Now that was a shocker. "Things haven't been going right for you?" Anna was one of those people who always seemed to land on her feet. Everything went right for her. At least that's how it always seemed to me.

She shook her head, and her eyes filled with uncharacteristic tears. She let go of my hand to wipe them away. "The last couple of years have been rough. I haven't been writing. When Todd and I separated...oh, I can't explain it without sounding fucking pathetic, but something went out of me. I stopped caring. About anything. I didn't want to write. I didn't want to teach. I didn't want to see people or go anywhere."

I automatically reached for the white velvet side chair that was still near the bed, and sat down. "That sounds familiar." I probably sounded bitter. I probably was bitter.

Anna nodded. "I knew if anyone could understand, it would be you. I know I tease you, but you're much more sensitive and insightful than people give you credit for, Christopher."

I did my best to look suitably sensitive and insightful, but the resulting expression probably resembled a case of mild indigestion.

Anna continued, "I don't know if it was a bad case of burnout or that I loved Todd more than I realized, but after he left, nothing seemed to matter."

Ah yes. How well I remembered those long, lonely days after David left. How the days had dragged. And the nights. Probably because he took my PA with him. I'd spent a lot more time talking to Dicky than I had David. I really missed Dicky.

With difficulty, I held my tongue, which I was guessing was what a sensitive, insightful person does in that situation.

"Nothing gave me joy. Nothing fueled my passion. But over the last few months, that's begun to change. I'm writing again, I'm getting a kick out of teaching, and I've begun to think that maybe I'm not too old for love. So to have this happen now...this fear that someone I know may hate me so much they want me dead...it's shattering."

I could see that. It's one thing to find out you get on people's nerves. That's part of the human condition. The idea that someone actively wanted you dead would be...er, a trifle discomfiting. As Miss Butterwith would put it.

"You don't have any idea who might want to hurt you?"

"I swear I don't."

"Let's look at it logically. Who has motive?"

Anna gave me a grim look. "It's not easy to be quite so cold-blooded when it's your own life at stake."

"I know. But think about it like a mystery writer. You're one of the best out there. Who gains by your death?"

"It's relative, darling. Rival mystery writers? Literary critics?"

I said with my usual tact, "You're rich. Who's in your will?"

Anna glared at me. "Lots of people. I've left most of my friends small mementos."

"How small?"

She said dryly, "I've left you an antique writing desk."

"Oh. Thanks." Was I supposed to reciprocate? My will currently left everything to my parents. That was one thing I'd seen to right away after David's departure. No way did I want that cheating bastard benefiting by a dime if I happened to be hit by an asteroid. Which had been a real possibility, the way my luck was going then.

"I don't plan on your collecting for some time."

"Of course not. Where would I put an antique writing desk anyway? What about the bulk of your estate?"

"The house itself will go to the Mystery Writers of America along with sufficient funds for it to be used as a writing retreat for the next decade. I've left financial bequests for all the servants—and before you say anything, yes, I've made substantial provision for Sara."

I hadn't been about to say anything, but I certainly found that an interesting tidbit.

"How much is substantial provision?"

"None of your goddamned business. A lot."

"How long has Sara been with you?" I knew the answer, but I was on a roll now being sleuth-like.

"For nearly five years. I sincerely doubt she's suddenly taken it into her mind to knock me off. I'm not *that* difficult to work for."

"Does she know about your will?"

"No. Absolutely not." Anna made a face. "I'm too much of a mystery maven to go around advertising the specifics of my will."

"Could she have found out?"

Anna shook her head. "It's not impossible, but once you get to know Sara better, you'll see how very unlikely that is. It's simply not the way she thinks."

"Okay. We'll put the high-minded Sara to the side for now. Who else did you leave money to?"

"Rudolph. That is to say, I didn't leave him money per se, but I left him the rights to my literary estate. All my work. Past and future."

"*Wow.* Nice."

"He deserves it. But Rudolph is very comfortably off. He might have wished to kill me a number of times over the past years, but it would be for missing deadlines, not financial gain."

"What exactly *is* your relationship with Rudolph?"

"None of your fucking business." She said it without heat.

"You asked me to help, Anna. I can't help if I don't know who all the players are and what their role is."

"Take my word for it, Rudolph has absolutely no reason to want me anything but alive and healthy."

"What it is to be universally beloved. So what about these students of yours? How well do you know them and are any of them in your will?"

46

Her face softened. For an instant she almost looked maternal. Only for an instant, because she was about as maternal as Hulk Hogan. "There's a bequest for Nella. The money is to be used for a topnotch MFA program. All expenses paid. And no, she doesn't know about it. And in any case, I'm going to give her the money next fall."

Very generous. Maybe a bit controlling too. That was the other thing about Anna. She liked to manage. Not that Nella would likely object to having to enroll in a nice MFA program.

"What about the others?"

Her brow creased as she considered the other members of this year's Asquith Circle. "I know them. I don't know them well."

"You've known Rowland for a few years, haven't you?"

"Rowland." She smiled dismissingly. "Yes. He was a clerk at the real-estate office when I bought my house. Now he works in a bookstore in Nitchfield. Blackbird Books. I've known him for about ten years, I think. I probably know him the best of any of them, barring Nella, of course."

"Who do you know the least?"

"Arthur. He's...a very interesting man. Much more intelligent than you might think."

A ringing endorsement if I ever heard one. "And how did he break into the sacred circle?"

Anna looked vague. "He's got a certain flair—and an original voice. Plus, I try to make sure we always have a balance of male and female students. You know what these writing weekends can be like otherwise."

Only too well. Like a slumber party on steroids.

"What about Poppy Whatshername and Victoria?"

"I met Poppy through Victoria. They were members of a

local women's writing group. Defunct now. I spoke at one of their luncheons, which Victoria organized." She shrugged.

"Have you ever had problems with any of them?"

"Nothing that would lead me to believe one of them wants me dead. Rowland was a little disappointed when I declined to write him a letter of introduction to my agent. Arthur doesn't take kindly to writing advice. Probably any advice. Poppy and I have occasionally had our difference of opinion. Victoria's a sweetheart. She rents a cottage on the back portion of the estate. She's a lovely tenant and I've never had a single difficulty with her."

"*Guilty*," I pronounced. "I can pack my magnifying glass and go home now. Beneath that mild exterior, Victoria is a raging, homicidal maniac."

Anna laughed, though it sounded strained. "I'm probably jumping at shadows. The more I think about this, the more ridiculous it seems."

I stood up and slid the velvet chair to the side. "Let's hope. We'll approach this as preventative medicine, how's that?"

She smiled faintly.

"You should probably sleep. I should probably sleep. I've got that mountain of manuscripts you left for me. Maybe it'll help me sleep."

Her chuckle was wicked. "Don't worry. I've already read through them and made notes, but yes, you should at least glance over the first and last few chapters. It'll be an experience for you."

"I am nothing if not a man of experience." I moved toward the door.

"Good luck tomorrow, darling," Anna called sweetly.

Chapter Five

Back in my room I made myself comfy on my funeral bier and settled down to do my homework.

The hefty stack of manuscripts before me represented the final drafts—as if there could be such a thing—of the five student members of this year's Asquith Circle. Anna had printed everything out for me because, throwback that I was, I preferred to read the old-fashioned way. Okay, not hieroglyphics on walls, but close.

If only Anna's guestrooms came stocked with minibars. But they didn't. I would have to face the task before me stone-cold sober. It had been a very long time since I'd read anything straight from the flames of inspiration that weren't part of my own barbecue, and I was nervous.

I was prepared for anything. Entire novels in present tense. Entire novels without dialog tags. Entire novels in second-person POV. *You are reading this book. You are not happy about it. You are not happy about much these days.*

Because it was the shortest in the stack, I started with Rowland Bride's *Came Tumbling After*. It wasn't bad, but it wasn't great.

Damon was trying to ignore the voice in his head....

Oh boy. Keeping in mind that these stories were by Anna's handpicked favorites, her top students, I had to wonder if Anna was less choosy now days or if the pool of talent was shrinking.

Then four pages in, my attention was caught by the fact that the narrator was killed in a fall down some icy stairs.

Not that a murderous fall down stairs wasn't a time-honored tradition in mystery fiction—it was right there with the voices in the head—but this did seem a wee bit coincidental. I continued to read. The story was about one of those spinster ladies Poppy Seed looked so disapprovingly on. The spinster was named Bess and she lived with her elderly invalid mother with whom she liked to share her observations and speculations about their small-town neighbors. Bess was too curious about her neighbors, as a matter of fact, and one of them didn't like it. He began to harass our heroine. What this big bully didn't realize was that Bess was a serial killer.

That wasn't bad, as far as it went, but Bess was the most boring serial killer in the literary history of serial killers. Well before the crucial fifty-page cut-off point, I was longing for Bess to meet a bigger, badder serial killer who would put us both out of our misery. My attention wandered to the night-blackened window and its view of starless sky.

Friday night. I sighed. *Friday night's alright for fighting.* If I hadn't agreed to help Anna out, J.X. and I would be having dinner right now. Or maybe we'd be back at my place and I'd be checking how he looked out of professional context. As I recalled, he looked pretty damn good.

I glanced automatically at the bedstand. An ornate globe lamp, a small plate of chocolate truffles I was earnestly doing my best to ignore, and a couple of books I'd brought including *Oscar Wilde and a Death of No Importance* and Adrien English's latest. No phone. It wasn't a hotel. Anna didn't furnish every bedroom with phones any more than minibars.

I didn't carry a cell phone. What would be the point? I

never went anywhere. If someone needed me, I could generally be found without expending much effort—the real test was getting through my call screening.

Still, it wouldn't be hard to locate a phone around here. I could call J.X. just to say...hey.

We were still friends, after all.

Not that we had ever exactly been *friends*, but surely he wasn't cutting me entirely out of his life.

I climbed out of the bed and threw on my robe. It was a snazzy red wool affair with my initials monogrammed on the pocket. It looked like the kind of thing gentlemen wore in 1930s films, and I confess it gave me a kick although it really wasn't practical for my normal Southern California work routine which basically consisted of me sitting around in jeans and flannel shirt or jeans and tee shirt for eight hours a day. Often the same jeans and shirt day after day after day until I moulted. The writing life isn't how it looks from the outside. Hemingway and Fitzgerald set up some very unrealistic expectations.

I opened my bedroom door, double-checked that the coast was clear, and made my way down the long hallway. I crept down the marble staircase beneath the disapproving painted faces of all those adopted ancestors of Anna's and an assortment of weaponry that could have equipped a small standing army. As I crossed the shining parquet floors I could hear screams and shrill bird cries drifting from the home theater. Things were going downhill fast in Bodega Bay.

Memory had served me correctly. There was a phone in the library. I sat down behind the grand desk with its burl wood inlays and decorative brass hardware. Picking up the handset, I began to dial.

On the other side of the country the phone rang with brisk efficiency.

Once.

Twice.

I glanced at the grandfather clock in the corner. Nearly eleven. J.X. should still be awake. He rarely went to bed before midnight. Wait. He was in California. Eight o'clock on his side of the continent. He would definitely be up and about.

Thrice...

Of course he might not be home.

It was Friday night and he was footloose and fancy free. I'd slipped the halter off him myself. Given that gorgeous rump a slap and said, *Be free.*

So what was I doing now?

Abruptly, I grasped how this was going to look. I didn't want to advance our relationship, but I didn't want to let go either. That wasn't fair to J.X., which he could hardly fail to notice and being J.X., hardly fail to mention in that direct ego-bruising way he had. I wasn't sure my ego could take a lot of bruising tonight. I missed him.

Very gently, very quietly, I replaced the handset.

It seemed a much longer trip back to my room.

An eerie silence issued from the home theater as I slunk back across the vast, slippery expanse of enough parquetry to make the Boston Celtics feel at home. Past the suit of armor guarding the marble staircase, up, up, up to the uncanny silence of the second floor, and back into my lonely bedchamber. And if there was ever a bedroom that deserved the title "chamber", it was this one.

I flopped down on the bed, which made an almost human sound of discomfort, and determinedly picked up the next manuscript. Arthur Gohring was apparently planning a series about a crime-solving ferret named Farrell. I sighed and started to read. The novel turned out to be funny and horrifically violent. One chapter into Farrell the Ferret and *Monkey Matters*, I understood why Anna thought Arthur needed to be part of the group even if he was an uncomfortable fit.

When I next looked up, it was past midnight and I still had four manuscripts to get through. I skimmed the ending of *Monkey Matters*—I'd been wrong about Arthur going for a series—shook my head over the bloody demise of Farrell, and reached for Sara Mason's *Death and Her Sisters*.

I hadn't realized until then that Sara was an active participant in the group. No wonder she'd seemed sort of, er, phlegmatic when I'd asked if she wrote too.

Three hours later, shocked and envious, I finally, reluctantly, set the manuscript aside, wondering what the hell Sara Mason was doing working as Anna's PA. Not that PA wasn't an admirable profession—when it wasn't engaged in spouse stealing—but Sara was the real deal. This went beyond talent and hard work, this was gifted. This was the kind of acuity you were either born with or you weren't. Like having perfect pitch or Brad Pitt's cheekbones.

The words flowed. The story was gripping, but the prose was mesmerizing. I didn't want to put the manuscript down. I could easily picture a bidding war breaking out for *Death and Her Sisters*. Sara Mason was a real find. She needed to be encouraged, nurtured, shepherded. Not by *me*, naturally, but by someone who knew which way was up. Anna. Which, unless Anna had changed a lot through the years, was already happening.

And that was a pretty nice perk for any PA. To have Anna Hitchcock as your mentor? No wonder Sara didn't mind organizing the occasional writing seminar.

I set Sara's manuscript aside to finish later. No way was I

spoiling it by skimming or glancing at the ending. I picked up the next manuscript.

Drive by Nella House. I began to read.

Ten minutes later, I began to skim. Nella was talented, no question, but I couldn't understand, at least from this particular work, why everyone from Anna to Rowland thought she was a force to be reckoned with. I'd probably read a dozen books similar to *Drive* in the past couple of years. Sure, the kid had a nice turn of phrase and some great imagery, but the themes were well-worn and the characters' motivation and psychology was about what you'd expect from a twenty-year-old.

One of these days Nella was going to be a fine, strong writer, but she wasn't that writer yet.

Maybe it was her age that was confusing everyone. She did write very, very well for a twenty-year-old. I wish I'd written half that well at twenty. If I compared her work to that of the average twenty-year-old, she shined bright. If I compared her work to the average mainstream published author...she showed a lot of promise.

Granted, this was one book. The rest of the writing group—certainly Anna—had seen more of Nella's work and maybe she *was* as good as I had the impression everyone believed.

As I picked up Victoria's manuscript, a noise from outside caught my attention. The hair on the back of my neck prickled. It sounded like someone was knocking against my window.

I set the manuscript aside, crawled out of the linen-lined crypt once more and went to the window.

I relaxed as I made out a tree branch, its twisted twig-fingers scraping at the edge of the window frame. What had I expected? One of the gulls from *The Birds*? Or Poe's raven tap-tap-tapping at my window?

The terrace below was blanketed in soft white, glowing preternaturally in the night. I realized the lights were all out downstairs. I hadn't heard anyone returning to their rooms after the movie ended, but the party must have broken up while I was engrossed in my reading. Staring down, I could pick out the shapes of flower urns, finials and steps beneath the frozen white velvet. The lawns beyond the terrace glittered like fields of crushed milk glass.

Wait a minute... I bent closer to the window, my breath misting on the dark surface. Someone was coming up the steps from the bottom garden. A large, bulky figure appeared at the top of the flagstone steps.

My gasp of shock fogged the whole damn window, or enough of it that I couldn't see for a few vital seconds. I wiped it clear with my sleeve and peered more closely.

Now the bundled figure was making its way along the path away from the house, heading toward the front drive perhaps.

Male or female? Male, I thought, though it was hard to get an idea of size let alone sex given the cumbersome snow wear.

He was not moving with any particular haste or stealth. If he was aware of me standing in this lighted window, he gave no sign. Maybe this was a household staff member who had every reason to be prowling around at this time of night. I tried to think of any maintenance jobs that were best performed in the dead of night. The only thing that came to mind was knocking down wasp nests. That was much better done when wasps were slow and sleepy—as I had good reason to know as a So Cal homeowner.

Anyway, I figured that was probably not the issue here at Chilblain Manor. I watched the figure slowly dissolve into the darkness.

I continued to wait at the window in case the mysterious

other reappeared, but even a few seconds or so of standing there in your bare feet at three o'clock in the morning—a morning in February at that—is a loooong time.

After about four very dull, very cold minutes I gave it up and jumped back into bed, pulling the bedclothes up around my shoulders.

Miss B. would have been disappointed in me, but she was elderly. She didn't need much sleep. She could spend entire nights watching her criminous neighbors through her bird-watching field glasses and nobody the wiser. I, on the other hand, required a full eight hours to be at my peak.

I clearly wasn't going to get them tonight. I still had two more manuscripts to wade through before the next day, which was already slinking up on me, ravening maw salivating in anticipation of my morning agonies.

I settled my reading glasses more firmly on my nose and reached for the next manuscript.

Chapter Six

Don't get me wrong. I like morning. Perhaps I'm not what you might call a *morning person*, but I'm okay with a.m. And I really like breakfast.

I like hot coffee and bright sunshine and the promise of a new day—even if the day is going to be exactly like all the other days that preceded it. That's kind of reassuring, frankly. I like those raisin cinnamon swirl bagels from Panera Bread, or maybe a mushroom and spinach omelet, and I like sitting in the honeysuckle-covered arbor that overlooks my sparkling swimming pool and watching the hummingbirds brawl and the bees drown.

"Look to this day! For it is life, the very life of life." That's according to the poets, and they ought to know all about positive attitude, given what poets earn.

Even when David and I were together, he usually left for the office and a busy day of chasing office staff around the file room before I peeled off my sleep mask, which is to say that I'm used to greeting the day in a state of mandarin-like serenity.

What I'm not used to is being social or even coherent before ten o'clock, and finding Poppy glowering at me over the coffee urn in the dining room at seven thirty was sort of...blighting. Especially since at four o'clock that very morning I'd been reading the gruesome thing her heroine did with a pair of gardening clippers to her ex-husband.

Even minus nightmares about pruning shears, I never sleep well in strange beds. Which is why I diligently stick to my own.

"Morning," I managed.

"Good morning." She sounded as crisp as a drill sergeant greeting the new recruits over three sets of pushups.

I didn't try to speak again until I'd downed a couple of reviving sips of very hot and very good coffee. In fact, I probably wouldn't have spoken at all, but Poppy fastened me with that hypnotic gaze of hers. She clearly expected something of me. What? Chitchat? Surely not.

I took another sip of coffee and cleared my throat. "Where is everyone?"

"Getting ready for class, I guess."

Class. It sounded so formal. "Is there a lot to get ready?" I asked uneasily.

She smiled. I've seen wolverines with more engaging grins.

Today's ensemble was jeans and a man's sweater vest over her tailored shirt. In fact, apart from the sweater vest, we were pretty much dressed alike. I like to think I filled out the jeans better, but I wasn't fully confident.

"Right. When do the festivities start?"

"Eight."

I shuddered.

She studied me with those striking blue-green eyes and smiled. "Didn't you sleep well?"

"I never sleep well away from home."

"My husband was the same." It was clearly a sign of weakness.

I didn't miss the *was* either. Well, I could see why Poppy's literary views on domesticity might create some tension behind the white picket fence.

"What did—does—he think about you writing murder mysteries?"

"He died in a sailing accident last year."

This is why I generally steer clear of small talk. I didn't get that gene.

"I'm sorry," I said.

"That's all right. More to the point, what do *you* think of my writing?"

Now I understood the air of expectancy. The feedback frenzy had already begun. I opened my mouth but did a rethink and instead poured in more coffee. What I thought of Poppy's work was that it had been years since I'd read anything that disturbing. And that was simply the overuse of adjectives. Never mind the violence her heroine perpetrated on her hapless ex in the name of self-assertion.

Rescue came in the shape of a handsome young man in a red parka. He had curly long brown hair and a ruggedly handsome profile which I beheld as he passed in front of the dining-room picture window carrying a long metal ladder. I did what any red-blooded hero would do when facing insurmountable odds. I pointed behind Poppy and exclaimed, "Look! Who's that?"

Naturally, Poppy glanced around. "Oh. That's Luke." She added, with that disturbingly feral smile, "Anna's handyman."

"Her...?" And then with the disapproval of any Victorian papa, "Exactly how handy is he?"

"Very, from what I understand. Well, why not? They're both adults."

In fact, Anna was adult enough to be Luke's mother. Age differences being something of a sore point right then. Not that five years was quite the same thing as forty.

Poppy looked at the clock hanging above the sideboard and said, "I'll start down to the cottage now. Shall I tell everyone you're going to be late?"

"I'm not going to be late." I gulped the dregs of coffee in my cup. "I'll meet you down there. I have to grab the stories out of my room."

As I raced back upstairs to my room, I couldn't help noticing how very quiet and empty the big house was. Of course, that was probably the mark of a well-organized household, a home as efficiently run as any Fortune 500 business. You had to admire that even if my own preference was for something cozier—and a lot more manageable.

Reaching my room, I paused. The door was ajar.

I pushed the door open. The obvious explanation was the maid had been and gone. Except...the bed was still unmade. I'd spread it up, but it hadn't had the official treatment from someone who knew a hospital corner from a thirteen-year-old-trying-to-hide-his-porn-mags tuck.

Maybe I'd forgotten to close the door properly after me. That was pretty unlikely though. I'm nothing if not paranoid about my privacy.

I walked into the adjoining bathroom. The towels were still on the floor where I'd left them to sop up the water that had pooled from the shower. My kit bag sat on the marble sink counter. My electric razor lay next to it. I stared and stared as though a baby cobra curled there.

Surely I'd dropped the razor back in my kit bag? It was second nature to me to do so. Then again, I'd been in a rush that morning, having overslept. Maybe I'd distractedly set the razor down.

In a puddle of water?

That *really* didn't seem like something I'd do, but equally I couldn't think of a reason anyone would want to search my things. It's not like I was carrying top-secret microfilm or fabulous stolen jewels in my luggage.

Too many late-night mystery stories. That was the most obvious explanation.

Nothing else struck me as wrong and nothing seemed to be missing, so...yeah. Too much imagination and too little sleep. I grabbed the stack of stories, shoved two of the smaller manuscripts in my laptop case and, carrying the others in my arms, hightailed it back downstairs.

Again I was struck by how still the house was. There was no sign of anyone. Not a creature was stirring. Not even a minion.

I wandered around till I found the kitchen, and from there I was directed out the back to a large, frozen herb garden. I followed a newly cleared path through snow-laden fruit trees until I came to the stairs leading down to the lower garden.

The garden steps looked freshly swept of any snow and ice, but I took them cautiously, clutching my armload of manuscripts. At least this wasn't the good old days when there might have been a horrible chance I was carrying someone's only copy, and if I did happen to slip I could make my crash landing on a bed of manuscripts.

Below me I could see lights on in the cottage. A wisp of smoke rose from the chimney, like ivory feathers against the slate sky.

I was out of breath by the time I crossed the garden. Reaching the cottage, I eased open the door. In the alcove near the window, this year's Asquith Circle was seated around the round table like the dwarves waiting for Snow White to make her appearance.

The babble of voices cut off sharply when I slithered in. Literally slithered in. The soles of my boots were soaked. I'd forgotten about changing them for the snow boots until it was too late. I skated to the table, dropped the armload of manuscripts with a thud and exhaled my relief.

"Better late than never," Rowland greeted me cheerfully.

Arthur grunted something that sounded unconvinced on that score.

"Sorry," I said. "I forgot the stories and had to go back and get them."

The seven members of the AC eyed me with various degrees of skepticism. All except Rudolph, who was smiling sympathetically.

"You're here now," he reassured. A man well used to dealing with frazzled writers.

"Would you like coffee or juice?" Sara rose and went into the small kitchen which was divided from the main room by a rustic-looking bar. "There are pastries. Or fruit and yogurt if you prefer."

Sara was eating fruit and yogurt. Everyone else was downing pastries like there was a moratorium on calories. Victoria had compromised by taking a few pieces of fruit, but clearly the pineapple was merely serving as garnish for her baklava.

To stall as long as possible I helped myself to coffee and a lemon tart and then I took my place at the table. I wouldn't exactly pronounce the silence *dead*, as I shoved the stack of papers aside and pulled my laptop out of the case, but it did feel uncomfortably like a pride of junior high school students was waiting to devour a stray substitute teacher.

I smiled nervously. "It's been a long time since I attended one of these shindigs, let alone conducted one." I groped for my reading glasses, more as stage prop than anything.

"You don't find it necessary to upgrade your skills in such a competitive field?" Poppy asked.

"Have you been talking to my agent?"

Not a smile. I was starting to feel like XP at a Vista class reunion. Jeez, one thing I've learned is you need a sense of humor to survive the publishing industry.

Nella said, "Last time we each read our first chapter and then we all commented on it and then Anna and Rudolph gave us their feedback."

The others concurred.

"Okay, that's fine by me." I hastily dusted pastry crumbs from the stack of manuscripts. "Who wants to go first?"

"I'll go first," Nella offered.

"No, no," Rowland said. "Save the best for last."

Nella blushed. The others looked less enchanted but tried to be pleasant about it.

"I'll go first," Poppy said, clicking keys on her notebook. Everyone settled back, coffee cups and pastries in hand.

Twenty shell-shocked minutes later no one was eating and Nella faintly excused herself to go to the washroom.

"You've got balls, I'll say that for you," Arthur said. "Unlike that poor bastard in your story."

Poppy laughed heartily. She looked inquiringly around the table.

Victoria said in her mild way, "Of course, I've read it before. I think this draft is cleaner, crisper."

"It seemed florid to me," Rowland said, with unexpected

aggression. "Too many adjectives and adverbs. Too many dialog tags. Too many exclamation points and italics. And I didn't like the main character at all. If you're going to start with something that violent and gross, you've lost me as a reader."

"You're not my target audience."

"Who is your target audience?" Sara asked.

Nella returned from the bathroom. Her face looked bloodless. Rowland smiled at her and she smiled weakly back.

"My target audience is women readers and mystery readers."

Sara replied, "That's too broad."

No pun intended? I held my tongue.

"I get the feeling you don't like men very much," Arthur said, maybe reading my mind.

"I'm not my characters or my story."

"I liked it," Nella said faintly. The kid had courage.

Poppy beamed at her.

Sara stated in her precise way, "I think it's violent, self-indulgent and unrealistic. The characters *sound* like characters in a book. And the entire book can't be a flashback."

Poppy turned to me. "Can the entire book be a flashback?"

"Uh...if you can make it work."

She turned away, satisfied.

At that point the Asquith Circle took their gloves off, metaphorically speaking, and the critique began in earnest.

In the end Rudolph merely had to say a few diplomatic generic comments, although when pinned, he straightforwardly admitted it was not a book he would buy.

That left my turn. "It's not a comfortable read," I said, "but I don't need a comfortable read so long as you make me care about the characters or tell a story so interesting I have to know how it all turns out. To be honest, that didn't really happen for me here. I have to agree that the characters didn't seem recognizably human."

I felt that was a gracious compromise to *I'd prefer to claw my eyes out rather than read your work again.* Poppy, unimpressed, curled her lip.

"I don't believe that woman would kill her husband," Sara said. "I think she would talk about it and fantasize about it, and never do anything about it."

"That's how much you know."

Sara raised her brows. Victoria said staunchly, "Well, I like it. I think it's your best work yet."

We hastily moved on.

Afterward I didn't remember much of the morning. Everyone read, everyone got their feedback. Nella got rave reviews pretty much all around. Even Rudolph seemed fondly paternal in his comments. Sara, by far the best writer in the bunch, went last. She was treated with scrupulous politeness and a distinct lack of enthusiasm. Even Anna hadn't bothered to make notes on her manuscript, which seemed more than tactless. I'd have been interested in hearing Rudolph's thoughts—I was surprised he didn't make Sara an offer then and there—but Sara herself cut him off by suggesting that we break for lunch.

I suspected that she couldn't take one more chilly kiss of death. Anyone who wrote as well as she did was obviously passionate about the work and her craft, and this kind of indifferent reception had to be soul destroying.

So, although I am rarely mistaken for one of those warm-and-fuzzy, teddy-bear guys, I blurted out, "Lunch sounds great, Sara, but I want to say I thought your book was amazing. I literally couldn't put it down last night. I thought it was beautifully written. The word that comes to mind is lyrical."

Rudolph seemed startled. The rest of the AC looked blank. Sara, for one split second, looked touchingly unguarded.

"Thank you."

"It's a wonderful book," Rudolph said quietly.

She gave him a very brief, shy smile and then she was back in snow-princess guise, informing us that, per tradition, we were on our own for lunch, but would be meeting back at the cottage at two o'clock sharp.

On cue, everyone rose, closing laptops and notebooks, picking up purses and pulling on jackets.

Sara had it all so perfectly under control I wondered why Anna hadn't had her run the seminar in her place. Except, I remembered with a flinch, after lunch I was supposed to give the first of my talks from the viewpoint of the nominal successful writer present.

With that recollection went my appetite for lunch, but Victoria and Poppy hailed me as I was buttoning up my Burberry.

"We're driving into Nitchfield," Poppy said. "There's a place there that does a real old-fashioned English high tea, and we thought that might be fun since you write a series about a British biologist."

"Botanist."

"Right."

Nella was with them and all three eyed me expectantly. I couldn't remember the protocol. Hazily, it seemed to me that Anna had made a point of lunching with different groups of students throughout the weekend of the seminar. That was part of the fun, right? Getting to pick a professional writer's brain in an open, casual atmosphere?

I glanced around for guidance. Sara was cleaning up the plates and crumbs from the morning session. Rudolph was speaking to her quietly. It was clearly a private discussion. Hopefully one in which he was offering her a publishing contract.

Was that perhaps part of the problem? Did the other members of the circle feel that Sara already had an unfair advantage because of her position? Did they think Anna had helped her with her story? Or was it simply that Sara's reserve didn't encourage people to like her? Whereas Nella was such an eager, enthusiastic kid it would take a harder heart than mine to squash her.

Speak of the devil. "I wanted to ask you about your agent," Nella said as my gaze happened to meet hers.

"Uh, sure." What the hell. I didn't have plans for lunch and if I was going to do a good deed, I might as well do it to the hilt. "High tea or lunch or whatever sounds great."

They made sounds of approval. Victoria called, "Rowland, did you want to join us for lunch?"

Rowland shook his head regretfully. "I was thinking I should check on Mother."

Victoria looked disappointed, although she said cheerfully, "Maybe next time."

Rowland nodded. He smiled at Nella, who blushed and smiled back.

Ah-ha, I thought. Followed by, *Uh-oh*. Didn't anyone want to date in their own age bracket these days? He had to be twenty years her senior, and yes, Nella was technically an adult, but the memory of how naive I'd been at twenty didn't fill me with confidence.

We trailed out of the cottage in a procession, Rowland walking ahead of us. By the time we reached the stairs he was well in the lead, moving with surprisingly brisk purpose.

Poppy remarked, "I don't know why he doesn't put that old bat in a nursing home."

Nella, several steps behind, made a sound of protest. Victoria shushed Poppy.

"He can't hear me." Poppy said to me, "Rowland lives with his mother, in case you couldn't guess. She's like those broads in Victorian novels who get everything they want by playing sick all the time."

"She has fibromyalgia," Victoria said.

"Fibromyass."

Nella's nervous giggle floated behind us.

"You think we're awful," Victoria said, glancing at me.

"No." That was the truth. I didn't care what they said about Rowland's mother. She probably *was* a total PitA. That didn't mean Rowland didn't love her dearly—I suspected from what I'd read the evening before, he did indeed love her—and it didn't mean she didn't deserve that love.

There's nothing more puzzling than human attachments.

I was preoccupied with trying to think of a way to ask if they suspected anyone of wanting Anna permanently out of the picture. It seemed sort of awkward to bring it up out of the blue. Somehow Miss Butterwith always knew how to segue any conversation into talk of death and disaster. Since I was the hand behind the puppet, I couldn't understand why I didn't have the same ability. Everything I thought of was liable to trigger the very thing Anna wanted to avoid.

"Chris could care less," Poppy said. "You should read the mean things he writes about people."

"Huh?" I stared up at her.

"I started reading one of your books last night. You're mean."

"Mean?"

"The little things you say about people. Those barbed what-do-you-call-'ems? Asides."

"I'm not mean," I protested. "Which book was it?"

"*Miss Buttermilk Has a Case* or something like that."

Oh. "*Miss Butterwith Closes the Case.*"

"That sounds right."

I'd been editing that one as things were falling apart with David. It probably *was* more astringent than some of the earlier books.

"You don't like people," Poppy observed.

"Yes I do. I like some people." Admittedly, I was less and less crazy about *her*.

"Ignore Poppy," Victoria told me.

I smiled politely. I had a feeling that was probably easier said than done.

Rowland had widened the gap between us by the time we reached the top level. His bright blue jacket was the only splash of color as he strode across the white lawns.

I wasn't as out of breath as Nella, but not by much. I really did need to make an effort to get myself in shape again. Not that it mattered, since the only one seeing my shape would be me.

Victoria asked, "Does anyone need anything from the house?"

We all agreed we didn't need anything from the house and struck off down the side path to the front drive. I remembered the shadowy figure I'd seen walking that way the night before.

That hadn't been a dream, right? A heavy dinner, a couple of glasses of vino and too many mystery stories in a row?

Overhead, a plane droned high in the granite sky. Ahead of me, Victoria and Poppy chatted about some mutual acquaintance, and a few steps behind, Nella was huffing and puffing. Yet my overall impression was of how still it was. The snow seemed to swallow sound in a vast white hush. In the distance I could hear the sharp insect buzz of Rowland's car falling away.

"How long did it take you to get published?" Nella asked.

"A few years." I smiled faintly at the memory of all those earnest attempts at the Great American Novel. All those passionate and utterly corny stories of coming out and coming to terms. Thank God no one had given them a second look. "I wrote my first novel the summer before I started college." It was still buried somewhere in a box in my parents' garage.

"But you didn't get published until after college?"

"I didn't get published until I finished my MFA."

"Do you think you need to complete an MFA to get published these days?"

"I don't think you ever needed it to get published. I wanted it because...I like structure and organization and it gave me a starting point."

"I just want to start writing," Nella said passionately. "I don't want to wait to start my career."

I thought about Anna's plans for Nella. Well, that was life. The thing that happened while you were busy making other plans.

Chapter Seven

The Tudor Teashop was a largish building with black-and-white decorative timbering, fake chimneys complete with fake chimney pots, and long, narrow windows with flower boxes containing perky plastic blooms.

Inside, it was quaintly decorated in ye olde pseudo-English style complete with Staffordshire pottery and pictures of the queen. It was packed on this Friday afternoon, but we found a table near the fake fireplace and sat down to order our lunch.

The ladies went for various cakes and dainties. I opted for the most substantial selection on the menu which turned out to be three different kinds of finger sandwiches: smoked salmon, watercress and walnut. I don't think any of it was true British fare, but by then I was starving and I'd have been willing to eat soggy cucumbers or anything else my system could digest.

"Can I ask you a question?" Victoria asked diffidently once we'd given our orders to the tiny brisk Englishwoman who owned the Tudor Teashop. "How did you get an agent?"

I opened my mouth. Closed it.

"Remember," Nella told her. "He wrote letters to everyone in *Writer's Market*."

I said, "Huh?"

"Oh, I must have missed that," Victoria said.

"Me too," I said.

Nella turned those wide blue eyes my way. "Isn't that right?"

"Well, I mean it's sort of right. I didn't write *everybody*. I tried to target agents who handled my kind of thing. Agents I had a chance of scoring with."

"How many rejections did you get?"

"It's a long time ago."

She said with disarming honesty, "I always remember the rejections better than the good news."

I thought of the recent rejections in my life. Maybe my perception was wrong, but I felt like even though I received fewer rejections these days, my bounce back had been better when I was younger. Part of that was probably spending nearly twenty years at the same publishing house with the same editor. Not to mention the thirteen years I'd spent with David. Although "spent with" was maybe looking at it through rose-colored reading glasses.

I said, "I was lucky. My agent was starting up and she was what's known in the industry as *hungry*. She signed me before the others had a chance to reject me."

"Is she looking for clients?" Nella asked.

"You know, I'm not sure." It was the truth.

Her gaze fell, her cheeks turned pink, and I knew she felt she'd been brushed off, which was kind of true, but not entirely.

To my astonishment, I heard myself saying, "If you want to mail me a copy of your manuscript, I could send it on to Rachel with a note of recommendation."

She lit up happily.

Yeah. No good deed goes unpublished.

"What's to stop you from stealing Nella's story?" Poppy

broke in.

"I'm sorry?"

"You could steal Nella's story and submit it as your own, right?"

"*Wrong.*" One cold, compact ice cube of a word cracked out of the frozen tray I wanted to dump over her head. I was too offended to let it rest there. "First of all, *ideas* aren't the hard part. Secondly, there are no new ideas, only the author's unique execution." I think I spoke the word *execution* with more fervor than strictly necessary. "Thirdly, why the hell would I want to submit Nella's book as my own when I—like every author in the world—like my own work better?"

"I guess I hit a nerve," Poppy said, amused.

"Nerve is the right word. I'm offering to do Nella a favor and you're basically—" I stopped there. He who argues with a fool is a bigger fool. Or drunk. And I was neither. I wasn't drunk, anyway. Worse luck.

I said to Nella, who was staring wide-eyed from me to Poppy, "Do what you want. If you feel safer sending the book on your own, you can let Rachel know I recommended you."

Our food came at that point, which was probably as well. I occupied myself with the triangles of sandwiches and did my best not to grind my teeth.

Victoria cleared her throat. "How long does it take you to write a book, Christopher?"

"Six months." Three of which were spent on research and convincing myself I still had one more Miss Butterwith in me.

I stopped chewing. Where had that thought come from? That almost sounded like I was tired of writing Miss Butterwith, and of course I wasn't. I adored her. I adored Mr. Pinkerton. I adored Inspector Appleby—even if he was in the closet.

I finished chewing, swallowed the last bit of sticky walnut sandwich and reached for my teacup.

My expression must have been peculiar because Victoria asked even more meekly, "Do you use an outline?"

"Yes."

Poppy opened her mouth. I leveled an austere look her way, and she subsided.

For a couple of minutes we all applied ourselves to sipping and chewing, but eventually I got over my ire. If I was fair, a lot of this publishing stuff seems complicated and mysterious when you're on the outside of it. You hear horror stories about crooked agents and insolvent publishers and nefarious writing partners. A lot of misinformation floats around, not to mention flat-out misunderstanding, rumor and speculation.

"So tell me about this guy, Luke," I asked.

They turned to the change of topic in relief.

Poppy laughed. "What's to tell? He's sex on legs."

Nella's cheeks went rosy again. I suspected that explained the awkwardness of her sex scenes.

Victoria said, "Now there's a story."

"Really? What is it?"

"He's an ex-con." That was Poppy.

I managed to drain my cup of Earl Grey without spilling a drop. "What was he convicted of?"

"Armed robbery," Poppy answered.

Victoria objected, "I heard it was assault and battery."

"I heard it was vehicular manslaughter." Nella reached for another frosted cake.

"Are you sure you're talking about the same guy?"

"Whatever it was," Victoria said, "Anna heard about his

case and worked to get him out on parole. I guess the evidence used to convict him was pretty shaky, and that factored into his being released early."

"Interesting. And you think they're having some kind of relationship?" I did my best to look innocent and inquiring.

Victoria's expression was uncomfortable. Poppy, however, could always be relied on. "If you ever see them together, you'll know it in a minute."

I could see Nella was about to protest. I cut her off. "How long has he worked for Anna?"

"It's been a couple of years now," Victoria said. "She hired him before she and Todd divorced. I think it was part of the condition of Luke's parole."

I returned lightly, "That Anna get divorced?"

They all laughed, though uneasily. Victoria spoke. "That Anna offer Luke a job. I'm not sure how it works. But it seems to be successful." She looked at the other two for agreement. Poppy shrugged. Nella looked vague.

Having given up on finding a subtle way to introduce the subject, I joked, "Is Luke the one responsible for keeping the garden steps cleared of ice?"

Nella swallowed a bite of cake the wrong way and began to cough. Both Victoria and Poppy patted her on her back.

"That was *awful*," Victoria said. "I actually saw it happen."

"You did?" Poppy looked startled.

Nella was still spluttering and coughing. Poppy absently thumped her again.

Victoria explained to me, "I live in a cottage on the estate. In the woods. It's about a two-mile walk to the house. It's really pretty and I find it calms my mind to walk rather than drive sometimes. Anyway, that morning I'd strolled over to bring

Anna some rutabagas from my winter garden. I was cutting through the lower garden when I heard her scream." She shivered. "It was terrible. I thought...I don't know what I thought. That she'd been attacked. She sounded like she was being murdered."

"It's amazing she hasn't been," Poppy muttered.

"So you actually did see her fall?"

Victoria nodded. "That is to say, I saw her roll to the bottom of the steps. I ran to her and saw that she was conscious. I told her to lie still and then I ran up the stairs to sound the alarm. Luke had heard her scream too, and he was already on his way down."

"That's why you should carry a cell phone," Poppy told her.

Victoria made a face. "I hate the damn things."

I considered her story. "Did Anna say anything when you found her?"

"Just that she'd slipped on the ice. She was in a lot of pain as you can imagine."

"Did Luke say anything?"

Victoria's brows drew together in an effort at recollection. "I think he asked what had happened. To tell you the truth, it's all kind of a jumble. I was so shocked."

"Could you tell where she'd slipped?"

"Look at you making like Miss Butternut." Poppy seemed tickled.

"Butter*with*."

"Same difference."

Why was I wasting my breath? I turned to Victoria who said apologetically, "I didn't notice. I was only thinking about getting help as fast as possible."

Nella said, "We should be getting back or we're going to be late."

Her shuttered expression caught my attention. Generally her face was as open and guileless as a little kid's.

"They can't start without us," Poppy replied, reaching for the last blue iced cake. "We're holding the teacher captive."

Next came the inevitable tussle over the bill. I was prepared to pay for everyone's lunch. I had some vague idea that this was what Anna had done back in my day, but to my surprise Poppy graciously insisted on picking up the check.

"Don't worry about it." She brushed aside my thanks. "My old man left me a big fat insurance policy when he kicked off."

I recalled that her spouse had died in a drowning accident. I wondered if anyone had thought to investigate possible suicide.

The bill paid, we trudged out into the elements once more. It was starting to sleet as we piled back into Poppy's battered Mercedes.

"Victoria's the tallest. She should sit in front," Poppy said when Victoria tried to offer me the copilot position. Victoria looked apologetic, but I was only too happy to yield to her. I squeezed in the backseat with Nella and we had a moment of awkwardness as I had to ask her to shift so that I could find the other half of my seat belt. Having driven into town with Poppy, no way was I risking the return trip without buckling up.

As we left the parking lot and hit the slushy, crowded streets, Nella said softly, "I'd like to send you my manuscript."

"Sure."

"How much do you earn per book, Chris?" Poppy questioned.

"Not enough."

"But you get an advance, right?"

Less at Millbrook House than I was used to receiving from Wheaton & Woodhouse, but beggars can't be choosers. Not that I liked to think of myself as standing at the transom, cap in hand, but for a while there that had been uncomfortably close to the truth.

"Yes."

"And do you have to pay that back if you don't sell all the books they print?"

"Sell through my print run? No. The only way you pay back an advance is if you don't deliver the book or the deal falls through for some reason."

Nella asked, "Can you live on an advance?"

"If you're willing to give up eating." Realizing that I was being a bad author ambassador, I amended, "It depends on the size of the advance and where—and how—you live. I have a large backlist by now, so I earn significant royalties. My advances tide me over between royalty checks."

"I'll say you have a lot of books," Poppy commented. "I don't know how you keep them straight. The book-jacket blurbs all sound the same."

I sighed and gazed out the window at the picture-postcard landscape gliding past. I was already starting to feel queasy thanks to the walnut-paste sandwiches. Poppy's driving wasn't helping. We don't do a lot of traveling through snow in Southern California, and I don't like being a passenger under the best of circumstances. And finding myself as Poppy's passenger was not the best of circumstances. She had a habit of frequently taking her eyes off the road to converse with Victoria—or even me and Nella in the backseat.

We left Nitchfield in the soft and snowy distance, and Poppy shifted into high gear as the road opened up before us.

The other three chattered about people unknown to me, and I tuned out, watching the dark ragged outline of pines, ice-limned chestnut and maple trees, the occasional tall stalk of grass poking through the blanket of snow.

There was scant traffic and the highway was mostly empty, though snow lined the shoulders in tall drifts. I could see glimpses of a frozen lake or reservoir over the top of the ice wall.

I was thinking that there was a very good chance that Anna had simply slipped on the icy steps. If Victoria had gone up the stairway immediately after, there couldn't have been anything obviously wrong with the stairs or she would have fallen too.

That didn't explain those other near misses, though.

"How long did it take you to be able to support yourself with your writing?" Nella asked me.

I turned to answer her—and so did Poppy.

The car swerved slightly, the tires failed to grab and we slid sideways. There were gasps all around, me included. Poppy instinctively slammed on the brakes, and we began to skid in horrifying earnest.

Victoria screamed. Nella cried out as Poppy wrenched the wheel against the skid. The fishtailing rear end of the Mercedes pitched violently away in the opposite direction, and now we were spinning, spinning like a top across the black and shining road. The trees and frozen hills went whirling by, the white wall of snow loomed up and we crashed into it.

Crashed into it—and ploughed right through.

The three women were screaming as we sailed out into empty air. For a moment we seemed to hang in the nothingness. Clumps of snow slid down the windshield and then blew away as we smashed down the hillside.

Chapter Eight

The next time I opened my eyes I was being whooshed along in a wheelbarrow. A crowd of excited gardeners surrounded me, shouting confusing questions.

That was...odd.

I ignored the hollow, booming voices, and stared up past the hovering green pajamas and smocks to the white ceiling and light panels skimming swiftly past like train tracks.

Train tracks? No. That wasn't it...

"Can you hear me, Mr. Holmes?" one of the gardeners yelled in my ear. Loud, annoying man.

No. Not a gardener. And not a wheelbarrow, although it was uncomfortable enough for one. A trolley of some kind...

"Are you allergic to any medications?"

No mistaking that sickly, antiseptic smell. I was in a hospital. Why?

What had happened to me?

The doctors or nurses or ambulance attendants—who *were* all these people?—continued to propel the gurney along, yelling tiring, silly questions.

"I'm allergic to cantaloupe." It seemed important that they understand this. "Maybe honeydew."

Perhaps they *were* gardeners because someone pinched

me. Hard. I objected forcibly, and then, suddenly, it didn't matter. I was gliding along and everything was pleasantly quiet once more.

I closed my eyes.

I didn't think I lost consciousness—I would have sworn I didn't—but all at once it was very bright and very noisy. I was so *tired* and it seemed to me that quite a long time had passed, yet there was only a blur where my recent memories should be. That worried me because there was something I should be remembering, something I urgently needed to tell someone.

What?

I said, "The pumpkin soup was very good."

A voice murmured in reply.

No, it couldn't be that because we were all agreed on that. And then I remembered the important thing I'd been waiting to tell someone.

"I want to talk to J.X."

The voice sounded like it was hushing me.

I persisted anyway. It had been on my mind and my sense of being wronged was strong. "It wasn't fair. He didn't give me a chance to explain."

I couldn't tell if the voice responded or not, but I was relieved to have that off my chest. Now I could sleep.

I closed my eyes.

"Christopher, darling, I'm so goddamned sorry," Anna said when she came to see me Saturday morning.

By then I was back in my right mind—if you could call it that—though still stuck in the hospital with a broken collarbone, a mild concussion and a wildly colorful assortment of bruises and contusions. None of which was making nearly

81

the impression on me they should have thanks to a blessedly generous dose of painkillers.

I made another try for the cup of water next to my bed, and this time I managed to snag it. I said around the straw, "The accident wasn't your fault."

I wasn't even sure it was Poppy's fault, terrible driver though she was. Anyone could have hit a patch of black ice—which was apparently what had happened to us. Admittedly, my recollection of the accident itself was vague. According to what I'd been told, we'd hit the ice, spun out and gone over the side of the embankment. The car had turned over twice before coming to a stop a few yards from the reservoir.

Anna took the chair by the hospital bed. She was using crutches—using them expertly, as a matter of fact. But she was obviously in pain.

As no doubt would I be once I came down from the chemical cocktail I'd been served with my cold breakfast. I was being kept over one more night because of the surgery on my clavicle. Apparently when the paramedics had reached us, the bone had been sticking through the skin—which I was delighted to have missed seeing. The surgery was relatively minor, but when it's your body being operated on, it always feels like a big deal.

"I can't help feeling..." Anna stopped. I managed to replace my cup on the bed cabinet—my spatial perception seemed off—and regarded her more closely. She looked dreadful. The only color in her face was her red-rimmed eyes and her red nose. For the first time in all the years I'd known her, she looked old.

"What can't you help feeling?"

Her mouth trembled.

Cold apprehension coiled through my gut. "How *are* the others, Anna? No one around here will tell me anything."

Her face worked. She sucked in a long, wavering breath. "I shouldn't— You should be resting, Christopher."

"I *am* resting. I'm lying right here resting." I gestured impatiently to my blanketed legs and feet. My mouth was dry again, but it wasn't the medications this time. "What is it you aren't telling me?"

It took her a moment. "Like you, Victoria was wearing her seat belt. She got off with some cuts and scratches. Poppy has a broken nose, a broken leg, fractured ribs, some cuts and lacerations. Nothing that won't heal. Nothing that bitch doesn't deserve."

That shocked even me. "Anna."

Color flooded her bone-white face. "She's a goddamned catastrophe on the road, and we all knew it. How many times did we all laugh about her fucking fender-benders and near misses? I should have warned you not to get in a car with her. I should have warned you *both—*"

The coil of nerves and worry in my gut twisted into something more like the Gordian knot. "How's Nella?" I made myself ask.

Anna tried to speak and had to stop as she struggled with tears.

"Oh God," someone said faintly. I realized it was me.

Anna managed at last, "Nella wasn't wearing her seat belt. She was thrown forward and...and broke her neck."

"Wait a minute. You mean she's *dead*?"

Sometimes people survived breaking their necks, right? It didn't have to mean...but Anna's face told me it did.

"She died instantly."

I didn't know what to say. I kept thinking there had to be some kind of mistake. Something we could do over. The idea that the kid was *dead*...

Just like that? From alive to not in a matter of seconds? All that enthusiasm and energy and excitement. All those hopes and dreams and aspirations. All the stories she would never have the chance to tell.

"I can't believe it." People always said that, didn't they? And yet if there was one certainty in this life, it was that we would all die. But when it happened to someone so young...when there was no warning. Humans were so fragile. So easily broken.

Watching Anna, indomitable Anna, struggle not to cry, I said, "I'm sorry. I know you cared about her."

"I'm an old fool," Anna said, wiping her eyes. "I told myself I wasn't going to do this. Especially with you. Christ knows you've been through enough."

I waved that away. My hand hit the bed railings. Yes, my perspective was definitely off.

"I've never thought of myself as the sentimental type. I never wanted children. But to see such promise...lost. Such a bright light extinguished."

"I'm sorry, Anna." It seemed to be all I could come up with. I was still having trouble taking it in.

She wiped at the tears with the heels of her hands and cursed quietly.

Out of the corner of my eye, I noticed someone had paused on their way into this private room. This private room that Anna was insisting on paying for. I glanced over, expecting to see another nurse bearing more chemical relief or the ever-efficient Sara waiting to take charge of her mistress.

J.X. stood framed in the doorway.

J.X.

Not a dream. Not a mirage. J.X. Tall, spare and, um, supple

in boots, jeans, and a Nordic blue Eddie Bauer parka. His dark hair was a little longer than I remembered it and matched with the perfectly groomed Van Dyke mustache and beard, it made him look like one of those dashing young explorers of days gone by.

"I'm sorry to interrupt," he said awkwardly, taking in the bedside tableau.

Blame it on the pharmaceutical companies, but I heard myself make a choked noise. I sat bolt upright, ignoring the pain flashing through arm, shoulder, ribs, back and butt as I stretched my arms out to him like the final frame in a cheesy medical drama.

But it wasn't cheesy. It was just...Jesus, I was happy to see him. I can't remember ever being so happy, so grateful to see someone. Someone I'd been afraid I was never going to see again.

J.X. reached the bed in three steps, but then he sort of hovered as though not sure how to hug me without doing damage. I wasn't having any of that. I wrapped my arms around him and as much as it hurt—and it did hurt plenty—it was nothing to the pleasure of being in his arms once more.

"Jesus, Kit." His husky voice, warm against my ear, sounded shaken, unfamiliar. "What the hell have you done to yourself?"

I could feel him trying to be careful of the various bandages and IVs, but then his mouth found mine and I think he forgot all about my weakened condition. I responded to that fierce gentleness to the best of my bruised and battered ability. I'd have had to be comatose not to respond to J.X.'s kisses.

Spots were dancing before my vision when he finally raised his head. His long-lashed dark eyes regarded me with emotion. "You look like a goddamned train wreck." He sounded winded and angry.

"You should see the other train." Then I remembered how really not funny the situation was. My glance fell on Anna who had got to her feet with the speed of a much-younger woman. She was leaning on her crutches, studying J.X. with open surprise.

"J.X., this is Anna. Anna, J.X. Moriarity."

"We met at Left Coast Crime about two years ago," J.X. said. Even distracted he had very nice manners. When he chose.

"I remember." Anna shifted her crutches. "I didn't realize—"

"Neither did I." I dropped back against the pillow, reluctant to let go of J.X. for even the length of time it would take him to shake Anna's. Jeez. What was wrong with me? I'd never been one of these sloppy, sentimental types. It was just...I was so happy to see him. So touched that he'd done this—flown clear across country to yell at me in my hour of need.

He was gazing down at me again with that flattering mixture of worry and aggravation. There were lines of weariness in his face and shadows beneath his eyes as though he hadn't slept in a while. "Is there a part of you that isn't black and blue?"

"My eyelids?"

"No. You've got a black eye."

"My mouth?"

"I'll leave you two alone," Anna interrupted when it looked like J.X.'s inspection might turn interesting. "Christopher, darling, the police will want to question you about the accident when you're feeling stronger."

I nodded. "I don't remember much of anything after we got in the car."

"I'll ring you this evening. Lovely to meet you again, J.X." Her smile was a brave effort.

J.X. made some distracted reply, and before I could think of what to say to her, Anna crutched her way out of the room. I'm ashamed to say I'd forgotten her before she was through the doorway. All my focus was on J.X.

He leaned over the bed railing again. He smelled pretty much like you'd expect from a guy who'd been traveling all night, but on him it was wonderful. Mixed with it was a hint of the John Varvatos fragrance I now associated with him: leather, tamarind leaves and auramber. His hands were cold as he brushed his knuckles against my cheekbone, a touch as light as a feather. Even so, I winced.

He said softly, admiringly, "That is one hell of a shiner."

"Color coordinated to match my hallucinations. Are you sure you're really here?"

"I'm sure." He leaned down. I closed my eyes as his lips delicately nuzzled my eyelids.

Eyes closed, I murmured, "Are you kissing it better?"

"Am I?"

"I think so. My lips hurt too."

He was smiling as he kissed me again, still restrained and tender, but with a hint of better things to come.

Abruptly he drew back. When I dragged open my eyes, it was to find his black with emotion.

"What is it?"

"Kit..." His Adam's apple moved as he swallowed.

"What's wrong?" Startled, I realized what was wrong. "It's okay. I'm okay." I watched in fascination as J.X.'s chiseled nostrils flared. He clenched his strong jaw. Yep, he was pretty worked up in his manly way and I was probably a dork to feel so pleased about it, but there's no denying that there's a certain appeal in knowing it would really ruin that special someone's day if you checked out early.

"When I got that call—"

In the middle of my smile, I yawned. For all the sleeping I'd already done, all at once I was so tired I could hardly keep my eyes open.

"I'm glad they called you."

"I'm glad you told them to call," he replied with quiet intensity.

Had I? If I had, it had been post op when I was out of my skull on painkillers. I nearly volunteered that unneeded info but had the wits to shut up in time. What did it matter how he'd got here? I *had* wanted him, and the only thing that mattered now was he was here.

Instead, I asked, "Did they tell you what happened?"

He nodded, looking somber. Yeah. Of course they had. Poor Nella. Poor kid. Another wave of lassitude swept over me, and this time it seemed to knock the legs right out from under me. Poor Anna. So far I hadn't been much help to her.

My fatigue must have showed. J.X. lightly touched my face again. "You look beat, honey. Why don't you sleep," he said softly.

Honey. That was nice. He'd never called me that before. Not that I'd ever encouraged the use of pet names. But for now...it was nice. I gave him a spacey smile, let my eyelashes fall shut and mumbled, "I hope you're not a dream."

He was not a dream. J.X. was sitting beside the bed the next time I opened my eyes. He was reading the latest Miss Butterwith, *The Moving Finger Writes for Miss Butterwith,* and frowning disapprovingly.

I sighed inwardly. Not that I wasn't glad to see that one of us was feeling better. He looked disgustingly refreshed for someone who had traveled cross country, and if he was back to criticizing my work, things were rapidly returning to normal.

At the rustle of sheets, his head jerked my way. He tossed the book aside—a bit too forcefully in my opinion—and rose to lean over the bed again.

"Hi. How are you feeling?"

"Like someone threw me over a cliff. What time is it?"

He glanced at his watch. "A couple of minutes after one."

"In the *afternoon*?"

He nodded.

"Jeez. You shouldn't have let me sleep." I sat up incautiously, gulped, and lay back, breathing hard.

"You have big plans, do you?" J.X.'s voice inquired from somewhere overhead.

I opened my eyes and scowled at him. "That fucking hurt."

"I bet." He casually brushed the hair out of my eyes. "Do you remember the accident at all?"

It was sort of ridiculous how good even that casual touch felt. Like my hair had nerve endings; I could feel him to my roots. That hyper-receptivity was probably due to the years of sensory deprivation that had passed for my marriage.

I realized I still hadn't answered his question. "Not really. I was talking to Nella in the backseat, that much I recall."

"Nella is the woman who died?"

"She was really just a kid. Maybe twenty or so." I swallowed hard, remembering. "God."

"Sorry, Kit." He said it gently, seriously. I regarded him

curiously. I never thought of him as particularly sensitive. My young, tough ex-cop. Maybe I didn't give him many opportunities for softness.

I was contemplating this new idea when he said, "They're letting you out of here tomorrow morning. What do you want to do?"

"Do?"

"If you feel well enough to travel, do you want me to see whether I can get you on an earlier flight? Originally you weren't leaving until Tuesday, right?"

"Right." And now I remembered why Anna had wanted me to stay that extra couple of days. Everything I'd conveniently forgotten came rushing back: like the real reason she'd dragged me out here to the Berkshires.

For all the good it had done.

A dreadful thought struck me. Wasn't this car accident *too* convenient? After all, Anna had had a close call a few weeks earlier when the brakes of her Mercedes had failed. Could someone have mixed the cars up?

No. That was unlikely. Not only was Poppy's Mercedes thoroughly thrashed, she had parked along the drive to the house. Anna's car would of course be in the garage. Even the stupidest would-be murderer had to know that much.

Right?

But I *had* seen someone suspicious wandering around the grounds the night before.

At least...post-midnight solo strolls seemed suspicious to me.

Even acknowledging that Anna couldn't have been the target this time—at least directly—wasn't this still a big coincidence? The accident had happened after leaving the

Asquith Estate, and Anna's own protégé had been killed.

"What's wrong?" J.X. asked, watching me closely.

I looked up at him uncertainly. "I don't think I can leave yet."

"Why?"

"Because...well, it's kind of a long story."

His face set in that mulish look he gets sometimes. Intractability was one of his less charming traits, although I bet it had made him a good cop.

"Anyway," I said, hoping to change the subject. "It'll wait. You haven't said how your trip was." I tried to turn it into a question.

"Kit." I'd known that solicitousness was too good to last. "Start talking."

Chapter Nine

"Aren't I supposed to get one phone call?"

"Quit stalling."

I quit stalling.

"So to recap," J.X. said when I'd finished relating everything Anna had told me when I arrived at the Asquith Estate, "your kindly old mentor, who sounds even loopier than you, dragged you back here in the dead of winter so you could play amateur sleuth?"

I could feel myself getting irritated, even though I knew he was right. "She's afraid for her life."

"Then she should go to the police."

"With what proof? Any one of those attempts could have been an accident."

"That's exactly right. And that's almost certainly what they were."

"Oh come on. What about the law of coincidence? What about the shadowy figure I saw wandering around the night before?"

"Kit." I could see him struggling for a tactful way to say it. "This sounds like something you'd write."

He should have kept struggling.

"Oh. Right. This from the grand master of the Bang Bang,

You're Dead school of crime fiction."

J.X. reddened. "Look. All I'm saying is, this sounds farfetched."

"Yes," I said huffily. "I understand *exactly* what you were saying. I'm a hack and you're the real deal."

"I didn't say that."

"You didn't have to."

"I'm not talking about that at all. Where is this coming from?" He seemed genuinely bewildered. But then he was thirty-something and still at the top of his game. The critics loved him and everything he wrote shot straight to the top of the bestseller lists—*all* the bestseller lists. In the last year alone three of his books had been optioned for film.

It was coming from jealousy and frustration and bitterness. It was coming from the heart of darkness. The same heart that yearned for him even while resenting him and his condescending attitude. And if that wasn't a recipe for romantic disaster, I didn't know what was.

Even so, my own aggression—not to mention my lack of timing—caught me off-guard. Maybe it was the meds I was being fed, but without warning it was all pouring out. "Look. We both know what you think of my writing. You think I write the equivalent of literary junk food. Brain lint. Disposable fluff."

"That is *not* what I'm saying." J.X. was so vehement I *knew* I was right. "I did *not* say that. I have never *once* said that."

"Yeah, you did, actually. When we were stranded in Northern California. You said I cranked them out in my sleep and that I'd been doing it for years."

I knew by the flicker of his eyes I'd cornered him. Not that it gave me any pleasure. I was startled at the painful accuracy of that particular memory. I don't think I'd accepted how much it hurt until this very moment.

"Anyway, whether you said it in so many words or not, you certainly think I'm a hack."

He stopped wasting time trying to defend the indefensible and went on the attack. "I don't think you're a hack. I think you're afraid to write anything that challenges you or that means anything to you."

"As opposed to you and your high-octane literary masterpieces about the straight, gun-toting Inspector Dirk Van de Meer?"

J.X. bit out each word very quietly. "You're a better writer than I am, Kit. You should be doing more with that gift. Instead, you're hiding behind Miss Busybody's skirts."

It was my turn for a red face. Not that he could tell beneath all the bruises, fortunately.

"Anyway," J.X. said, while I was still trying to come up with a response. "Like I keep trying to tell you, that wasn't what I meant. What I meant was, if someone really wants Anna dead, it wouldn't be that hard to arrange. They wouldn't have to go to all these elaborate lengths of icy steps and food poisoning and pushing flower urns off rooftops."

He paused to give me a chance to respond.

The choice was mine. We could continue to quarrel over what couldn't be changed or we could move on to a relatively neutral topic. I took a deep breath and let it out. "Clearly this person needs it to look like an accident."

Imperceptibly, the tension eased in J.X.'s frame. "There are easier ways to do it and simpler accidents to arrange."

He had a point. I was wondering myself why someone hadn't simply conked Anna over the head with the nearest rock. Maybe this person or persons unknown didn't intend murder.

Maybe they were trying to frighten Anna. But to what end?

With his disconcerting knack for reading my mind, J.X. said, "Are you absolutely convinced someone really is trying to kill her?"

"No," I admitted. "I also agree that it all sounds unlikely. Someone might be trying to give her a scare, but that seems pretty abstract. And equally contrived."

"It doesn't happen like this in real life."

"Hey, I watch *Snapped*. Truth is stranger than fiction. Look at that guy on the Food Network."

But it seemed J.X. didn't want to look at the Calorie Commando and his attempt to hire homeless hit men. "How stable is Anna?"

"*Stable?* What kind of a question is that? How stable is anyone? Being human is an unstable condition. Has she officially been diagnosed as nutso? Not that I'm aware."

"I mean, is she prone to exaggerate or dramatize?"

"No."

He looked skeptical.

"Well, she's a writer. Exaggeration is part of her job description. But not the way you mean, no. I don't think so, anyway. I know it's been a few years, but Anna always seemed pretty hardheaded to me. I don't think she's someone who's easily scared. I don't think she's someone who jumps at shadows. Is she a dramatic personality? Yes, I guess she is. She's used to being a media darling—as much as any writer can be."

"Okay, don't get so worked up. I'm only trying to narrow the possibilities."

"Fine, but whatever the possibilities are, I can tell you right now I can't abandon Anna. Not after what's happened. She asked for my help." Not something that happened to me very often, and I felt obliged to take it seriously.

"Kit, you're not in any shape to help anyone right now."

That was certainly true. I felt like shit. And, worse, I apparently looked like shit. Which made me feel worse. It was a vicious cycle.

"And you're going to feel worse when they let you out of here," Mr. Helpful couldn't help adding.

I asked irritably, "Aren't you supposed to be trying to cheer me up?"

J.X. had the grace to look sheepish, but he said, "I've had a dislocated shoulder before. I know how much fun that is. Never mind all the rest of it."

"Yeah, whatever. Word. Next time you ride *ventre à terre* to my death bed, you could at least bring me grapes."

I was kidding, naturally. Trying to, anyway. I don't even like grapes. But J.X. said seriously, "I was in a hurry to get to you."

That sincerity threw me off my stride. It seemed to require reciprocal honesty, but that's something I'm really bad at.

I said instead, "Anna asked for my help. If she still wants it, I'm going back to the estate."

"The seminar is over. What is it you think you're going to do? You're not exactly in shape to act as her bodyguard."

Let's face it. I've never been in shape to act as anyone's bodyguard. And there are fewer things I'd be less inclined to try. J.X. on the other hand...

I eyed him speculatively. "Since I'm laid up here for the time being, could you do me a favor?"

"Yes." He said it so gravely, looking right into my eyes—and this despite our recent spat—I felt a fluttering sensation in my belly.

"Could you trade on your cop pedigree and find out whether the police are investigating this accident as an accident?"

He hesitated. That was a given. J.X. was not impulsive.

"What I mean is, can you drop a word in the right ear, or an elbow in the ribs, or whatever it is brother law enforcement does, and suggest that they look closely? More closely. That they make double sure that it *was* an accident?"

"Yes. I will do that for you," he said like he was making a formal promise. It lifted an unexpected weight off me. Whatever J.X. thought, I knew that I could rely on him. If he said he was going to do something, he was going to do it, and to the best of his ability—or die trying. Believe what you will about tight abs and dark-as-midnight eyes, there's a lot to be said for reliability. To find them all in one package...well, perhaps better not to dwell on his package in my fragile state.

Not long after J.X. departed on his mission of mercy, I rang for a nurse and asked after Poppy. I wasn't sure she had been admitted to the same hospital as me, but I was informed that she was, in fact, conveniently located downstairs next to the frozen-foods aisle. Which is still better than *being* a frozen food.

One problem down. The next quandary was what did one inmate wear to visit another? I felt my backless ensemble was a trifle informal for the occasion, so it was a relief to find that Anna had brought a few essentials with her when she'd stopped by.

The effort of getting dressed—well, that was an exaggeration right there. The effort of pulling on my bathrobe nearly sent me whimpering back to bed on jellied legs. There was the problem of the IV too, which meant I had to drape my robe more or less toga style so as not to come undone.

Anyone who wasn't half-stoned on pain meds would have instantly realized what a really bad idea this plan was, but since that didn't include me, I didn't worry about it.

Off I sallied, dragging the IV stand rattling after me. I got some peculiar looks from staff and visitors alike, but no one challenged me, which is a statement as to what an air of confidence will do. Or how truly scary crazy people are.

Eventually I found Poppy sharing a room with a tiny Asian lady and her mob of equally petite relations. It was like a gathering of *yousei*. I determinedly weaved my way through the crowd, hauling my medical apparatus behind me like my little red wagon.

Poppy was lying in the bed staring bleakly up at the ceiling. She looked more bruised and battered than me, which is always a comfort. Her nose was taped up and her leg was in a cast.

"Hi."

Her gaze dropped to mine. Her eyes widened. "Hi." She sounded muffled due to the taping of her nose. "What the hell happened to you?"

"The same thing that happened to you."

"I mean..." She fell silent as I lowered myself painfully to the only available seating not taken up by the grandmotherly lady's family—a small chest of drawers beneath a mounted TV set.

"How are you feeling?" I asked.

"Like shit."

I nodded feelingly.

"You broke your arm?"

"Collarbone. Apparently I dislocated my shoulder too, but I can't tell one from the other."

"Oh. Are you supposed to be up and walking around?"

"No one told me I couldn't."

She seemed to think that one over and then abandon it as another thought struck. "I guess I should tell you how sorry I am you were injured."

I shrugged—or tried to. Either way, it was a really bad idea.

In the distance, I heard Poppy say, "Anyway, I *am* sorry and I hope you forgive me. But what I'd really like to know is, are you planning to sue me?"

"I hadn't thought about it." I steadied myself on the IV stand, but since it had wheels, I nearly pitched off the chest of drawers. That hurt too. A lot.

I tried to remember why it had been so urgent I get down to see Poppy that afternoon.

"Probably not," I managed, once I'd regained my balance. "It's not like you were drunk or criminally negligent."

"No, I'm just a lousy driver."

What could I say to that? She *was* a lousy driver and we'd all paid the price—unless by some chance that accident had not been an accident.

She watched me, her brows drawing together. "Are you sure you're okay?"

"Why do you ask?"

"Erm...you seem kind of..."

How could she hope to be a writer when she had problems formulating the simplest thoughts? I tried to get the conversation back on track. "Do you remember what happened? I don't."

This seemed to be familiar ground. "I explained it to the police. I hit a patch of ice. Black ice. The car spun out—and kept spinning. I couldn't get it back under control and we went over the edge of the embankment." She closed her eyes. "My airbag went off. That's the last thing I remember."

That was more than I remembered. That wasn't unusual with concussion, but it was weird to have that gap.

"Did the car seem...I don't know. Did the car seem all right?"

She opened her eyes, the only color in her waxen face. "What do you mean?"

"Just that. Did the car seem okay? The brakes and everything?"

"It happened so fast." Poppy thought it over. "I don't think there was anything wrong with the car."

Would she necessarily know?

Into the silence that fell between us I could hear the grandmotherly lady complaining in what sounded like Japanese and the muted sounds of a busy hospital afternoon: the rattle of carts, the beep of monitors, suspiciously calm voices over the intercom. My shoulder was hurting. My ribs were hurting. My head was hurting. I wanted to go back to bed. As soon as I got the energy to stand up again.

Poppy said, "Nella's mother is suing me. Anna's helping her. She told me herself when she was here earlier."

And I'd thought J.X.'s bedside manner needed some work. What was there to say to that? Anna's anger at Poppy had taken me aback that morning, but I could understand that her feelings would be different from my own. She'd lost someone she loved. I didn't think Anna had many people to love.

Since some response seemed to be required, I said, "Maybe they'll see things differently later on." That was about as much comfort as I could offer.

Her smile was bitter. "If you think Anna will change her mind, you don't know Anna."

"*Mr. Holmes*, what on earth are you doing down here?" demanded a scandalized voice.

Both Poppy and I jumped. The IV stand rolled and once again I had to fumble for it while not managing to overbalance.

A formidable-looking nurse stood in the doorway, the grandmotherly lady's family parting before her like the Red Sea before Moses. Grandma Moses in her case.

"Oh. I—" I began guiltily.

She didn't give me a chance. "You need to return to bed *at once*." She advanced on me.

By the time I shuffled back to my own room, Nurse Hellhound nipping at my heels, I found a youthful and very handsome state police trooper waiting for me.

His eyes popped when I clattered through the doorway like Jacob Marley lugging his chains—I may even have been moaning—and he jumped to his feet.

"What on *earth* could you have been thinking?" Nurse Hellbound demanded, still in hot pursuit.

After two floors of it, I knew the question was rhetorical, and I wouldn't have bothered to answer even if I'd had breath. Which I hadn't.

I nodded to the trooper, dropped my robe on the floor and crawled awkwardly into bed.

There were loud gasps behind me, but I was preoccupied with not detaching any vital equipment, my own or the hospital's. I lowered myself slowly, carefully, to the spinning bed of nails they supply to all the patients they hate and closed my eyes.

"...Trooper Scott's questions?" Hellsound was asking when I tuned back in after the commercial break.

I pried open my lashes and took in Trooper Scott's ruddy countenance.

"Do you feel able to answer a few questions, Mr. Holmes?" His eyes were doing a jittery sort of back and forth away from my face to my... *Was he checking me out?*

Weird.

"What do you want to know?" I asked.

"Anything you can remember about yesterday's accident."

Was it only yesterday? It seemed a lot longer ago than that.

Trooper Scott had a small pad and a sharp pencil. He licked the tip of the pencil, which was something I'd only seen people in cartoons do, and gazed at me inquiringly.

He was cute and I wanted to be helpful. I told him everything I remembered, which wasn't a whole hell of a lot. I suspect that even what there was, wasn't the most coherent recital I've given. There may have been a brief, acerbic side commentary on the lunchtime fare at the Tudor Teahouse, but I'm not sure.

Scott asked me a few questions, which seemed to literally go in one of my ears and out the other. I was having a lot of trouble focusing by then. I felt truly awful. Tired, sick, shaky, but I did my best to respond sensibly.

The interview was short, civil and clearly routine. The police believed Nella's death was simply another tragic traffic fatality. And maybe it was. Certainly Scott seemed startled when I asked if he'd considered that it might be anything but an accident.

"Why would you think that, sir?"

"I think it's too much of a coincidence."

He reminded me uncomfortably of J.X. as he said, "What does it coincide with?"

"Everything else that's happened."

"What else has happened?"

"The attempts on Anna's life."

"Who's Anna?"

"Anna."

"I think that's going to have to be all for now." Frau Blücher intervened, busily checking and reattaching the jumper cables.

Trooper Scott looked relieved. I could see him eying the clear fluid trickling into my veins from the sack o' fun hanging next to my bed.

"You get some rest, sir," he said kindly. On the way out, he added, "You sure were lucky."

"I hear you mooned a state trooper," J.X. cheerfully informed me when he returned.

I dropped my fork on my dinner tray.

"It's not nice to tease invalids," I said.

"It's not nice to tease state troopers either." He kissed me hello, lingering a little. "Mm. There's something about a man who tastes like Salisbury steak."

I leaned back against the sponge pancake they laughingly called a pillow and studied him. "You seem to be in a good mood."

J.X.'s face was creased in that oblique white smile that always made him look like a wicked Spanish grandee skulking behind an arras, but at my words, his smile faded. "I am. I saw the Clark woman's car."

"Oh."

His lean brown throat moved. "I don't know how you're not dead, Kit. Your part of the car smashed into a boulder and the side was crushed in like tin can."

My ribs twinged, and I shifted uncomfortably. "I'm happy to say I don't remember."

I couldn't seem to look away from those dark solemn eyes. I could see from J.X.'s expression how close it had been. Oddly enough, my uppermost thought was not that I would have been dead. It was that I'd never have seen J.X. again.

Not good. Not good to care this much.

To break the moment which was becoming awkward in its gravity, I gestured to the dinner tray. "Would you like some of this?"

He lifted an eyebrow at the remains of the day. "No thanks. I'll grab something later."

"I don't offer to share my lime Jell-O with just anyone, you know."

"I realize that. Beneath my stoic exterior I'm very moved."

He didn't look particularly stoic. His eyes were crinkling at the corners and his teeth were very white as he grinned at me. He looked...happy. My throat tightened in response. I didn't want that responsibility. I wasn't good at making people happy.

I cleared my throat. "So what did the cops say?"

"They said three of you were very lucky."

"Was the car tampered with?"

"No."

"Are you sure?"

"They are."

I insisted, "Are you sure they checked everything?"

"They checked. They double-checked after I spoke to them. It was an accident, Kit. The car hit a patch of black ice. Clark was going too fast, she jammed on the brakes and lost control of the wheel. It's that simple."

I absorbed this silently. It seemed like too much of a coincidence given Anna's close calls and the figure I'd seen prowling the estate the night before, but accidents *did* happen.

"Nobody tampered with the brakes? Nobody messed with the steering column?"

"Honey. No. It was just a terrible accident."

There it was again. *Honey.* What was up with that? I manfully swallowed my objection, mostly because I realized it had slipped out without J.X. noticing. Anyway, "honey" was what I'd heard him call his four-year-old nephew Gage when the kid had phoned crying on one of the weekends I'd stayed over. But it made me nervous. David and I had not gone in for lovey-doveys. I'd never thought of myself as anyone's honey. What was the expectation for someone's honey?

Instead, I said argumentatively, "It's too much of a coincidence."

J.X., however, declined to argue. He didn't say anything at all. I stared at him. "Don't you think?"

Finally, he said, "Are you determined to stay on here?"

I nodded, qualifying, "If Anna wants me to. I don't know that she will. She's grieving."

He seemed to be consulting some inner voice. I waited.

"Okay. Well, if you're staying, I'm staying too."

This was not a possibility I'd even considered. I wasn't sure what to say. All I came up with was a lame, "You don't have to."

"There's no way I'm leaving you on your own."

That sounded more parental than loverly, but I was still sort of touched. I felt that, at the least, I owed him honesty. I said, "The thing is, J.X." I drew a deep breath. "I'm...not very good at relationships."

"That's the understatement of the year."

All my good intentions evaporated. "I don't know that you're such an expert either."

Now why he should find that funny, I've no idea, but J.X. said way too gravely, "That's fair."

"What I'm trying to tell you is..." I stopped. The fact was I had no idea what I was trying to tell him.

J.X. said calmly, "You know what, Kit? I'm a big boy. I can look after myself. I know that right now the idea of a relationship paralyzes you. But I think you do care for me, or you wouldn't have had the hospital contact me when you were hurt, and I'm willing to hang in here for a while longer. You're worth it."

My heart was hammering as though I was having a panic attack. "What if I hadn't called you?"

"I don't know. I can't do this on my own, obviously. I wanted you to try and meet me halfway. Or as close to halfway as you could handle. That's what this feels like." He shrugged. "So we'll see how it goes. Either way, I'm not leaving you to play Lord Peter Wimsey on your own."

"My accent's all wrong."

"Among other things." But his smile seemed to be telling me all that was right. "So tell me about this lewd and lascivious behavior charge."

I eyed him suspiciously. "You better be kidding."

He laughed.

Chapter Ten

Anna called around eight o'clock that evening.

J.X. and I had been watching TV and holding hands. In the interests of accuracy, I'd been mostly dozing, but the point wasn't the attentive viewing of *COPS* (which J.X. criticized in an under-his-breath commentary), it was the hand holding. Just as I couldn't recall exchanging pet names with anyone before, I couldn't remember sitting around holding hands with anyone before. I'm not sure David and I ever held hands, other than to slip rings on each other's left fingers. For sure not in a serious, prolonged, clasped-hands, linked-fingers, old-fashioned-courtship kind of way.

It was...nice.

And alarming.

But mostly nice.

The phone shrilled next to the bed and I started out of a confused but pleasant dream where J.X. and I stood in an open snowy field making snow angels. I happened to land on top of him. His breath whooshed out on a warm laugh—

"It's okay," J.X. reassured from somewhere overhead.

My eyes jerked open. I watched him reaching with his free hand for the phone.

Anna, he mouthed to me. I blinked dopily at him. Wiped at

the snowflakes, er, sand in my eyes.

After a few polite words to Anna, J.X. handed the phone over. Pressed the button to raise the bed slightly. "Got it?"

I nodded and felt another flash of discomfort. Emotional, not physical. I wasn't used to anyone taking care of me, of caring *so much*. It had almost been easier when we'd been at loggerheads. At least I knew how to do that—and do it well.

"Christopher, darling." Anna's voice was her old, firm, crisp one. "How are you feeling?"

"Better. Good. Almost like new."

I glanced at J.X. He arched one skeptical eyebrow.

"Excellent. I know, after everything that's happened, I don't have any right to ask, but would you consider staying at the house for a few days while you recuperate?"

I'd told myself this was exactly what I planned to do, but now that the moment was here I felt an intense longing for home. For my own bed. For my own company. Though J.X. beside me whispering sweet nothings wouldn't come entirely amiss.

But how could I walk away? I'd told Anna I'd help. Was I going to back out because it turned out she really *did* need my help? I have my faults, but so far running out on my friends isn't one of them. Granted, keeping the number of my friends to a minimum helps.

I lowered the handset. "She's asking me to stay on for a few days."

"If you're staying, I'm staying." Uncompromising. It should have been annoying, but oddly enough I didn't mind. I picked up the handset again. "If you don't mind an extra houseguest. J.X. and I are flying home together."

There was a pause. Anna said smoothly, "Of course,

darling. It was obvious today that he's very much in your life. I hadn't realized before."

"Probably because I said there wasn't anyone."

"That might have had something to do with it."

"We had some problems." My eyes went automatically to J.X.'s. "We're trying to work them out."

"I'm glad," she said with her old warmth. "You deserve someone who appreciates you. David was always going to have an eye out for someone younger, handsomer and more exciting."

I knew what she meant, but it still stung. Especially since J.X. was that someone younger, handsomer and more exciting.

"True," I said.

"And of course J.X. is welcome. Did you tell him—?"

"I did, yeah. I don't know if you recall that he used to be a cop."

"Oh." Her voice changed. "No. I don't think I ever knew that."

I remembered how determined she'd been to keep the police out of it, and I decided I'd better come clean.

"Yeah, he gave it up for fame and fortune, but he used to swing the old blue lantern." I glanced at J.X. who shook his head resignedly. "Anyway, you're probably not going to like this, but I asked him to go trade on his former badge and find out from the local fuzz if there was any chance the accident wasn't an accident."

"But that's it," Anna exclaimed. "The more I think about it, the more convinced I am that it *can't* have been an accident."

"Well, but the thing is—"

"It's too much of a coincidence. The car *must* have been tampered with while it was parked on the estate."

"The police don't agree," I interrupted before Anna got too carried away with her theory. Granted, it had been my theory too.

"But they're wrong. They must be. They're not looking carefully enough."

"I think they're looking pretty carefully, Anna. Especially after J.X. asked them to take a closer look." I sucked in a deep breath. "I think we're going to have to accept that it's merely a very tragic accident."

"I don't believe it."

I closed my eyes. I really didn't have the energy to fight her on this. "Okay. Maybe you're right. We can talk about it tomorrow."

She said in an urgent, shaking voice that revealed how much stress she was under, "Christopher, *please* believe me. I'm not making this up. Someone is trying to kill me."

I opened my eyes again. J.X. was frowning at me. "I do believe you."

"There was nothing wrong with that car," J.X. said.

I shook my head at him. I spoke to Anna. "I'll call you as soon as I'm officially released."

"Don't worry about that," she responded. "Just come. As soon as you can." The receiver clicked.

I handed the phone to J.X. "We're supposed to drive out there as soon as I'm released."

"Don't get sucked into her paranoia."

"Look, if you're going to dismiss her as a nut job, you might as well go home."

"I'm not staying for her. I'm staying for *you.*"

I sniffed disapprovingly, but really...it was hard to maintain appropriate levels of aggravation if he was going to say things like that.

Being J.X. he couldn't let it go. "Think about it. What would be the point of sabotaging someone else's car? Was there a chance in hell Anna was going to climb in that vehicle?"

"No."

"No. So the dumbest criminal on the planet would know he had nothing to gain. I agree it's an odd coincidence, but the fact that this woman with a history of bad driving had an accident on a dangerous road during poor weather conditions isn't that amazing."

"Agreed. But Anna's frightened. And she's grieving."

"I get that."

"Just...tone down the skepticism around her, okay? Because regardless of what you think, something *is* wrong at that house."

He was silent.

"I can't explain it, but all the time I was there I felt an undercurrent. I'm not explaining it well, but if I felt it, it's there." We both knew what I meant: that my unease was significant not because I was especially sensitive, but because of the exact opposite.

"You're really fond of her."

I forgot and shrugged. When I got my breath back, I said, "Yes. She's a big part of why I have a writing career. Such as it is. I owe her."

"That's good enough for me. We'll do what we can for her."

I admit that it wasn't easy climbing into J.X.'s rental car the next morning.

In fact, if it had been anyone but J.X. driving, I'm not sure I could have done it, but the idea of letting him know how

111

freaked I was, combined with the fact that I really did believe he was a very good driver, gave me the necessary backbone.

Even so, I wasn't sure I would be able to ever ride in a backseat again. My hands were ice cold as I buckled the seat belt, and that was nothing to do with the new snow drifting lazily down.

I thought I was hiding my tension pretty well as we left the city and headed out into the scenic hills and valleys of the Berkshires, but J.X. glanced over at me and said, "Okay?"

"Fine."

"If you want me to pull over, say the word."

What word would that be? *Mommy?*

"No. I'm fine." If I kept telling myself so, it was bound to eventually be true.

I was grateful that he left it there. Too much sympathy was going to make it harder. The white fields and dark woods flashed by as we drove.

The previous driver of the rental car had left a CD in the player. Jack Johnson's *To the Sea*. About as far from Connecticut as you could get. I focused on Johnson's laid-back tunes of sand and sea.

Eventually the landscape began to look familiar, and I knew we were coming up on the site of the accident. My stomach began to bubble unpleasantly like overcooked Cream of Wheat.

The car slowed a fraction. J.X. said nothing, but I knew he was unobtrusively watching me. It only served to make me more tense.

Up ahead I could see the skid marks in the road, black quote marks standing out sharply against the dull pavement, a statement of disaster. Police tape marked where the car had crashed through the wall of snow along the embankment, and I could see the gray frozen lake beyond.

And then we were speeding past and the scene of the accident was growing smaller and smaller in the side mirror, until it was lost around the next curve in the road.

As we headed up the long drive to Asquith House we passed Luke riding along the side of the road on one of those snowblower tractor thingies. He eyed the car with a dark, unblinking gaze as we tooled past.

"There's someone it might be well worth checking out," I said.

"I'd just as soon not hear about other guys you want to check out."

"I don't mean check out as in check *out*, I mean check out as in run a background check. He's supposed to be romantically involved with Anna, but he's an ex-con of some kind. His name is Luke."

"What was Luke in for?"

"It's not exactly clear. I've heard three different stories. The only thing everyone seems to agree on is Anna managed to convince the parole board to release him early, and apparently one of the conditions of his release was that she provide him with employment."

J.X. raised his eyebrows but didn't comment.

"He's also a beneficiary of her will, although that's not saying a lot. Her will seems to include everyone on the planet."

"All right. I'll ask around." Meeting my gaze, he smiled wryly. "The sooner we figure out what's going on here with Anna, the sooner we can go home."

Home. It sounded nice the way he said it.

I said rashly, "I'll make it up to you."

"Could that be the pain meds talking?"

I studied his face. "Actually...no."

I wasn't sure, but I thought he might have blushed.

Chapter Eleven

I was obscurely pleased to see that even J.X. wasn't able to defrost Sara.

"How's Anna doing today?" I asked after the initial greetings were out of the way. I use the term "greeting" lightly. I didn't get the impression Sara was any more overjoyed to see us than I was to see her.

She hesitated. "At the moment, she's resting. I'm sure I don't have to tell you what a terrible shock this has been for her. She's not a young woman."

No, she didn't have to tell me. It had been a terrible shock for me too and I wasn't a young woman either. I refrained from saying so. I'd already noticed Sara wasn't much for funning, and my tendency to inappropriate humor was a nervous tic I was trying to break.

"Is anyone from the writing group still staying at the house?"

"No. They've all gone." She clarified almost immediately, "That is, Rudolph is still here. He's leaving Tuesday." She added without expression, "And Ricky's here."

"Who's Ricky?" There were some gaps in my memory, but I was pretty sure there hadn't been a Ricky taking part in the Asquith Circle.

"Richard Rosen. Anna's stepson." Though Sara's expression gave nothing away, I had the distinct impression she disapproved of Ricky. "Everyone else left yesterday. Victoria lives on the estate, of course."

Two miles from the house. Within walking distance. I did remember making a mental note of that.

"I don't think Ricky and I have met," I said.

"He's Miles's son. Anna's first husband."

I'd never met Miles Rosen, but I knew of him. He had been another mystery writer, best known for a very dry but award-winning series about a Midwestern school teacher. He'd died of cancer a couple of years after he and Anna had divorced.

Before I could come up with any further questions about stuff that was none of my business, Sara said, "You're in the same room. If you'd prefer other arrangements, I'll be happy to see to it."

"Why wouldn't the same room be all right?" I asked, puzzled.

Sara looked at me like I was an idiot. "I mean, per Anna's instructions, you're *both* in the same room." She looked pointedly at J.X.

"*Oh.* Right. Yes, same room is fine."

It was, wasn't it? J.X. had said nothing, but when I glanced at him, he nodded.

"Of course."

Of course. 'Coz we were going to do that relationship thing for real now. I tried not to gulp.

After that, I ran out of things to say. That was okay, because I felt surprisingly tired, even shaky as we made the long trek from front door to second floor. It was funny the way getting thrown upside down a few times and partially squashed could take it out of you.

We reached our room and Sara said, "I know you're still convalescing, Christopher, but Anna will want to see you when she wakes up."

"That's why we're here." I was trying to be team-spirited, but I saw from the quick look J.X. threw me that I was probably supposed to be more discreet.

Sara didn't seem to notice, however. "Dinner is at seven. As before."

"Thanks." I wanted her to go away so that I could shut the door and formally introduce J.X. to the monolith. His expression as he took in the velvet draperies and twirling grapevines was priceless.

"Let me know if you need anything," Sara said. Her tone was not encouraging.

I nodded and kept nodding until the door closed behind her. I slumped against it, letting my head fall back. Between the strain of the trip and a certain amount of reaction, I felt whipped.

I jumped as J.X.'s arms went around me.

His breath was warm against my face. "What's wrong?"

I shook my head.

"Come on, Kit."

I grimaced. "It's occurred to me that we're probably in over our heads. I am anyway. Your head is...well, probably better at this." I told myself that I was thinking in terms of sleuthing, but I knew that wasn't all that was worrying me.

J.X. gave a sound somewhere between a snort and a laugh.

"Come and lie down, honey. You're all wound up."

I eyed him with exasperation. Typical guy. Hopefully he wasn't thinking we could get up to anything because I was

117

definitely *not* in shape for fooling around...

So it was as big a surprise to me as anyone when the next thing I knew I was lowering gingerly to the continental plate serving as our bed, turning cautiously—with much wincing and catching of breath—to watch J.X.

He was shaking his head at the production I was making but smiling at me with such affection that it started my heart pounding noisily in my ears. The bedclothes rustled, the old springs gave a rusty groan as he landed limberly beside me. He slipped a careful arm beneath me.

"Looks like we're getting our weekend together after all."

"Er, yes."

"Though I'd be happier if you didn't look quite so banged up."

"Did you know in Britain 'banged up' means to be jailed or locked up?"

"I didn't know that." He was still smiling. I smiled self-consciously back. I felt a startling leap of pleasure as he slid my jeans zip down.

"That's what *I'm* talking about," he murmured, and I gave a spluttery laugh.

"Well, enough with the talking."

J.X. grinned. He displayed such a touching tenderness, his fingers not quite steady as he reached in to touch me through the warm cotton of my briefs. The hardness he found there seemed to reassure. Him and me both.

Maybe I was in better shape than I thought. My breath expelled in a long, sighing gust, and I lifted my hips so that J.X. could pull my jeans wider, slip his hand inside the pants to take hold of me.

"Mmm." I closed my eyes, relying on the sensory impression

I was receiving as J.X. fondled me. That over-sensitized-skin thing was happening again as his fingertips trailed gently. Every cell seemed to vibrate. In fact, the intensity of my reaction to him was disquieting.

It seemed like at the least I should reciprocate, but he said, "Relax, Kit. Close your eyes. Let me do this for you."

It was only too easy to give in. I murmured in acquiescence. He had to shift around to get the angle right. My cock nudged him, trying to nestle into his palm. He rubbed me gently, and I reached out, showing him what I wanted, positioning his hand on my genitals which seemed to throb in heavy response.

That warm weight felt very good as he stroked me. "God, that's nice."

He made an inquiring sound.

"Oh, yeah. Just like that."

"Yeah? How about this?"

My breath caught. "*Yes.*"

His hand slid down, cupped my balls. Squeezed lightly.

"A little harder. I won't break," I urged as J.X. squeezed again. There was a funny fluttery feeling in my guts, like a swarm of butterflies tickling their way through me, filling me with ripples of startled reaction. I wondered if he was going to make me come like this. So much for my invalid status.

"Go on," J.X. urged softly. "Tell me what you want, Kit."

I opened my eyes. "Let me count the ways. Jesus, you turn me on." I pressed against him, needing more, needing this to be both of us together, not just him taking care of me. I suspected he was too often stuck in the role of responsible party. "Do you think you'd want to—?"

Two minds with but a single thought. He seemed to have arrived at the same idea.

He withdrew his hand, murmuring reassurance before disappointment could set in, unbuckling and unzipping his own jeans, shoving them impatiently down so he too was naked from belly to thigh.

"We can't get too elaborate. You're liable to be summoned by Her Majesty any minute now."

"Let's try this." I slithered over, ignoring the flash of pain at an unwise move, and spooned against him. He smelled so good, body heat and soap and aftershave, and his arms, closing around me, were muscular and comforting. I leaned my head back on his shoulder, wriggling so my buttocks accommodated the hard prod of his flesh without categorically throwing wide the gates to the city. I didn't quite feel up to handing over the keys, though I was surprised at how much I wanted to.

Nearly as much as he wanted it, but J.X. maintained his gentlemanly angle of approach though now and again the snub head of his cock poked the entrance of my body. I could feel the flush building beneath his skin, the damp of perspiration as he held me close-pressed against him. He kissed the side of my face, and I turned awkwardly to kiss him back. He slid his hands over my waist, avoiding my painful ribs and shoulder, veering in to take my cock once more from this more penis-friendly angle.

Yes, that was what I wanted. I sighed pleasurably and pushed upward into J.X.'s gripping, tunneled hands, relishing the friction—the exact right amount—while his cock slid rhythmically between my ass cheeks. That felt good too, that thick hardness pressing against the tightness of my asshole was exciting.

We'd never done that—but we were going to, soon. Again, it surprised me how much I wanted it. Especially as I didn't really have the energy for even what we were doing.

J.X.'s thumb rubbed over the sensitive foreskin of my penis, and it was so good, so sweet. I angled my face toward him, found his searching mouth. It was awkward for a real kiss, our mouths grazing as our bodies rocked against each other. His moist mouth touched the side of my throat, the curve of my shoulder. His heart pounded hard against my shoulder blades.

So little really, but with J.X. more than enough. My pleasure peaked and broke, spilled over into his warm, welcoming hands.

A few thrusts later I felt him tense, felt his rock-hard penis poking hard in the channel of flesh between my ass cheeks, his hands still cradling my limp softness, his thumb still gently, spasmodically stroking me. He was close, I could feel that. I tightened my buttocks, gripped him fiercely and gasped as his cock once more grazed over the pucker of flesh.

Yes, very soon I was going to let him—and I was going to ask for the same from him. I could hear his harsh breaths, hot against my ear as he surged up one final time.

He thrust, went rigid, and spurted out a slippery hot flood.

We drifted. As our bodies calmed, cooled, I thought we should retreat under the tapestry coverlet, but I hadn't the strength to move yet. I felt boneless, peaceful. J.X. was dozing, his breath light and warm against my ear, his arm possessively draped over my side.

From beneath heavy eyelids I watched the gilded dust motes sailing lazily through the air, watched the sunshine creep across the floor. The light seemed unnaturally bright and lucent bouncing off the snow outside the window. I closed my eyes.

It was some time later that I jerked awake, feeling the bed move as J.X. rolled away from me.

"What?" I asked foggily.

"Didn't you hear that?"

"Hear what?"

No need to ask again. A sound shattered the silence of the afternoon. From down the hall a woman was screaming.

Chapter Twelve

J.X. was out the door before I managed to get to my feet. I could hear the pound of his footsteps disappearing down the hall.

I dressed quickly, awkwardly, and followed him. The hallway stood empty. In the wake of the final reverberation of that scream, the silence seemed to hang, waiting...

As I reached the head of the staircase I spotted Sara running up.

"Was that Anna?" she gasped, gaining the top. It was the first time I'd ever seen her with a hair out of place. She looked almost disheveled, pale hair spilling over her shoulders, her face flushed.

"I don't know. I'm on my way to find out." If Sara hadn't screamed, my instant assumption was that it had to have been Anna, but of course it could have been one of the servants. I'd have screamed too if my daily duties had included dusting that much bric-a-brac.

I followed Sara along the gallery which overlooked the main entrance hall.

The door to Anna's room stood open as we burst in on her. She was sitting on the foot of her bed talking to J.X. At the sight of Sara and me, she gave a shaky laugh.

"False alarm, darlings."

J.X. stepped aside as Sara went to her, saying, "Anna, what on earth happened? What did you scream for?"

J.X.'s eyes met mine. I could see he was trying to tell me something, but I had no clue what it might be. My fly was unzipped? I checked surreptitiously.

"Don't fuss, darling. It was only a-a nightmare." Anna was so clearly lying I don't think any of us could come up with a response. There was an awkward silence.

"A nightmare?" Sara repeated slowly. "What did you dream?"

"It doesn't matter." Anna sounded almost impatient. "Anyway, really, I'm fine now. Don't let's make a production."

I started, "Did you want to—?"

"No, not right now, Christopher." She managed a smile. "I'd like to be on my own for a bit. I'll see you all for dinner."

There seemed to be no alternative but to leave her in peace and quiet. The three of us filed out.

"Is she all right?" I asked Sara as, at Anna's bidding, she eased the door shut behind us.

Sara shrugged. She seemed as puzzled as I felt. "I suppose so. If she says she is, she probably is."

J.X.'s hand rested briefly on the small of my back which I read as either he couldn't wait to get me back to bed or, more likely, he had something to say to me in private.

"I guess we'll see you at dinner," I said to Sara.

I don't think she even heard me. She was still standing in the hall, gazing thoughtfully at Anna's closed door as J.X. and I departed for our own room.

"What up?" I asked as we reached the sanctuary of our own bedchamber.

That distracted him for an instant. "You're so street, Kit," he said admiringly.

"Yo yo yo, homes. Now what did you see in Anna's boudoir?"

"Nothing. What I saw was a man leaving her boudoir in a hurry."

"What man?"

He looked heavenward, opened his mouth, and I interrupted, "All right, all right. Describe him."

"White male. Blond. Approximately six feet. Our age."

Not Rudolph. Not Luke either. So who the hell was it?

"I appreciate the tact of that 'our age'," I said. "But was he my age or your age?"

"Late thirties, early forties. It's pretty much the same thing."

"Hmmph." I thought it over. "Unless one of the servants is taking untoward liberties, it must be the stepson. Richard Rosen."

"There's something else. When I walked into Anna's room, she was rubbing her wrist. Her arm was red as though someone had grabbed her."

"You think Rosen manhandled her?"

"If it was Rosen, it looked that way to me. Anna had the sleeves of her robe down by the time you and Sara arrived."

"Did you ask her what happened?"

"I got the same story you did. She didn't bother to try and explain the guy running from her room."

"Maybe it's a common occurrence." I wasn't serious, just letting my mouth flap while I thought—a bad habit of mine.

J.X. asked quite seriously, "Is Anna promiscuous?" It

seemed to put a different slant on the matter.

"I don't think so. I don't know, to be honest. I wasn't genuinely speculating. I don't think she's seduced her stepson or anything like that."

"But you don't have any idea what their relationship is like?"

I shook my head.

"It might be worth finding out."

He was right, of course, but I had an uncomfortable feeling, call it an instinct, that despite having asked for our help, Anna was not going to appreciate any digging into her private life. You don't have to be a detective to know we all have things we'd rather not share.

I was considering whether it would be better to try and approach Anna directly or circumvent her by talking to Rudolph or Sara when J.X. said, "You feel up to showing me these garden steps Anna fell down?"

"Sure. I don't know what you'll be able to tell from looking at them."

"I want to get a feel for the lay of the land."

I opened my mouth, caught his gaze. "Naughty," he said with a grin.

The sky looked heavy and gray, like a sagging pillow about to burst. An occasional snowflake swirled in the breeze as we started down the flagstone steps. About midway down, my foot slithered on the slush, and J.X.'s hand shot out, wrapping around my biceps.

"Careful."

"Yes." I was a little breathless. I told myself it was the cold air and not fright, but the thought of a tumble down those murderous stairs was alarming. "Obviously, she *could* have fallen," I said. I glanced at him. "And thanks, by the way."

"Yes, she could have. And by the way, you're welcome."

I wasn't sure that we would find the cottage unlocked, but the handle turned and the door swung open.

Victoria stood at the table in the alcove. She was gathering up manuscripts, which she promptly dropped as we walked in on her.

It's hard to say who was more flabbergasted, her or us. Well, me. J.X. did not flabbergast. At least I'd never seen any indication of it and I knew the signs firsthand.

"My God, you frightened me. What are you doing here?" Victoria's voice was uncharacteristically shrill.

"I came down to get my laptop."

I'm not sure where the lie came from because if I'd thought about my laptop at all since the accident, I'd assumed the ever-efficient Sara had picked it up and safely stowed it. I was nearly as surprised to spot it lying amidst the papers and electronics still scattered over the round table as I was to find Victoria in the cottage.

"That's why I'm here," she said quickly. "To get Poppy's notebook. She's staying with me for a few days."

"I didn't realize the hospital had released her so soon."

"Yes. Yes, they don't hold people long these days. Not if they can possibly turn them loose."

"How is she?"

"Oh. You can probably imagine."

Not really. I'd made some mistakes in my life, but so far none of them had caused anyone's death. That was a terrible burden Poppy was carrying. I didn't envy her mornings.

I moved toward the table. Victoria was staring at J.X., so I

127

made the introductions although I admit I was vague about why he was with me.

"I've read your books," she told him. "*So* exciting."

J.X. never had the problem I did of readers not recognizing his name or work. He made the usual deprecating noises.

"I'm glad you're all right. I meant to stop by and see how you were," Victoria said awkwardly to me. "Things have been...hectic."

"I'm sure they have."

"You're staying on at Anna's?"

"For a few days."

"I guess you probably don't feel up to that long flight home."

"Right."

She hesitated. "Well, I'll take..." She gestured to the papers and Poppy's notebook.

I couldn't see any reason she shouldn't take the things belonging to her and Poppy, although the snoop in me would have liked a chance to look through everything. Of course, I'd already seen the stories, and anything else was not my business, but minding one's own business is not part of the sleuth job description.

We watched Victoria self-consciously gather the papers again and shove them into a backpack. She told J.X. what a pleasure it was to meet him, told me she hoped we'd see each other again before I left, and she hurried out. The door banged shut behind her.

"What was that about?" J.X. asked.

"I didn't imagine it then? She *was* acting strangely?"

"She was acting guilty as hell. She's the one who lives on the property?" J.X. asked. "The one with the cottage in walking distance?"

I nodded, glancing over the remaining manuscripts. I saw that Nella's story was one of the ones Victoria had initially scooped up. I flipped through the pages absently. Knowing now that there would be no other stories from Nella gave me a different perspective on *Drive*.

"What do you know about her?"

"Nothing, to be honest. She seems perfectly pleasant. No one has a negative word to say about her."

"Guilty," J.X. pronounced.

I laughed. "That's what I said when Anna was telling me what a great tenant she was. The least likely suspect and all that jazz."

"Yeah. That's not how it works in real life," he couldn't help pointing out. "In real life, nine times out of ten, the most likely suspect *is* guilty. We—the police—might not always be able to prove it, but we almost always know the bad guy."

"I know. I'm kidding," I said kindly. "I don't know if it means anything, but she started to take Nella's story in that stack."

"Could it have been a mistake?"

I mentally pictured the table on the day of the accident. Everyone's papers had been spread out in front of them.

All but four places had since been cleared—along with all the dirty cups and crumb-strewn plates, probably by Sara after we'd left. I could guess what had happened. The others would have returned following lunch, heard about the accident, gathered their belongings and left. The remaining papers and electronics belonged to me, Poppy, Victoria and Nella. We hadn't been sitting near each other and I couldn't see Sara shuffling everything into one big disorganized pile.

I shook my head. "No. But she might have been curious." I thought back to the interactions between the members of the AC that fateful morning. I'd had the impression that Victoria had feelings for Rowland. Rowland, it had seemed equally clear to me, had feelings for Nella. Given the knack people had for inflicting pain on themselves, I could imagine Victoria wanting to read Nella's completed story, especially since Rowland had thought so highly of it.

Or was I the only one with neurotic self-punishing tendencies?

"What was Victoria's story like?"

I made a face. "The usual chick fantasy. Beautiful, kick-ass lady bounty hunter fucks and shoots her way through a series of misadventures. I skimmed a lot of it. Not my kind of thing, and to be honest, it was getting late. Anna was supposed to send me the files earlier in the week, but in the end she printed everything out for me. She'd already done the real evaluations. I was basically a guest speaker."

"And Anna's relationships with these people?"

"I didn't pick up anything amiss. She had her favorites, and being Anna she didn't bother to hide them. But I doubt if that would be cause for—"

"Motive is the least important aspect of any murder investigation."

"Right." I did know that, though in the Miss Butterwith books motive was everything. "We don't really have much of a starting point without it."

"From the standpoint of means and method, Victoria looks like a likely candidate. She's right on the estate and it looks like she comes and goes as she likes."

"That's true of Luke too. And *he* does have motive and a criminal record, although it might not be pertinent."

"Criminal record is always pertinent." That was the ex-cop talking.

I flipped through Nella's manuscript, read a few lines. It was illogical, but it did affect my opinion of the work knowing that Nella was dead. But was that sympathy or was that merely a more open-minded reading? I wasn't sure.

I wasn't sure it mattered.

I was pretty sure Nella had not been anyone's target. Why would she be? Besides, a car accident was a pretty dumb means of trying to commit murder. There were too many things that could go wrong. In this case, four people could have died, and that seemed a bit too much like whole-scale slaughter.

Any way I looked at it, it didn't seem to make sense.

Chapter Thirteen

"Anna wants to see you," Sara greeted me when we returned to the house.

"Now?"

"Now."

I looked at J.X. His eyebrows lifted. "I'll see you back at the clubhouse."

I nodded and followed Sara upstairs. It was the usual wordless trek across hill and plain and antique carpet. She tapped on the door, stepped aside as Anna's muffled voice bade me enter.

Anna, wreathed in a cloud of smoke, was seated on the loveseat in front of the bay windows looking over the frozen ornamental lake. She wore a peach silk dressing gown. The leg encased by the cast was propped on pillows.

"Darling." She patted the side of the loveseat. "Come sit down."

I was fairly sure she didn't expect me to leap to the cushions and curl up beside her. I sat on one of the companion chairs.

"I have to apologize for earlier," she said. "Not for the lie, but for the lameness of the lie."

"That's all right."

"I don't think you ever met my stepson Ricky, did you?"

"No."

"He's what's known as a rotter in the kind of books you write."

I've never used the term *rotter*, but I didn't see the point in debating it. "Did he threaten you? J.X. thought he saw you holding your arm as though you'd been hurt."

She made a sound that fell somewhere between derision and irritation. "Ricky has a temper. So do I. It doesn't mean anything. I know how to handle Ricky."

I repeated, "Was he threatening you?"

"He was asking for money. That's nothing new. Ricky comes home for one reason and one reason only. When he's short of funds."

"So he *was* threatening you."

"You say potato, I say potahto."

"I say rice pilaf. I say you're trying to distract me with talk of side dishes. I say it sounds to me like Little Ricky has a motive for wanting you out of the way, assuming you included him along with everyone else in your will."

Her mouth tightened. "Ricky is in my will, naturally. In addition, upon my death he inherits Miles's literary estate as well as Miles's share of our joint holdings."

"How old is Ricky?"

"About your age."

Interesting. Forcing Ricky to wait until Anna's death before inheriting from his father seemed like a guarantee for resentment. Not that it was necessarily pertinent, but I wondered whose decision that had been. Anna's tendency to want to control people was liable to prove a contributing factor in someone wanting to get rid of her. I wasn't tactless enough to say so, of course.

One thing that did strike me was that Anna and Miles had been divorced for a couple of years by the time Miles died, yet he'd left Anna as Ricky's trustee. I guess that was a vote of confidence if there ever was one. Unless Miles had forgotten who he'd named Ricky's trustee. Hard to believe.

"Was Ricky here when you had any of your other accidents?"

Her face took on a stubborn expression. "I don't remember."

"Well try, Anna."

"Ricky is not to be considered a suspect."

"That's logical."

"Logical or not, Ricky is family. I don't want you to include him in your...your speculations."

Funny how my investigation became speculation the minute Anna was annoyed with the direction I was moving in. "You said yourself he's a rotter. And he's got the best motive of anyone so far."

"I'm serious about this, Christopher. You must trust my instinct on this. Ricky is not trying to kill me."

"Okay. Next theory. Could it have something to do with the writing group?"

"Such as?"

"What about the stories themselves?"

Anna blinked. "The...stories...themselves? You mean one of the Asquith Circle wrote something that he or she later regretted letting me read?"

She articulated the theory so quickly I had to believe the idea, however fanciful, had already occurred to her.

"Is it possible?"

She didn't answer immediately, further confirming my suspicion. "It's not very likely, is it?" she said finally.

"I don't know. With the exception of Victoria, they all wrote about small-town murders that are, in theory anyway, plausible. Rowland's story about a fall down a staircase sounds pretty similar to the tumble you took. Sara wrote about one sister using insecticide to get rid of another."

"Sara?"

"Sure. *Death and Her Sisters*."

Anna still looked uncomprehending. "Sara had a story?"

"Yeah, she had a story. She had the best story in the group. You didn't know?"

She shook her head.

"I guess that explains why you didn't make any notes or comments on her manuscript."

"No..." Anna seemed to gather her thoughts. "That is, I knew of course about the novel, but I didn't realize she was going to show it to the group. She was so adamant about *not* showing it."

"Why? The book is brilliant."

Anna's expression was troubled. "I don't know why. And I agree with you about the manuscript. I only know that Sara was very definite about not showing the novel to the group. I'm...astonished to hear that she apparently changed her mind."

"Don't you think that's suspicious?"

Anna laughed with genuine humor. "Not really. Sara is a very private person. To be honest, I'm sure she would never seriously consider publication."

"You've got to be kidding."

"I'm not. Sara really does write solely for herself. At least...until now."

"But she's shown her work to you?"

"Yes. I've mentored her to the best of my ability. I've encouraged her to publish for years." She fell silent.

"Well, she's taken the first step. Now my next question is, is it possible one reason Sara didn't want to publish her book is because it's based on something in her own life?"

Anna opened her mouth and then closed it. Opened it and closed it again. Seeing that she was not getting past the codfish impersonation anytime soon, I said, "Or what about Rowland with his mom-loving serial killer?"

"There's never been a serial killer in Nitchfield, and to return briefly to the topic of Sara, she doesn't have any sisters living—" She stopped abruptly.

"She had a sister who died?"

Anna put her face in her hands. Her voice was muffled as she said, "This is *crazy*."

"Crazy is as crazy does. Did Sara's sister die under suspicious circumstances?"

Anna looked up. "I don't know. I know nothing about it. I swear."

"All right. Maybe J.X. can talk to his pals in the local PD and find out for us."

Anna said urgently, "Until we know something for sure, you mustn't let on in any way that Sara is under suspicion. She's not merely an employee, she's a friend."

"Understood."

"I'm serious, Christopher. Not by word or deed or—or even facial expression. I know you. You're not good at hiding your feelings."

"I'm not *that* bad at hiding my feelings," I said, peeved. In fact, I thought I'd done a pretty decent job of hiding my feelings from the minute I'd arrived at the Asquith Estate.

Anna looked tolerant but unimpressed. She said with what I thought was unseemly lightness, "Anyway, if someone—and I don't mean Sara necessarily—did realize he or she was under suspicion, they might...retaliate."

"Retaliate?"

She said succinctly, "Well, think about it, darling. If someone starts to view *you* as a threat, you might find yourself in the same danger as me."

"She said that to you?" J.X. looked sternly handsome—as stern as a man dressed in nothing but his underwear and goose bumps can look—as I related my talk with Anna while we dressed for dinner.

"Well, it's common sense."

"Nothing about this weekend is common sense," he had to point out.

"All right, but it's logical that if someone is willing to kill to protect him or herself once, they won't hesitate to remove a nuisance like me." I paused to watch him pull up his Diesel black jeans. It was a sight worth savoring.

"Yeah, what bugs me is that Anna knowingly dragged you into a situation that could prove hazardous to your health."

I nodded absently. I wasn't seriously worried. Besides...J.X.'s thighs were long and muscular, his ass was trim and tight, and the hand-brushed denim encasing both had a cool, worn-in look.

"Kit?"

"Hmm?"

He turned to face me, and the view was even better before he zipped it away. "You're not listening."

"Yeah, I am. You don't like Anna."

I don't know why I said it. It wasn't something that had been on my mind. I'm not sure it had even consciously occurred to me, but the minute I said it—and saw his expression—I knew I was right. "You really *don't* like her."

J.X. said awkwardly, "That's putting it too strongly. I don't *dis*like her. I don't know her. I don't like the way she's using you."

"How is it using me to ask for help? We're friends. Friends help each other."

He nodded. The fact that he wasn't arguing as he normally did made me more uneasy. It wasn't like J.X. to tiptoe over my tender feelings.

"She's scared. She's—"

He gestured at the clock, cutting me off. "We should get down there."

I said slowly, "Right." I finished buttoning my shirt and slid my arm back in its supportive sling.

I wasn't aware that J.X. was watching me until he said, "Don't worry about it, Kit. I don't have to like her. I'm sure you won't be crazy about all my friends either."

Well, that went without saying. I made a face and he chuckled. Unconcerned as usual.

"What's with you and black?" I inquired as we started down the stairs. I nodded at his black lambswool turtleneck. "I thought you were one of the good guys?"

He grinned. "Hey. Black is the new white."

I was still thinking over that philosophical statement when we joined the others for cocktails in the drawing room.

I was sipping my gin and tonic as Anna, assisted by Rudolph, joined us. She looked spectacular in an aquamarine sequined pantsuit, and if she privately feared for her life, she hid it well—as good at applying the emotional concealer as the other kind.

"How are you feeling, Christopher?" Rudolph asked. He appeared to be going for aged collegiate in a red cashmere pullover.

"Lucky," I answered.

"Yes. That was...truly terrible."

"I need a drink," Anna said, lowering to the blue velvet sofa before the fire.

Sara, elegant and cool in gray silk, brought her scotch and water. To Rudolph, she said, "Bourbon on the rocks?"

He smiled faintly. And smiled again when she brought his drink. She didn't exactly warm up, but she wasn't as frosty as usual.

A silence fell, broken only by the chink of ice in glasses and the crackle of the fire in the fireplace.

"Ricky, darling." Anna smiled in welcome at the young man who appeared in the doorway.

I say "young man", but he was my age. Clearly he spent a lot more time at the gym and the tanning salon. His hair was the shade of gold that comes from a bottle. I recognized it because that's the same place I get my stylish highlights. And lowlights. His eye color was lapis lazuli. I was guessing tinted contacts, because that's a color Mother Nature generally reserves for non-humans. His clothes were expensive and well cut, but for all the time and effort spent, Ricky wasn't handsome, just...well-crafted.

Anna made the introductions. Ricky was pleasant and

smiling as he promptly forgot all our names. I admit I was predisposed not to like him after J.X.'s speculation on whether Ricky had grabbed Anna, but he seemed a nice enough guy. Maybe a bit too slick, but that's not hard in a gathering of writers. *Savoir-faire* and *author* are not generally what you'd call synonymous.

"Writers!" he said. "A houseful of writers. Whoa, baby."

"What do you do?" J.X. asked.

"I sell company-certified pre-owned Mercedes-Benz cars." The used-car salesman offered a big, bright smile. "How successful a writer are you?"

J.X.'s smile was considerably cooler.

"You're wasting your time. He's Ford tough," I said.

Ricky laughed like that was the pinnacle of humor. Maybe around the dealer showroom it was. He said to Sara, "Can you get me a beer, babe?"

God. Why was no one trying to kill *him*?

Sara bestowed a smile that should have paralyzed Ricky as effectively as curare, and departed to get him a beer. Dinner was announced and the rest of us shuffled off to the dining room. Things immediately began to look up. Whatever Anna paid her kitchen staff, they were worth every penny.

Green salad with artichoke hearts was followed by chicken breasts crusted in pistachio nuts and shallots served over wild rice with a creamy white wine sauce. Once again there was a quantity of wine, both red and white. Conscious that I had enough physical aches and pains without adding a raging headache to my problems, I stuck to the chardonnay. The others opted for Beaujolais.

J.X. sat directly across from me. His eyes met mine periodically, a wry smile in their depths that inexplicably cheered me. Occasionally, his foot brushed mine. However weird this setup was, I wasn't alone, and that cheered me more than I'd have expected.

The mealtime conversation was polite and innocuous, which seemed weird to me, but also understandable. It might have been different if members of the Asquith Circle had still been present, but only Anna had any real link to Nella. Perhaps if she hadn't been at the table, the others would have discussed the accident. As it was, the topics of conversation encompassed the weather, everyone's travel plans, and—inevitably with writers—what we were all working on.

There was the usual excitement over J.X.'s latest project. He was working on a standalone thriller, his first. I'd already had a sneak preview the last time I'd spent the weekend. The book was an unholy, riveting, utterly readable page-turner involving unwed mothers, Russian mobsters, ecoterrorists and a small-town sheriff with Issues. It had bestseller stamped all over it, and I preferred not to think about it.

Not that I was jealous or anything.

"And what has Miss Butterwith planned for us next?" Anna inquired of me, after J.X. had finished modestly brushing the acclaim the best he could off his broad shoulders. It tended to stick to that dark material.

"Nothing. I'm not working on anything," I said in answer to Anna's question.

I felt the quick look J.X. threw me. Anna said, "Oh fuck! Surely there's *something* you haven't put the old girl through yet?"

I smiled. Reached for my wineglass.

"You haven't done anything with soccer or hockey themes, have you?"

I shook my head.

Anna was enjoying herself. She raised her hand as though checking perspective on a painting. "I can picture the title now. *Miss Butterworth Kicks the Bucket.*"

There was laughter around the table. I laughed too.

"What are you working on, Anna?" J.X. sounded terse enough to be grilling a suspect. Anna looked mildly surprised, as though one of the candelabra had spoken up a la Lumiere in *Beauty and the Beast.*

"*Ah.* Thank you for asking. As I was telling Christopher the other day, I'm very happy, very relieved to say my own dry spell is over." She raised her glass in a toast and the rest of us followed suit although I couldn't help noticing the surprised exchange of glances between Rudolph, Sara and Ricky.

Anna said to me, "I do feel your pain, darling."

Startled, I said, "I'm not having a dry spell."

She didn't hear me. "What's it been, Rudolph?"

"Five years."

"Five fucking years." Anna shook her head, sipped her wine. "It felt like twenty."

"Anna, that's marvelous. I didn't realize." Rudolph was smiling—beaming, in fact.

"You haven't been listening, darling." There was the faintest edge there.

"Here's to another blockbuster from the American Agatha Christie," Ricky said. "And here's to the movie rights!" He raised his glass in a toast.

We lifted our glasses. The bell-like chime of crystal rang up and down the long table and filled the silence.

I woke to the unpleasant sound of someone being sick.

Fortunately not me.

Unfortunately someone nearby. I raised my head cautiously. The adjoining bathroom door was closed but I could see the band of light beneath it. I could hear the muted hum of the fan and the less muted and distinct sounds of J.X. paying homage to the porcelain god.

I swallowed hard. Did that in-sickness-and-in-health thing hold for dating?

Shoving aside the bedclothes, I tiptoed across the chilly floor and pawed faintheartedly at the bathroom door.

The resulting sounds were not encouraging but...

I pushed open the door.

J.X. knelt before the toilet, hands braced and white-knuckled, black hair drenched in perspiration. Perspiration sheened the muscular planes of his back too.

The animal scents of sweat and sickness knocked me to my knees beside him.

"Honey," I whispered, touching his ice-cold face. "What's wrong?"

J.X.'s dark eyes looked glazed as they met mine. His colorless mouth moved, but I couldn't make out the words.

"Hold on," I told him. "I'll get help."

Never underestimate the energizing benefits of sheer panic. I was up and sprinting down the shadowy hallway and across the gallery before my brain had a chance to catch up with my rarely used muscles.

I had no idea where I was going, but I was making good time when I tripped over something soft and warm and moving feebly in the same direction as me. Until I landed awkwardly, painfully on the expensive antique runner, I'd forgotten that I was still convalescent myself.

Fortunately my scream was buried in the velvety pile allowing me to retain whatever dignity was possible while rolling around on the floor swearing and moaning.

My outpourings blended inharmoniously with those of the person I'd stumbled over, who turned out, on peering inspection, to be Ricky.

He appeared to be suffering from the same malady as J.X.—and that frightened me like nothing else.

Poison.

I remembered Anna talking about a mysterious bout of food poisoning that had hit this house once already. Twice in the space of a few weeks was too much of a coincidence.

"Hang on. I'll get help," I told Ricky. I had no idea if he understood me or not. I was up and running once more, but only a yard or so down the next hallway I narrowly avoided slamming into Rudolph who had reeled from the shadows to clutch at me.

"Are you ill?" he gasped.

"No, but J.X. is." I didn't have to ask after Rudolph. Even in the poor light I could see he was gray-faced and perspiring heavily. "Have you checked on Anna?"

He shook his head.

"Do you know where Sara's room is?"

I didn't know if Sara was behind this sudden outbreak of food poisoning, but it seemed to me that it would be well worth keeping an eye on her—not that I had an eye to spare.

"I've already tried Sara," Rudolph whispered. "She's ill too."

Well, she would be, if she had any brains at all. But not *too* ill, I was willing to bet.

Rudolph said, "We need to call for help. We need to phone an ambulance or emergency services or—or something."

Yes to all of the above. But first things first. "I'm going to make sure Anna's all right," I said, gripped by sudden cold fear. I detached myself from Rudolph's limpet-like clutch, and continued on my way down the hall.

Anna's door was closed. I tapped a couple of times—no response—then pounded energetically.

Still no reply.

I pushed the door open. Moonlight flooded from the bay windows, spotlighting the crumpled figure lying on the floor.

Oh God.

"Anna?"

I knelt beside the cloud of lace and rayon, reaching for her arm. Her skin was still warm. Was she breathing? I couldn't tell. I felt around the delicate bones of her wrist, trying to find some kind of pulse. As my fingers closed around her wrist, she moaned and tried to raise her head.

The relief had me falling back on my ass. I'd thought for sure...

"Take it easy, Anna. Help is on the way."

"Poison," she wheezed. "I've been poisoned."

"Everyone has been poisoned." Everyone but me. What did that mean? What had everyone else eaten that I hadn't? Nothing as far as I could recall. I'd eaten everything and eaten heartily. What can I say? Death and disaster give me an appetite.

What had everyone drunk that I hadn't?

Cocktails. No. We'd all had different cocktails. And later everyone had red wine at dinner. Except me.

I'm not sure if Anna understood me or not. She writhed, for once too weak to swear, curling onto her side—or trying to. The cast weighted her down.

I pushed to my feet, went to the bedside table and turned on the lamp. I had to pick the princess phone up and hold it away from my face to read the tiny buttons. Perhaps I'd reached an age where I ought to start wearing glasses on a chain around my neck. Like a lady librarian. Not that librarians necessarily wear eyeglasses to bed—disconcerting to one's bed partner if magnifiers are required.

It occurred to me that my thoughts were spinning and I wasn't getting much mental traction. I concentrated on the task at hand, finally making out the button that read *housekeeping*. I pressed it.

On the end, the phone buzzed and buzzed and then picked up. A sleepy voice said, "Yes, ma'am?"

"Mrs. Hitchcock's ill. I need some help up here."

"Yes, Mr. Dunst. I'll be right there."

Mr. Dunst?

I said, "Before you do anything else, call 911. I think everyone has been poisoned. We need medical help ASAP."

She was still squawking when I dropped the handset on its hook and went back to Anna. I crouched down beside her.

"Anna?"

Nothing. Her breathing sounded weird.

"Anna?"

"Christopher..."

"Help is on the way."

She nodded feebly. "Help me...back to bed?"

"Maybe you should lie still. I'll get a bla—"

"I didn't break my other fucking ankle. I've been *poisoned*. Help me into the goddamned bed, Christopher."

By then I was desperate to get back to J.X., but I was

equally worried about leaving Anna on her own.

It wasn't easy between my bad back and injured shoulder and her injured ribs and cast, but at last, sweating and breathless—that would be both of us—I dropped her into the disturbed tangle of sheets and blankets. She moaned and swore. I pulled the bedclothes over her sprawled form.

She moaned again—more ominously.

I looked around for something she could be sick in and had to settle for a cloisonné flower vase. I threw the flowers and water in the fireplace and placed the vase beside the bed.

"Anna? Can you hear me?"

She started as though she'd drifted off. "Rudy?"

Or maybe she was hallucinating.

"No. It's me. Christopher. Listen, I have to check on the others. I'll be back as soon as I can."

"Don't leave me."

"I'll be right back. I promise."

She pleaded, "Don't leave me, Christopher. I'm in danger."

Who the hell wasn't at this point?

"Everyone is ill, Anna. No one will try for you now. I promise I'll be right back."

She clutched feebly at my hand, but I was already on my way toward the door.

Midway down the hall I spotted Rudolph. He was standing in the middle of the corridor, weaving slightly. His face was ghastly.

I went to help him. "Here, you'd better sit down before you fall down."

"Christopher." Rudolph stopped. His mouth formed a word, but I couldn't tell what it was. He tried again. "Sara."

I drew back, studying his bloodless face. His eyes looked like he was on dope—black and stunned. My heart thundered in my ears. I had to raise my voice to speak over it. "What about Sara?"

"Sara..." He reached out and touched my arm. His fingers were ice cold and trembling. I understood that he wanted me to follow him.

I didn't want to. I wanted to go back and reassure myself that J.X. was all right. I didn't want to see whatever it was Rudolph wanted me to see.

Somehow my feet were uprooting themselves, stumbling forward, following him as he half-walked, half-reeled down the long hallway. He was hunched over, one of his arms clutching his belly, clearly in pain, but he was determined.

That determination said more than any words could.

At last we reached a bedroom off the main hallway.

Rudolph didn't knock, didn't call out. He pushed open the door and led the way through the elegant, tidy bedroom toward the large bathroom. Before I was halfway across the bedroom I knew what we were going to find.

She was lying belly down on the tiles. Her gilt hair was tumbled over her shoulders, veiling her face. She wore a flannel nightdress and I remember staring at the tiny peach roses and blue stripes. Not what I would have expected somehow. There was something so normal, so ordinary and comfortable about a flannel nightie—and this situation was anything but normal, ordinary or comfortable.

Dimly, I was aware that Rudolph was crying. I couldn't seem to tear my gaze away from Sara. I kept watching her back, waiting for the rise and fall of her breaths. They didn't come.

There were no breaths.

Rudolph dropped down on his knees beside her and stroked her shining hair with a shaking hand.

"Sara," he whispered.

Sara didn't answer. Sara didn't live here anymore.

Chapter Fourteen

As bad nights go, that one was right up there. Or down there. Whichever. I felt at the time that it was the worst night of my life, which was saying something because I'd had some crappy nights in the last year.

I left Rudolph with Sara's body and ran on shaking legs for my own room. Bursting through the doorway, I had to hang onto the doorframe to keep on my feet as I stared and stared at the sight before me.

J.X. was lying on the stately bed, his hands folded on his chest like he'd been laid out for burial.

I stumbled forward.

J.X. must have heard the stricken noise I made because his long black lashes lifted and his dark eyes gazed up at me from his colorless face.

I could have cried with the relief of it. After the horror of finding Sara—

"Are you...okay?" I faltered.

He whispered, "I've been better."

I impatiently wiped the blur from my eyes. "Emergency services is on the way."

He raised his eyebrows.

I sat on the edge of the bed. He winced as I rested my hand

on his forehead. His skin felt cold. Was that a bad sign? I had no idea. The extent of my medical training involved Band-Aids and Bactine.

"Are *you* okay?"

I nodded. "Everyone who was at dinner is ill. Except me."

Apparently he'd been thinking about this too. He cleared his throat. "The wine. You had white. We had red."

I nodded. "That's my thought too." I took a deep breath. "Sara's dead."

"Jesus." He closed his eyes. With those long lashes and the unusual pallor of his chiseled features, he looked disarmingly young—though still heroic, of course.

He lifted his lashes again and said, "You need to secure the crime scene."

A slightly hysterical sound burst out of me. "The whole fucking house is a crime scene. I told you everyone in the place is sick."

"Sara's bedroom," J.X. said huskily. "Close it off and don't let anyone inside."

I thought guiltily of Rudolph who I'd left sitting beside Sara's body. "What does it matter? We already know how the poison was introduced."

He clenched his jaw against a stab of pain—whether from his gut or my obstinacy.

I don't know why I was arguing because I knew full well that, since Sara's was the only death so far, there could easily be some crucial variable in her case. I was hoping heart failure. I was hoping Sara was the poisoner and she'd had the bad luck to fall prey to the ultimate irony, but I feared that was too easy. I guess the truth was, I didn't want to leave J.X. Not that I was doing him one whole hell of a lot of good sitting next to him wringing my hands, but he was still alive and I wanted to make sure he stayed that way.

After a struggle for composure, he asked, "Have you notified the police?"

"I..." God almighty. It hadn't even occurred to me. What would Miss Butterwith think? "Not specifically. Nine one one." I swallowed. "Are you...okay on your own for a few minutes?"

He smiled wanly. Awkwardly patted my thigh. "I'm hanging in there. Go."

"I'll be right back."

See Christopher run. Run, Christopher, run, run.

I took the stairs at a fast hobble. By then I was starting to feel pretty rocky myself. Considering the fact that I wasn't twenty-four hours out of the hospital, I wasn't doing too badly, but adrenaline and alarm could only take one so far. I'd about used up my allotment.

Downstairs, the lights were all on and the household staff was rushing around in what looked to me to be complete disarray. I kept hearing Sara's name mentioned. Not because anyone yet knew she was dead, but because they were expecting her to show up and tell them what to do.

My arrival on the scene was greeted with more doubt than enthusiasm. I requested help for Anna and Ricky, who I'd last spotted crawling across the gallery, and then I went into the library, closed the door and phoned the police.

It didn't take long.

Once I'd given my information to the astonished police dispatcher, I returned upstairs to Sara's room. Rudolph was sitting right where I'd left him.

Oddly enough, the first thought I had was how much Sara

would have detested the indignity of her death scene. Not that dying is ever glamorous, but vomiting your guts out and expiring on a bathroom floor has to rank up there with freak accidents and celebrity overdoses.

I helped Rudolph to his feet, assisted him out of the bathroom. His knees seemed to give out as we crossed the beige bedroom carpet. I half-dragged him to the bed.

He fell back on the rumpled bedclothes. Whether physical distress or emotional trauma, either way he seemed to be in bad shape. I leaned over him, trying to determine if he was conscious or not.

"Rudolph? Can you hear me?"

He nodded. His eyes remained closed. He wasn't a young man. Regardless of what J.X. said, I didn't see how I could drag him out of here until he was ready to go. I straightened up, my hand going to the throbbing small of my back. My glance fell on the pillow which still carried the indentation of Sara's head.

I looked at the pillow lying next to it. It also carried the indentation of someone's head.

Of course, Sara could have been using both pillows. I slept alone and I used two pillows, but I scrunched them up into one big ball. I didn't divide the night up and spend it lying neatly on each side of the bed.

Sara had had company last night.

I turned back to Rudolph. The vision of him sitting on the bathroom floor stroking Sara's hair flashed into my memory. At the time, I'd put that and his other reactions down to shock.

Now I wondered.

Were Sara and Rudolph—?

But if that was the case, why were the housekeeping staff apparently not surprised to hear Rudolph calling from Anna's bedroom?

I gazed at him with disbelief. The old *dog*.

I'm a law-abiding citizen, so I don't know why the police make me nervous. I know cops are supposed to be sexy and all that, but something about a man in uniform makes me wonder if I've forgotten to pay any recent parking tickets.

However, given the unglamorous activities of the emergency services upstairs, I was glad to be occupied answering questions in the library.

I'd been through the drill once before three months earlier when I'd ended up involved in a murder investigation at a writing retreat in Northern California, but I didn't find it any more comfortable the second time around.

First, we went through who I was and what I was doing at the Asquith Estate. The easy questions. We moved on to my relationship with Anna, the other guests and, of course, Sara.

I thought about going with my cover story, such as it was. I knew how ridiculous the truth was going to sound: Anna had coerced me—a fellow mystery writer—into flying out to Connecticut because she thought someone was trying to kill her. Plus, Anna had been so adamant about keeping the police out of her private life. But a woman had died tonight, and although it was far too soon to know by what method, I was positive Sara hadn't suffered a natural death. Not with everyone else in the house keeling over.

"This is a new one on me," Detective Eames said, after I'd finished making my statement. He was short and stout with a little black Hitler mustache and the palest blue eyes I'd ever seen. "You're claiming that Ms. Hitchcock hired you—"

I corrected quickly, "She didn't hire me."

"Okay. *Enlisted* you because she feared her life was in danger?"

I nodded.

"If that's true, why wouldn't she come to us?"

"I told you. Anna was afraid that you'd think it was a publicity stunt."

I've seen floorboards with more expression than the face Eames was offering me.

"And," I added, "she wasn't absolutely *positive* someone was trying to harm her. I think she thought having an extra pair of eyes couldn't hurt."

"It didn't help," Eames said bluntly.

That was unanswerable. I scratched my nose.

"And your theory is the red wine at dinner was poisoned?"

"It's the only thing that everyone else had that I didn't."

"Hmm." Eames regarded me without pleasure. He asked me to give him my account of the events of the evening, which I did. I stuck to the bare facts—mostly—so it didn't take long.

"So, in this amateur sleuthing you were doing—" Eames said *amateur sleuthing* in the same tone most people would say *exposing yourself in public*, "—did you reach any conclusion as to who the bad guy or girl might be?"

It wasn't a serious question. Or, rather, it was serious in as much as he was too good a cop not to cover every angle, but he was clearly not expecting anything helpful. And he was right. When I'd gone to bed that night I'd been convinced Sara was a shoo-in for Psycho of the Year. Now it appeared she had fallen victim to that Psycho—or to her own machinations. Either way, that wasn't a theory I was about to offer up.

"Er, no. Not really."

He looked astonished. "No? And you've been here how
155

many days?"

Ah. Sarcasm. And unfair sarcasm at that. I didn't pretend to be a trained investigator. Plus, I'd been sort of preoccupied with my own near-death experience.

I explained about the car accident and that did catch his interest. He heard me out in attentive silence.

"And you still have no idea who this mysterious person you saw skulking around the night before the accident might have been?"

"No. Shadowy figures all look pretty much the same."

He refrained from making whatever his first comment was going to be. I appreciated that. I'd had a rough night.

It occurred to me that one thing I had got right in the Miss Butterwith books was the point about people never telling the cops the whole truth and nothing but the truth.

Which is to say, I'd told the truth, but I'd left out all kinds of things that might—or might not—have proven useful to a homicide investigator because they were either embarrassing to Anna or she'd asked me not to speak of them. I'd left out my theory that Sara was trying to kill Anna because it sounded so farfetched. Besides…Sara had been one cool, efficient woman. I found it difficult to believe she'd have fallen into her own trap. But I'd also left out the fact that J.X. thought he'd seen evidence of Ricky manhandling Anna earlier that afternoon. I'd left out my suspicion that Rudolph and Sara had been having a thing. Also the indications that Rudolph and Anna had also been having a thing. Granted, there were other reasons the housekeeper might think Rudolph was in Anna's bedroom summoning help. Next to Sara, Rudolph *was* the person Anna was most likely to turn to for help.

At least, before Anna had suspected one of her nearest and dearest of trying to knock her off.

That was a peculiar thought right there. Okay, maybe Anna had—and maybe rightly—suspected Sara of trying to do her harm. But Rudolph? She and Rudolph practically went back to when time began. Their relationship had outlasted all the others in her life. And Rudolph...well, let's just say that no one would believe a book where Rudolph was the murderer. He simply wasn't the type.

Sure, in mystery novels anyone can be the killer. That's part of the fun. But in real life? No. Not everyone is murderer material. Capable of killing, yes. I think pretty much everyone is capable of killing given the right—extreme—set of circumstances. And certainly, given how vulnerable humans are, everyone is capable of killing by accident.

No, Anna *couldn't* believe Rudolph was involved in any plot to murder her. Of course, to hear Anna tell it, she couldn't believe anyone she knew wanted to get rid of her, but I took that with a grain of salt.

So why *hadn't* she gone to Rudolph for help? Assuming that she'd told the truth about that. Had she held her own council because she knew Rudolph and Sara were involved? That sort of made sense to me. I hadn't got the impression that she was aware of anything between Sara and Rudolph, and I thought I probably would have if only because—gut feeling—I suspected Anna wouldn't approve of such a relationship. It was definitely awkward having one's editor and old chum banging one's PA. Granted, not as awkward as having one's husband banging one's PA.

Perhaps I was projecting.

"What do you know about the relationship between Ms. Hitchcock and her stepson Mr. Richard Rosen?" Detective Eames's voice snapped me out of my thoughts.

I must have looked instantly guilty.

"Mr. Holmes?"

I was conscious of Anna saying that Ricky was not to be considered a suspect, but Anna had pretty much said that about anyone I asked her about. I understood and even sympathized with her squeamishness, but unless Anna was fabricating all these attempts on her life, *someone* had to be a suspect. And Ricky—well, in my opinion, Ricky looked pretty good for it.

I said, "I know that he stands to inherit a lot of money after Anna's death. I also know that their relationship is occasionally difficult."

His tone was so neutral I knew it had to be significant as he asked, "Have you overheard anything in the nature of threats from Mr. Rosen?"

"Me, no. But my—friend, Mr. Moriarity, believes he saw Rosen leaving Anna's room yesterday afternoon after we heard her scream."

"Scream?"

I nodded.

"What reason did Ms. Hitchcock give for screaming?"

"She didn't."

He considered this. "A number of the servants commented that Rosen and Ms. Hitchcock have frequently quarreled over money."

I conceded, "Anna said that Ricky had asked her for money. She also indicated that it was a common occurrence. She said it wasn't a problem, but...she did scream."

"The scream, yes. All right, Mr. Holmes, thanks for your help. If I have any further questions, I'll let you know. When are you planning on flying back to L.A.?"

"Are we free to go?" I asked, surprised. "We're not

suspects?"

"You're not a suspect, Mr. Holmes. Neither is your friend Mr. Moriarity. For one thing, these attacks on Ms. Hitchcock—assuming there were any previous attacks on Ms. Hitchcock—predate your arrival at the house, right?"

"Right." It wasn't that I wanted to be considered a murder suspect, but I could see Eames wasn't taking my theories nearly seriously enough. In fact, unless I was mistaken, he was struggling to preserve a suitably grave expression at the notion of me as a serious contender for killer.

I said, "Then I guess as soon as my—Mr. Moriarity is well enough to travel, we'll be on our way."

Chapter Fifteen

I woke to bright sunlight and a soft, insistent tapping at the bedroom door.

I couldn't have been deeply asleep because memory came rushing back the minute my eyes jerked open—including the recollection that I'd spent the early hours of dawn poised over J.X.'s sleeping form watching like a hawk for any signs of distress after the paramedics had finished their unlovely business.

I could feel the slow, steady beat of his heart against my back. His hand rested on my flank. His skin felt warm, but not feverishly so, and neither too dry nor clammy. He was making peaceful snuffling noises into my hair. Probably endearing if you were the sort of guy who was moved by that kind of thing.

The knocking at the door was getting louder. After last night, whoever was outside likely feared we were both dead in here.

Gently, I lifted J.X.'s arm and slid out from under, doing my best not to hurt my shoulder or wake him. Throwing aside the blankets, I staggered over to the door.

It was funny what you could do when you had to. Yesterday at this time, I'd felt like a complete invalid, fit only for crawling into bed and pulling the covers over my head. If anyone had told me I'd spend last night running up and down stairs and doing my impersonation of an action hero, I'd have requested a reality check.

A rain check at the very least.

I finally inched the door open and the maid eyed me doubtfully. It might have been *The Spiral Staircase* eyeball I was giving her through the crack between door and frame. Speaking for myself, after the horrors of the night before it was almost shocking to see someone looking so...normal.

"Ms. Hitchcock would like to see you, sir," the maid whispered.

I threw a quick look back at J.X. His weary, drawn face reminded me of a young, handsome Don Quixote. I wouldn't have been surprised to spot pieces of broken windmill scattered in the sheets around him.

"I'll be right there." I retrieved my red wool bathrobe, tying the tasseled belt around my waist and easing out of the room.

As I made the now-familiar trek to Anna's room I could see the gruesome signs of last night's catastrophe—and the markers of a police investigation in progress.

I shivered, pulling the robe more tightly about me.

The drapes were drawn in Anna's room. One soft light illuminated Anna sitting propped up in a nest of pillows and pastel cashmere throws. She appeared to be trying to force down tea and toast—and not making much progress. When she saw me, she pushed the tray away.

"Christopher." She held out her hands and I hiked around the bed. "It's too terrible to believe. First Nella. Now my poor Sara."

There were tears in her eyes when she released me. I'd never seen her without makeup before. She didn't appear to have eyebrows or eyelashes and the effect made her look very odd, like a mournful alien. Or possibly Elizabeth the First without her wigs.

"How are you feeling?"

"Grateful to be alive." Anna made a face, a ghost of her old charming moue. "Guilty."

"You don't have anything to feel guilty for."

"I know. But inside…" She put her hand to her eyes. It took her a moment to regain her composure. "I can't help believing that if I'd gone to the police when this all started, Sara, at least, might still be alive."

I wasn't convinced either way. I said, "Have the police confirmed that the wine was poisoned?"

Anna shook her head. "I haven't heard anything. I was too ill to talk to anyone last night. I'm sure they'll be up here any moment. According to the servants they're prowling all over the house. Evidently, Sara's room is sealed off."

That made sense. It was inconvenient but not unexpected. "I wouldn't know. I've only woken up myself."

"How's J.X.? I can't tell you how sorry I am that he was caught up in all this. That you both were."

"He's okay. He's pretty tough." I believe I sounded convincingly blasé for a guy who had spent the wee hours of the morning panicking every time J.X. hitched a breath or shivered.

"That's the advantage of youth."

I smiled wearily. Nodded.

"You were an absolute hero last night, Christopher."

That got a splutter out of me. "No way. I just happened to be the last man standing. Literally."

She ignored that. "I knew I made the right decision in asking you to come back to the house."

"For all the good it did."

"Now, Christopher." She sounded like the old Anna. "You keep telling me not to feel guilty, but I'm far more culpable than you."

We could have played ethical ping-pong all morning. I didn't have the energy. Abruptly my aches and pains were catching up with me. I pulled over the white velvet side chair and sat. "Anna, what do you think is going on? None of this makes sense to me."

"Nor to me."

"The police are certain that Nella's death was an accident." She started to speak. I forged ahead. "Obviously that can't be true of Sara's. At least, I don't see how it can be. That would be one helluva coincidence. But what the connection can be, I sure don't see."

"The connection is *me*. Someone is trying to kill me."

"But there's no way you could have been the intended victim of Poppy's auto accident. Even if it wasn't an accident, you couldn't have been the target."

She drooped back against the pillows and stared despairingly at the ceiling. "I don't pretend to understand the reasoning of a homicidal maniac, but obviously there's a connection between the car accident and last night's poisoning. Anything else defies logic."

"But how can any of this be the work of a homicidal maniac? These attempts aren't random and...last night proves that they're coming from within the house."

She shuddered and drew the comforter up around her shoulders. "I know," she said almost inaudibly.

"Who has reason to want to hurt you?"

"No one. *No one.*"

"Then we're back to looking at other possible motives. And financial gain is the most obvious."

She shook her head.

"What about Ricky?"

She stared at me as though she didn't understand the question.

I persisted. "I know what you said yesterday, but the whole house has heard you two arguing about money on other occasions. Obviously your relationship has its ups and downs."

She made a graceful, dismissing gesture.

"Anna, he needs money and you're currently standing in the way of that. Frankly, I think the way Miles set up Ricky's trust fund was an invitation to murder."

"Nonsense." She was shaking her head again, very definitely. "Ricky wouldn't hurt me. We have our differences, but he'd never—"

"Someone would."

She was silent.

"How *does* Ricky fare in your will?"

"I told you. Obviously...I've made provisions for him. He's my stepson. He's entitled to that."

"He's your stepson and he has financial problems. When, aside from you dying, does he inherit his father's property?"

"When he turns fifty. Unless, prior to that time, I agree that he's responsible enough to take control of his finances."

Fifty? "Which you're not about to do."

"Absolutely not."

If I was Ricky, I'd probably want to conk her over the head myself.

"So he doesn't inherit for another ten years?"

"Twelve, to be exact."

"Was he here when you had your fall down the garden stairs?"

"No."

"Was he here for any of your other close calls?"

"I don't remember." Her chin rose mutinously. "Ricky is not trying to harm me."

"Have it your way. Maybe Rudolph is trying to knock you off."

I'd been thinking she couldn't get any whiter, but she went the color of dirty linen.

"Rudolph would never…" Her voice gave out.

I agreed with her. I'd never met a more kind and gentlemanly man than Rudolph. I was playing devil's advocate as I said, "Rudolph was here when you fell. Was he here when you had any of your other accidents?"

"Yes. *No.* You're mixing me up, Christopher. Stop this."

"How can I? It's not like I'm enjoying this. You brought me here to help you. What am I supposed to do now? Pretend nothing happened? Nella's dead. Sara's dead. I nearly died. J.X. could have died." With surprise I heard the wobble in my voice when I said J.X.'s name.

"I know."

"That's not easy to ignore. The police sure as hell aren't going to ignore it."

"Did you share any of this…ridiculous speculation about Ricky with the police last night?"

"I didn't have to. The detective in charge of your case brought it up."

She stared down unseeingly at her breakfast tray.

"I asked you once before and you basically told me to butt out. I'm asking you again. What's your relationship with Rudolph?"

She closed her eyes. Her head fell back on the mound of pillows. "You're not naïve. You know what my relationship with Rudolph is."

I considered her unhappily. I really *wasn't* enjoying this. Anna had asked me to help her, and the only way I could see to do that was by ferreting out the truth.

"Okay, but there's also local speculation that you're having some kind of affair with your gardener."

Her head lifted. "*Luke?*"

I nodded.

"You didn't share *that* with the police, I hope?"

"No." I hadn't bothered because one thing I was quite sure the police would turn up all on their own was Luke's criminal record.

"You mustn't—*must not*—mention Luke to the police. Not in any context."

"Why's that?"

"Because he's an ex-con. And if you introduce his name into this case, the police will give up looking for anyone else. Promise me you won't mention Luke's name."

"You can't ask me to do that."

"I *am* asking you. I'm insisting."

"Anna." I shook my head. "I'm sorry. No. I can't make you that promise. Besides, if the police aren't complete incompetents, they'll already have that information."

"They *are* incompetents. That's obvious from the fact that they believe Poppy's crash was an accident."

We were back to that. One thing about Anna, she was a tireless advocate. Which is a nice way of saying she didn't know when to give up.

"Is Luke in your will?"

Her mouth tightened. She didn't reply.

"Let me try it from this angle. Is there anyone on the planet who *isn't* in your will? Did you maybe forget to mention some gal in Vanuatu? It would be nice to cross *someone* off our suspect list."

Anna said tartly, "You're assuming the primary motive for wanting me out of the way would be gain. Perhaps it's something else. Revenge. Lust. Fear. Jealousy."

"I'm open to suggestion here. Feel free to tell me who wants revenge on you."

She shook her head.

I sighed. "Out of curiosity, why was Luke in prison?"

Anna struggled inwardly. At last she said huskily, "He was convicted of attempted murder."

J.X. was awake and dressing when I returned to our room.

"Hey, what are you doing up?"

"There you are." He'd clearly had a shower. Drops of water beaded the bare honey-brown planes of his chest and shoulders. His hair was black and sleek as seal fur. Dark shadowed his chest and groin. "I was coming to look for you. You okay?"

"Me? Fine. I wasn't the one throwing up my guts last night."

He looked briefly self-conscious. Having excellent self-esteem, he shrugged it off as efficiently as his digestive tract had thrown off poison. "I'm fine. I'm a quick healer."

No kidding. He still looked pale, but other than that he seemed to be his normal exhaustingly healthy self. His expression was grim, though, his face set in tough, unfamiliar lines. His cop face, I thought.

"What's the situation this morning?" he asked.

"I'm not sure." I tossed my robe over a chair. Sadly, it appeared we were not going to hide in our bedroom all day. "I haven't had much chance for reconnaissance. Anna's freaking me out." I headed for the bathroom.

J.X. disconcerted me by stepping into my path and pulling me into his arms. "How so?"

It seemed only polite to reciprocate.

In the course of reciprocation, I lost the conversational thread.

"I'm very glad you didn't die last night," I told him a short while later.

"Thanks. Me too." He kissed the bridge of my nose. "What were you saying about Anna?"

I had to think.

"*Oh.* I have this bad feeling that she knows who's behind these attempts on her life. Or that she at least strongly suspects. Yet she won't speak up. Won't even seriously discuss the possibilities. She keeps insisting Poppy's car crash is somehow related. That it wasn't an accident. And she made some weird comment about revenge being a possible motive."

J.X.'s dark brows formed a straight line. "Well, the car wasn't tampered with. Is she suggesting the Clark woman tried to commit suicide?"

That was an angle I hadn't considered. "I don't know. She's not exactly suggesting anything. She's insisting that it wasn't an accident. And that she was the intended victim."

I expected J.X. to scoff at this, but he seemed to consider it. "I guess it's not impossible if you buy the attempted-suicide theory. The House kid was a favorite of Anna's, right? So if Clark did want to hurt Anna for some perceived wrong, taking the girl with her—and let's not forget *you*, Anna's old friend—might have been a way of settling scores."

"If it is, it's the dumbest plan I ever heard. Poppy would be dead. How would that be a satisfying payback?"

"It wouldn't be, not to a balanced mind, but whoever is behind these attempts isn't hindered by a balanced mind, if you know what I mean."

Here I'd insisted to Anna that we weren't dealing with a homicidal maniac. J.X.'s mouth twisted at whatever he read in my face. "When I was with SFPD, very early in my career, I was involved in a suicide-by-cop shooting. Do you know what that is?"

"Yeah. How do you mean *involved*?"

"Involved. I was a participant."

I admit I was mildly shocked. You don't expect your significant others to have blood on their hands. Unless they cut themselves shaving.

"It's one of those things you pray will never happen on your watch. I happened to get called out as backup on a domestic. We had a complaint that an ex-SWAT officer had beat up his wife. Not for the first time either. There was a history of domestic violence at that address. Anyway, when the first responders went to the door, the guy pulled what they believed to be a rifle. He aimed it at the officers, wouldn't put it down despite repeated warnings, and...we shot him. It turned out later that he was brandishing an air rifle, but there's no way anyone could have known that at the time. Somebody's pointing a rifle at you—someone who knows how to use it—" J.X. shook his head. "We were all cleared, but I can tell you I thought long and hard about resigning. The officers who first responded both ended up taking early retirement."

"Jeez." I had no idea what to say to that. I had no idea J.X. had anything like that in his past. It was a reminder of how much we still had to learn about each other.

"It's hard to comprehend the way a disturbed mind works. But disturbed people often seem perfectly rational until they finally snap. We all have our methods for coping and they usually happen behind closed doors."

I recalled a few of my own methods for coping after David had left. "Okay. But Poppy couldn't have doctored that bottle of wine last night."

"You won't know that until you know *how* the wine was doctored—if whatever substance made us sick was even in the wine. But it's not impossible that a guest in this house could have tampered with a bottle of wine, any bottle, knowing that sooner or later the poisoned bottle would be selected. The more time that passed, the stronger this person's alibi would appear. Especially if he or she could avoid returning to the house."

"Great."

J.X. grinned. "Nobody ever said being a master detective was easy."

Chapter Sixteen

As much as I generally enjoy breakfast, I can't say I had much appetite for eggs and bacon in a house where a fatal poisoning had occurred a few hours earlier. I wished I could have ordered in pizza, but it was liable to send a negative message.

A more negative message than the cops roaming the stately halls of Murder Manor.

J.X. had even less appetite for breakfast. He sipped tea while I bravely poked hardboiled eggs and nibbled on the corners of bacon.

We had the dining room to ourselves. I don't know what Tim Gunn's take is on such situations, but I was relieved to not have to make polite breakfast conversation with people I suspected of trying to bump off my hostess.

"You want some toast?" I inquired. "You should probably eat something."

He shuddered like a horse trying to rid itself of flies. "No thanks."

I gave up trying to pretend I was eating either. "I've been thinking. Since Poppy is staying with Victoria, maybe we should walk over there."

I had his full attention. "And do what?"

"Ask her if she's feeling suicidal?"

He choked on his coffee, but recovered. "If you want. But it would make more sense to drive."

"Actually, I think I'd like to be outside for a while."

"Are you sure you're up to a walk in the snow?"

"I am if you are."

He shrugged off the idea that he might not be up to anything. His gaze, meeting mine, was thoughtful. I was afraid he understood my reluctance to get in a car again only too well.

Since we practically live in our cars in So Cal, I knew I'd have to get over that, but for now I preferred the idea of walking. It helped that, as battered and bruised as I was, I seemed to have a constant supply of sheer nervous energy that was keeping me on my feet and moving. Since I'm usually about as big a baby as you can find when it comes to my own physical woes, I was a little surprised at my macho-man impersonation. Though probably not as surprised as J.X., who'd witnessed me canceling one of our three weekends midway through because of a migraine.

Maybe the tough guy thing was catching.

Probably not.

We were finishing up our tea and coffee when a uniformed officer requested J.X. accompany him to make his statement. He rose at once in a spirit of cooperativeness, although I'm not sure how much of a statement you can get out of the single word *ralph.*

I went upstairs to change into something warm enough to walk across the north forty without developing pneumonia.

As I was checking my wallet I noticed the In Case Of Emergency card had been tucked in with the bills. Probably when the emergency technicians or hospital staff were trying to identify us after Poppy's car had gone over the side. I stared at the small, Day-Glo green card.

The wallet was only a couple of months old, and I hadn't bothered to fill in the emergency card until after I'd returned from my adventures in Northern California. I'd forgotten all about it, in fact, but right there in the field where it asked who to contact in case of emergency, I'd written J.X.'s name and phone number. There was no mistake. It was my handwriting.

As horrible as that writing-retreat weekend had been, I'd come back from it feeling newly confident and even happy. And a large part of the reason for both those emotions was J.X.

It was later on that I'd got cold feet, that I'd kept trying to stall and delay the relationship from progressing.

Why?

Clearly I'd been feeling confident enough to list J.X. as something pretty darned close to next of kin.

Nor had I been wrong. When I'd needed him, he'd dropped everything to fly across country to my bedside—and this after I'd basically blown him off.

I slipped the card back in my wallet. That was one mystery solved, anyway. Maybe it hadn't been conscious, but I *had* asked for J.X. after I'd been injured. I had certainly wanted him.

I still did.

Sliding the wallet into my back pocket, I dragged a heavy blue and green tweed pullover over my shirt and headed for the door.

It opened before I reached it. J.X. looked in.

"There you are. Ready?"

"I think maybe I am."

He blinked as I walked straight up to him, wrapped my arms around his neck and locked my mouth on his.

When we finally, reluctantly broke contact, he said with a hint of unsteadiness, "What was that for?"

As I stared into his eyes I felt like I was seeing right into his heart, seeing the strength tempered by gentleness, the stubbornness balanced by loyalty and integrity, the honesty that didn't sacrifice kindness. "I missed you."

"Okay. I missed you too." He seemed bemused, but agreeable.

My normal self-consciousness reasserted itself. I started to walk past him and J.X. caught my good arm, swinging me back. He scrutinized my face for a long moment, then he kissed me again, quickly, lightly.

"I mean that," he said softly. I realized that once again he'd read me quite accurately. It was getting to be a habit with him. "I did miss you, Kit. But I won't push you for more than you can give."

It was absurdly hard to meet his eyes. I nodded.

It seemed like a very long walk to Victoria's, but that was probably more about snow than distance.

Or maybe it was more about how out of shape I was. Although, in fairness, I was in better shape than I had been three months ago—or at least I had been before the car accident. Once J.X. and I had started seeing each other—okay, perhaps "seeing each other" was an overstatement of three visits in three months—I'd made myself start swimming again and half-heartedly working out.

In fact, it occurred to me, as he was helping me over yet another fence stile, that maybe that sense of being unprepared, well, *unfit*, had been a factor in my reluctance to get involved with him. There was going to be a lot of competition for a guy like J.X. I'd already lost one lover to a younger, cuter rival. I didn't know if I could take having it happen twice. All the biceps curls in the world weren't going to turn me into Mr. Atlas.

Hell, J.X. was probably too young to even know who Mr. Atlas was.

I continued to brood as we walked down the snow-cleared dirt road past long white stretches of meadow and copses of dark evergreens. The air smelled of snow and pines. It burned in my lungs. My muscles burned too. It was a hike, not a walk, and a harder hike than I'd expected.

"Tell me about Poppy," J.X. asked, probably to distract me—much like the sheriffs do with their mortally wounded deputies in all those old westerns.

"She's...different. I couldn't really get a fix on her. Apparently her husband died in some kind of accident last year and left her a bundle. I don't think she likes men."

"You mean—"

"No. I think she's heterosexual, I think she just dislikes men. I think she's got a lot of aggressions for whatever reason." I described the story she'd contributed to the group for him.

"Wow."

"That was, in varying degrees, kind of the reaction of everyone else in the group. In fact, I think she made Nella sick to her stomach. Literally. The story *is* pretty graphic. Nella's story had a lot of violence too, but it was all lyrical and symbolic. Poppy's approach was what you might call cut and dried."

"Ouch."

"Yep. That was my reaction reading it." I hoped he hadn't noticed how hard I was breathing. My shoulder was aching like a sonofabitch. Why had I thought making like Scott heading for the South Pole was such a grand scheme? I was beginning to think I'd end this expedition the same way.

"Is there any conjecture her husband's death wasn't an accident?"

"I don't know. It didn't come up over the finger sandwiches and tea. She did make a weird comment when Sara was critiquing her story. I forget the exact wording, but Sara said something like the protagonist of Poppy's story would never have the nerve to commit murder, and Poppy answered to the effect that it went to show how little Sara knew."

"Hmm."

I knew what that noncommittal *hmm* meant. I said, "It's not what she said—well, it is partly what she said—but it was kind of the tone too. Like she let her anger get the better of her. And Victoria cut in right away, as though she was trying to keep Poppy from saying something damaging."

"You think Poppy killed her husband and Victoria knows about it?"

"Maybe. I realize Victoria could have merely been trying to keep Poppy from saying something stupid. She does present all the symptoms of terminal open-mouth-insert-foot disease." I added, "If Poppy did murder her better half, I don't see her killing herself out of remorse."

"But there might be other things going on that you're not aware of. Financial problems, legal problems, health problems."

"True."

"Did you want to stop and rest for a few minutes?"

"God *yes.*"

His laugh was not unkind as he brushed snow off a flat-topped rock that provided a natural bench.

After I saw Victoria's farmhouse I had to revise my idea

about possible motives for murder. It was one of those cute, rambling places that provide the domestic centerpiece of films like *Bringing Up Baby* or *Christmas in Connecticut*. *I'd* have killed for a place like that: old stone and dormer windows, Dutch doors and gingerbread trim. Lamps shone in welcome from behind the mullioned windows.

There was no front porch, only a stoop beneath the white-frosted overhang. We—okay, *I*—staggered up the single step and hammered at the wooden surface half-concealed by the enormous evergreen wreath.

The door swung open and Victoria gazed at us in open surprise.

"Chris!"

"Hi there. We were...er, out walking." As cover stories went, it wasn't much, but you have to work with the tools you have. In my case, hypothermia and blisters.

"Did you lose your way?"

I heard the small sound J.X. made behind me, but I ignored it. "How's Poppy? Is she still staying with you?"

"Well, yes. But..." Her gaze veered from me to J.X. and back to me again. Reluctantly, she stepped back, holding the door wide. "Poppy's feeling much better. Come in, both of you. You must be freezing."

The interior of the house lived up to the promise of the exterior: big rooms with open beamed ceilings, built-in bookshelves, old-fashioned wallpaper, comfortable chintz-covered furniture.

Victoria led us straight through to the front room where a fire was burning in the grate.

"I can't believe that you're out hiking after just getting out of the hospital."

"I didn't realize how far it was." That, at least, was the gospel truth.

"How are things over at the house? Is Anna feeling any better?"

"She's better, yes. Still weak, though."

"Weak?" Victoria sounded puzzled. "Well, of course it was a shock, and Anna was very fond of Nella."

I stopped walking and J.X. halted short of crashing into me. "Then you don't know?"

"Know what?" Victoria turned to face me. If she was faking it, she was a better actress than me. Er, than I'd expected.

In the wide room beyond her I could see Poppy. She lay on a long blue chintz sofa, her broken leg propped on pillows. She looked pretty comfy, all things considered. She was staring wide-eyed at us over the top of *Vogue* magazine.

"Sara Mason is dead," I said. "The whole house was struck with food poisoning last night. Sara had it the worst."

The magazine in Poppy's hand slipped and crashed onto the table, knocking her coffee mug and sandwich plate to the floor.

The two of them stared at us in open horror.

"I thought you knew," I said. "It didn't dawn on me that you might not." If I'd realized, I might have tried to break it more gently, though admittedly this did give us better opportunity to examine their reactions.

Victoria seemed to gather herself. "We've had the TV off all day. I don't listen to the radio and we haven't used our laptops since..." She cleared her throat. "No one called us."

"It's still pretty chaotic over there with the police and all."

"*Police*," they echoed.

"You said food poisoning." Poppy's tone was accusing.

"Did I?"

"Yes." That was J.X. Always a stickler for accuracy, that guy.

"I guess I did. I don't think the police have determined the exact substance used, except that whatever it was, it was probably administered through the wine we had at dinner last night."

"*Wine*?" Victoria whispered right before she fell over in a dead faint.

Chapter Seventeen

As you might imagine, J.X. is much better at scraping damsels in distress off the carpeting than yours truly. Even not counting the injured shoulder and bad back.

He scooped up Victoria practically before she hit the ground, well within the five-second rule. If she'd been a potato chip, he could have still eaten her. Not something I particularly wanted to contemplate.

Poppy was squawking as she hauled herself off the sofa and hopped out of the way. J.X. replaced her with Victoria who was already coming around all twitchy and fluttery.

"Where am I?" she breathed, gazing bewilderedly up at the ring of faces surrounding her.

Poppy ignored her—and with dialog like that, I couldn't blame her. "Is it true? Sara's dead? Poisoned?"

"It's true that she's dead. She appears to have been poisoned. I really can't say more than that."

"No, you can't." J.X. gave me a stern look. But if he'd had views on what I should or shouldn't say, he should have expressed them earlier. Like during our journey through the Northwest Passage.

"When did it happen?"

"She died during the night. We don't know anything else.

Not for sure," I added conscientiously.

"It doesn't make sense. Why would anyone want to kill Sara? I mean sure, she was a snotty, cold bitch—"

"*Poppy,*" moaned Victoria.

Poppy shut up.

"No love lost, huh?" I asked.

"I didn't like her, no. But I didn't kill her. How could I? Why would I?"

"Sara wasn't the intended victim. Anna was the intended victim."

They exchanged distressed looks. Victoria made more of those protesting noises. Poppy said nothing.

"Wait a minute," J.X. intervened. "This is all supposition. We don't know that it *wasn't* food poisoning; let alone who the intended victim might have been."

"It wasn't food poisoning if the problem was with the wine."

"We don't know that for a fact yet either. You're jumping the gun, Kit."

"It had to be the wine. That's the only thing all of you had that I didn't."

Victoria said faintly, "I brought Anna a bottle of red wine when I arrived for the weekend seminar."

Neither of us had an immediate answer to that.

Poppy said finally, "Oh."

"Where did the wine come from?" J.X. asked.

Victoria put a hand to her forehead. "I bought it."

J.X. and I asked at the same time, "Where?"

"I-I don't remember."

"When did you buy it?"

"I don't remember."

"You don't even drink wine," Poppy said.

Victoria lowered her hand and shot Poppy a look that would have shut anyone else up. Not Poppy.

"Well? You *don't* drink wine."

"It was a gift. I didn't plan on drinking it."

"Then you must have only recently bought it. How can you not remember where?"

Victoria looked outraged. "*Shut up*, Poppy."

"Do you have a receipt?" J.X. asked.

"No."

As I regarded her unhappy, angry face, a thought occurred. "Was the wine a gift to you?"

Score. I could tell by her red face. Regifting. You gotta love it.

"Who gave you the wine?"

"I don't know."

I could see by Poppy's expression that she and I were finally in agreement on something. "Why are you protecting this person?" I demanded. I really couldn't follow her logic. "You're probably next on her list."

"Kit."

"But she could be in danger herself." Assuming she hadn't bought and poisoned the wine and then concocted this story as a cover. J.X. was shaking his head.

"I *don't* know who gave me the wine. I *swear.*" Victoria sat up in her earnestness. "I never knew. I got it at Christmas in a Secret Santa gift exchange."

"A what?" J.X. and I shared looks.

Poppy explained, "It's where a bunch of people exchange

names anonymously and buy each other cheapo Christmas presents they'd be otherwise embarrassed to purchase. Victoria's always participating in that kind of thing."

I asked, "Don't you find out who your Secret Santa is after you exchange gifts?"

Victoria nodded.

"Then you must know—"

She was shaking her head. "No. That's what I'm trying to tell you. The name tag must have fallen off. I never knew who gave the wine to me. I belonged to two different Secret Santa exchanges last year. It could have been someone from either group."

I looked at J.X. He said, "Can you make a list of everyone who took part in the two gift trades?"

"Why should she?" That was, predictably, Poppy. She hopped over to one of the wide chintz-covered chairs and lowered awkwardly to the fat cushions. "What authority do you two have to start butting into this? Isn't this for the police to dig into?"

"Anna asked for our help." I could feel J.X.'s gaze. I ignored it. Anna was the queen bee in this circle, and the only person likely to thwart her wishes was, in my opinion, the person who wanted her dead. And even that person was unlikely to openly oppose Anna.

"I don't have anything to hide." Victoria lost what little color she'd regained. "I'll make the list. I can't believe that there was anything wrong with the wine. That would mean..." She stopped, swallowed, gazed at us all with wide, stricken eyes.

"You were the actual target," I said.

It pretty much took any pretense at social out of our social call.

"We never did get a chance to question Poppy." J.X. and I were back in our bedroom at the main house. He sat on the side of the bed tugging at his boots while I paced up and down.

He muttered, "It's moot, don't you think?"

"What is?" I stopped pacing.

We'd ended up calling for a ride back—I'd had to cry uncle, an elderly uncle, it felt like—and admit I wasn't up to another long walk through the snow. Luke had retrieved us in a rattletrap of a station wagon.

Initially it had seemed like a heaven-sent opportunity to question Luke, but he wasn't the chatty type. He had responded to all attempts to initiate conversation with grunts—when he bothered to respond at all. Short of an unvarnished interrogation, which we had neither time nor authorization for, there was no way to casually interview him.

I'd spent the entire drive gazing at the back of his head, staring at the rumpled Fabio-like mane while commenting fruitlessly on the weather and the road and life in general in a vain attempt to draw Luke out. J.X. had, unhelpfully in my opinion, gazed out the window at the white landscape bumping and bouncing by as the station wagon hit every snow-covered pothole and rock in the dirt road.

Anyway, Luke wasn't a major concern for me anymore. The police would surely investigate Luke more thoroughly than we could. I was now convinced that the lead to follow was Victoria's mysterious bottle of wine.

On that score at least, J.X. had seemed of the same mind. "I don't know about you, but Poppy didn't strike me as particularly depressed." He tossed his left boot to the side of the bed.

I absently considered that discarded boot. It seemed, I

dunno, sort of territorial the way he tossed his belongings around my room. Granted, it was his room too. That was the whole idea of sharing a room. But I wouldn't have been so comfortable so fast.

I said automatically, "Plus, it's hard to believe that if Poppy was involved she'd be so...indiscreet. If I'd killed someone, I don't think I'd go out of my way to point out how much that person needed killing."

J.X. shrugged. "The genius mastermind criminal is pretty much a myth. The average bad guy—or girl—is a lot more likely to be found trying to audition for *America's Dumbest Criminals*."

I snorted. "Either way, this anonymously gifted bottle of wine has to be significant."

"Maybe."

"There's no *maybe* about it. Either Victoria has been the target all along, or Victoria is the killer."

Hands locked around his right boot, he tipped his head, studying me. "Slow down, Kit. First, we don't know that the poison—well, to start with, we don't know that poison was involved—but if poison *was* used, we don't know that it came from Victoria's bottle of wine. We have no idea what bottle of wine was used last night. Secondly—"

"No," I interrupted. "I refuse to believe that. I refuse to believe that in the midst of someone trying to kill Anna, there are these two totally random accidents. That's just—it's just impossible to believe. It's...bad fiction. These things *have* to be connected."

"Truth is stranger than fiction."

I gave him a look of disgust.

"Okay, okay. But I find it equally hard to believe that someone is trying to knock off both Anna and Victoria."

He had me there. It did seem unlikely. I sighed. "I know. The car accident and the anonymous bottle of wine couldn't have been aimed at Anna, which means Victoria had to be the target—which is almost harder to believe than the idea of Victoria as a cold-blooded murderess willing to wipe out entire dinner parties to achieve her ends. No pun intended."

J.X. was grinning, though I failed to see what was so amusing him.

"Yes?" I inquired shortly.

"I don't know. It's just...you're cute when you're all worked up." He pulled off his boot and tossed it over with the other.

"Do you mind focusing here?"

He stretched out on the bed, propping his head on his hand. "Why don't you lock the door?"

"Huh?"

"We've got a couple of hours before dinner. Why don't we have a nap together and see what...transpires?"

I put my hands on my hips and scowled forbiddingly at him. My disapproval seemed to sail right past him. He smiled at me, his teeth very white against the outline of his beard. It was an appealing smile, I admit.

"You're not taking this seriously enough."

"Honey, the police are involved now. Our role is primarily moral support for Anna. If you want to bat theories back and forth, I'm fine with that, but—" A wide yawn cut him off. I had a front-row view of his epiglottis before he continued, "I'm running short of sleep. As are you. Why don't we discuss this lying down?"

"Hmph!" I replied.

J.X.'s smile went still wider—and seemingly whiter. "Come on, Kit. Relax for a few minutes."

I was very tired. I'd been tired before the two-mile hike to Victoria's. I probably hadn't had more than three hours sleep the night before. And not a restful three hours at that. The mere idea of kicking my shoes off and lying down was seductive—let alone the idea of lying down in J.X.'s brawny arms.

I went to the door and locked it. Returning to the bed, I tugged one-handedly at my own boots.

He raised his head. "You want some help?"

"No." I couldn't help the note of irritation. I've never been good at needing help, let alone asking for it. I finally got my boots off and flopped back on the tapestry coverlet.

J.X.'s hand closed on my good shoulder. "You're so far away. C'mere. Get comfortable."

I groaned, but moved with a great deal of wincing and flinching. I felt best on my back with a pillow bracing my injured shoulder, but even that wasn't comfortable. I was supposed to wear the damned sling for a minimum of six weeks and thinking of that put me in a horrible mood.

J.X. watched the production, still smiling. "How's the shoulder?"

"Terrible. How's the stomach?"

"Much better."

I sighed, settling down next to J.X. He wrapped his arms around me and pulled me closer, and despite the fact that my mending collarbone was not happy with that particular position, there was great comfort in resting in his arms. He leaned his face against mine. His lips were soft, so soft against my jaw. I could feel his eyelashes flickering against my skin, feel his warm breath.

"I knew it," I said. "We're not going to talk."

I felt his smile. He didn't even bother to answer.

I started to complain, but was caught mid-yawn. Who was I kidding? I also wanted to sleep. I closed my eyes. My lungs seemed to fall into the same peaceful rhythm as his own. I could feel his heart beating quietly, steadily against mine. I let my body relax, go heavy.

I think I was starting to drowse when J.X. murmured, "You know what I really want to do?"

"Mm?"

He whispered in my ear.

My eyes shot wide open.

Chapter Eighteen

I want to fuck you, Kit.

I raised my head, cleared my throat. "Come again?"

J.X. smiled at me, a lazy smile. His eyes were dark and tender. "And again and again and again." His voice was soft. It seemed to raise every hair on my body, like the drifting ripple of static electricity.

"Oh." I lowered my head to my arm, looked into the serious regard centimeters from my own. Well, good luck avoiding him at *that* distance. I redirected my gaze to his mouth. It was soft and moist and his lips were faintly pink as they shaped his words.

"You never let me before. Is it a problem?"

"Uh...no."

"You don't sound sure."

I wasn't sure. That is...the idea turned me on, no denying it. The idea of J.X. taking me, all that warmth and strength burying itself in me and making me his own—*bizarre* thought and yet...definitely a turn-on. Which was kind of weird because I'd never liked being fucked. Never enjoyed it. Found it uncomfortable, a little painful, and too much like subjugation. And David had felt the same way. So we'd taken turns with it, because that was the fair thing to do, but there had always been that niggling knowledge that both of us were never truly enjoying sex at the same time. That it was always a concession on someone's part.

J.X. and I hadn't really fucked since we'd got together. I wasn't sure what his feelings were now days. When we'd first hooked up all those years ago, he'd let me fuck him and he'd accepted without demur my refusal to reciprocate.

I mean, I'd tried to put it in more diplomatic terms than that, but the bottom line was...for me there was a bottom line. And I hadn't planned to cross it. Not for him and not for anyone else. Not ever again. I suppose it was all tied up with my feelings for what had happened with David.

Maybe it was still tied up with that.

Although, the truth was, I never *had* liked it. But recently I'd found the idea not merely acceptable, more and more I'd found myself truly excited by it. Which, frankly, made me sort of uneasy.

"Talk to me," J.X. said. My eyes were probably starting to spin—black and white swirls while my brain overheated.

I said, "I know it's only fair that we...trade off."

His brows drew together. "So you *don't* like the idea?"

"No. It's not that."

"Come on, Kit. Tell me what you think." Not impatient. Coaxing. I think I'd have preferred exasperation. Then I could have worked myself into a snit and we could have sidestepped the issue for the time being.

I rolled onto my back. "I don't know. It's never been good for me like that."

"Did someone hurt you?"

Startled, I turned my head. J.X.'s nostrils had a pinched look, his mouth a straight line. I realized he was angry on my behalf. Angry at the idea of this imaginary lover who had hurt me with his careless, selfish ways. J.X. not realizing that I had probably been as careless and selfish as any of my lovers. Not that there had been so many of them, though I'd indulged in the usual youthful experimentation before settling down with David.

"It's not like that," I said quickly, and I reached over to stroke his hair back from his serious face. The strands felt like silk—short, cool, black silk—and they clung to my fingers. "I mean it does hurt—"

"It shouldn't."

"But that's not really it. I don't mind a little discomfort if the payoff is worth—" I stopped in time.

Not really in time, though.

"But the payoff isn't worth it?" His tone was absolutely neutral.

I held his gaze with my own. "I think it would be with you, which is why, for probably the first time in my life, I'm starting to fantasize about it."

His face softened. "I think I could make it good for you, Kit. I'd make sure nothing hurt you. I'd take care of you every step of the way." His voice went dark and husky, and he put his hand to my crotch, feeling me up through my jeans with an expert, even possessive hand.

I heard myself make a sound in the back of my throat, and I closed my eyes, focusing on that touch.

"I love you," he said, and his mouth covered mine.

There was a lump in my throat. I wasn't used to someone...caring so much. It got to me in a way I'd never have expected. I made another of those freaky sounds— uncomfortably close to a whimper—and thrust against him.

J.X.'s tongue slipped into my mouth, wet, hot, intrusive. Another thing I'd never been crazy about. What can I say? There's a reason I chose to write about an elderly spinster and her cat. It wasn't just the, um, hygiene factor—although supposedly dogs' mouths are cleaner than humans—it was so *personal* having someone push his tongue into your mouth. Hard to think of other things when a guy's checking out your back molars.

J.X., however, French kissed me with delicacy and skill, and need bloomed like fever in my bloodstream.

"I do want it," I panted. "I want you to fuck me."

He groaned like I'd granted some amazing, impossible wish—which, frankly, was all the more exciting.

He kissed me again, broke the kiss with seeming reluctance. "Hang on. We need something…"

"Condoms. Hell. It's been years since I've had to—"

"No, not condoms. I mean, yes, condoms, but I've got condoms. I mean something we can use as lube."

I was still dealing with the fact that he evidently carried condoms everywhere like he was still nineteen, when the significance of the word lube hit me. I gave a shiver that was half excitement and half alarm.

Jesus, we were going to do this. I was going to let him push that long, thick cock right up my tight little asshole.

Wide-eyed, I watched him disappear into the bathroom and reappear a few seconds later with a bottle of Fekkai glossing conditioner.

I was still clumsily trying to peel off my clothes as he took his place beside me on the bed. Together we helped each other undress, warm hands lingering in unconscious caress, accommodating each other. My heart was going a million miles an hour as I leaned back against the pillows he'd propped up for me. I watched his face, so grave and absorbed as he squirted the pale, shimmering liquid onto his fingers.

The scent of sex mingled with that of sunflower and olive oil and citrus. Very California. Very us.

He leaned forward to kiss me again. As our mouths brushed, a thought occurred to me. "Not on this bedspread!"

He laughed against me, drew back. We did some frantic shoving and rearranging of bed linens.

"Anything else?" His eyes were crinkling at the corners, and the knowledge that he would deal patiently with any further minor uproars went a long way to relaxing me. What was the big deal after all? It wasn't like I'd never done this.

"Be my guest," I said.

He grinned, reached forward to stroke me, cupping my balls lightly in his hand. "And what a wonderful host you are."

I spluttered a laugh, let my legs fall wide, making a cradle for him as he lowered his lean, muscular length onto me.

"Am I hurting your arm?"

"It's not my arm I'm worried about."

I said it without thinking. His face was instantly serious. "We're not going to do anything you don't want to."

"I know. Don't listen to me."

He appeared to consider this. "Sometimes I think the words get in the way with you and me, but I always listen to you. I always will."

I nodded. "You're better at this than I am. I'm trying to learn by example."

He looked touched. "That's one of the nicest things you've said to me."

"I need to say more nice things to you."

I proceeded to turn over a new leaf. That led to some nuzzling and nibbling and other forms of unspoken communication. As J.X.'s clever fingers tweaked one of my nipples, I arched up. He watched me, his eyes dark and hooded, his mouth pink from kisses and love bites.

I knew what was next and I consciously relaxed my muscles as I felt his warm hand spreading the silky lotion in the cleft of my ass.

This was it. I shifted, allowing him better access, trying not to tense as J.X. pushed his finger through the tight band of muscle. It was invasive, certainly, but it was electrifying too. I bit my lip, trying not to make any sound that might be mistaken for pain. It was a bit uncomfortable, but the wicked pleasure of J.X. touching me there melted any resistance I might have had.

He worked his finger slowly, insistently, and my body had no choice but to adjust to that careful breaching of defenses. I'd stopped focusing on anything but startling sensation when I realized one finger had become two. J.X. waited, watching until I relaxed again and accepted that more intense pull and penetration before he pressed on. He flexed his hand and I could feel the muted sharpness of his fingernails—hell, I thought I could feel his fingerprints.

I heard myself make one of those sounds from the back of my throat as he pushed a fraction farther and pressed against the nub of my prostate gland.

I squeezed my eyes shut against that tiny exquisite explosion.

"Yeah, that's nice, isn't it?"

I nodded helplessly as the sparkles rippled up and down my nervous system.

Slow and easy J.X. continued, thrusting his fingers in and out.

"It's like watching a naughty little mouth sucking my fingers." His thumb traced the opening to my body.

I shivered, wanting more but not wanting to have to ask for it.

J.X. withdrew his fingers in a final, slick caress and I felt my body spasm around the sudden and disappointing emptiness.

But the disappointment didn't last long. I opened my eyes at the wet, brisk sound of skin slicking skin and saw J.X. slathering lotion on his already rigid cock. I swallowed at the sight of that sizable erection. Impressive by any standards.

By contrast my own cock was only partially committed to the proceedings. I gave it a reassuring stroke, resettling as J.X. knelt between my legs and carefully guided himself into my body. My muscles clenched in a kind of panic and then relaxed, cautiously accepting, shyly welcoming him.

It wasn't lack of preparation, unless it was the mental kind, that made this such a production, but J.X. seemed prepared to take all afternoon if necessary. Slowly, slowly, he pushed inside, pausing now and then to stroke my belly or flank.

Too much. Too deep, too thick, too intimate...and yet I kept yielding ground, falling back, watching from a helpless distance as he knocked my doors down one after another until there were no barriers left and we were locked tight.

I'd never felt anything like it. Frankly, never *wanted* to feel anything like it.

He gave a tentative thrust and my hips rocked to meet him seemingly of their own volition. I realized that the discomfort was gone and now there was only pleasure and a mounting excitement in my belly. I arched into his next thrust and let myself cry out.

He shoved back and I rose to meet him, wanting to feel him more deeply. Now we were finding a rhythm, our rhythm. Long, sweet and slow strokes that seemed to pierce me to my heart. I wanted to keep it up forever, that happy glide, the dulcet friction that was pleasure so extreme it was almost painful, but a frantic tension began to build in my body, and I knew I had to come or fly apart.

J.X. breathed warmly against my ear. "Let *go*, Kit. I've got you now."

It was like swinging out into the vast, light-studded night. Stars rained down around me. I let go and fell with them.

"Was it all right?" J.X. asked a couple of turns of the world later.

I turned my head on the pillow. Stared at him. He stared back. He was serious. In fact, he looked uncertain. Didn't he know? Couldn't he tell? Hell, if the writing career didn't work out, he could always—I stopped that thought, stopped that instinctive and automatic sarcastic distancing, and let myself absorb what had really happened between us.

It deserved my full consideration. I'd never felt anything like it, never responded to anyone like that. It was like J.X. had reached into me and turned me inside out. I felt weak and empty and at the same time utterly relaxed and peaceful. It was so *weird*. As he'd fucked me, I'd felt helpless and out of control with the intensity of my reaction, both physical and emotional, but I really was...okay now. Better than okay. I felt very good. Yes, my body was a little sore and I was very tired, but the aches were all the satisfying kind.

I said shakily, "At the risk of sounding like something out of *Ladies' Home Journal*, it's never been like that for me."

His face relaxed into a smile. A faintly smug smile at that. Well, perhaps he deserved to feel smug.

"I figured."

I raised my eyebrows. "Oh you did, did you?"

"Yeah. Sometimes you have to give up a certain amount of control to get what you want."

I swallowed. "Maybe."

He leaned over and covered my mouth with his own.

We drowsed. How long, I'm not sure, but the next thing I knew the room was in shadow and the dying sunlight burnished the furniture in a fuzzy glow. I listened, wondering what had woken me. I heard a cautious tap-tap-tapping at the door.

I moaned.

J.X. swore under his breath. He was up and off the bed in one lithe movement, scooping up my bathrobe and stalking to the door as he shrugged it on.

I dragged the blankets still higher. I couldn't remember what the rules were about houseguests having sex. Was it rude? Wasn't the fact that Anna had thrown us into the same room sort of tacit permission to go at it like college kids on spring break?

Anna was at the door. She sounded nonplussed to find J.X. answering her knock.

"*Oh.* J.X. I'd almost forgotten—how are you feeling, darling? I should have made the effort to find out sooner, but I've been...been feeling so goddamned *shattered.* I can't seem to pull myself together. Is Christopher—?" She let it hang delicately.

"He's resting."

Say what? I didn't think I imagined that undernote of

197

protective belligerence in J.X.'s tone.

I sat up quickly. "It's okay. I'm awake now."

J.X. stepped back and Anna came into the room, wielding her crutches with expert ease.

Her smile twisted. "I see my timing could use some work."

J.X.'s uncharacteristic silence seemed to agree with her.

Un-com-fort-able!

"No," I said. "We were only getting some shuteye."

Anna gave a disbelieving laugh, then murmured thanks as J.X. pushed one of the chairs forward. She carefully seated herself. "I spent most of the morning talking to the police."

Neither J.X. nor I spoke.

"The wine at dinner was tampered with." She wiped hastily at the corners of her eyes. "There were corncockle seeds at the bottom of one of the wine bottles used at dinner last night."

"Corncockle?" echoed J.X.

"It's a winter annual weed," I said. I was only too familiar with corncockle. I'd used it as a means of knocking off a particularly obnoxious character in *Sow Shall Ye Reap, Miss Butterwith,* the most literary entrée in all the Miss B. oeuvre. "Four seeds or more is usually deadly."

Anna nodded. "They found three seeds. There could have been more, but in that case..."

"Everyone would be dead." My voice sounded way too calm. "Instead of only Sara."

J.X. asked, "Did the police offer an explanation for why Sara died and no one else?"

Anna shook her head. "Perhaps she had a medical predisposition or unknown weakness. Her heart perhaps. I don't know. It seems unlikely. She was always in excellent health. In fact, she was a health nut."

"Where did the wine come from?" I asked.

Anna shook her head. "We used two bottles of red last night. One bottle came from the wine cellar. I have no idea of its provenance. I don't really keep track of things like that. Besides...I was distracted last night, not really paying much attention. The second bottle..." She hesitated.

We waited. I made an effort not to look at J.X.

"The second bottle was a gift from Victoria Sherwell." Anna added roughly, "Before you say it, Christopher, I don't believe for one moment that Victoria poisoned that wine."

"Was it homemade wine?" That was J.X.

"No. It was an ordinary bottle of medium-priced wine. The kind of thing you can pick up anywhere really."

"Did the bottle appear to have been tampered with at all?"

Anna gave him a fierce look. "The police asked the same question, and my answer to them is the same as it is to you. Do you *really* think I'd have served that wine to you all if I had *any* suspicion that it had been tampered with? Especially with the previous attempts on my life?"

"Hey, the question has to be asked." J.X. was cool in the face of her heated response.

Anna ignored him and turned to me. "What I really came here to tell you, Christopher, is I can't put you in danger any longer. I should never have sent for you. If I'd realized there was any danger to anyone else, I wouldn't have. I hope you believe that."

I waved that away impatiently. "It goes without saying, Anna."

"I want you to change your plane reservations again. I want you to leave as soon as possible. I simply couldn't bear it if

199

something else happened."

"We're not going to leave you in the middle of this." I glanced at J.X. for confirmation. It wasn't coming anytime soon. He looked back without expression. I frowned at him and the line of his mouth thinned, but that was it. He remained otherwise unmoved.

"I'm serious," Anna said. "It's too much to ask. Besides, my own stepson can't leave the sinking ship fast enough. Why on earth should you have to stay to hold my hand?"

"Ricky's leaving?"

"Yes. He lives in New Milford, though. It's not as though he were fleeing the country."

"We're not going to leave you, Anna." I glanced at J.X. again. His eyes would have had to be onyx for his gaze to be any stonier. I said slowly, "At least, I'm not."

She looked from me to J.X. "Well, perhaps you'd better talk it over. In the meantime...I confess I still don't feel very well. I'm going to have something on a tray in my room and make it an early night. I can have the cook do the same for you. Or perhaps you'd like to go out to dinner. I fully understand why you might not want to dine in this house again if you don't have to."

I opened my mouth, caught J.X.'s eye, and closed it again.

"We'll figure something out," I said.

When J.X. had safely closed the door behind her, I went on the attack. "What the hell was that about?"

"What?"

"Your attitude. You were one step from openly rude." And it was a baby step at that.

"So's she."

"No she wasn't. She was just...being Anna. She doesn't

mean anything by it."

He slipped out of my robe and tossed it over the back of the chair she'd been sitting on. Stalking over to the dresser, he pulled out clean jeans and a sweater. "You want the shower first?"

Apparently we weren't going to talk about it. Maybe that was as well. I didn't want to get into a big fight with him. Especially while I was still basking in the afterglow of some of the best sex of my life.

I asked instead, "Are we going out to eat?"

"Sure. If that's what you'd like."

"What did you want to do?"

He glanced over his shoulder and wriggled his eyebrows at me. I shook my head regretfully.

"In that case I could go for some Italian."

"Will a middle-aged WASP do instead?"

His cheek creased in a smile. "Don't flirt with me if you're serious about leaving this room."

"I'm serious about finding somewhere to eat where the only thing I have to worry about is MSG. Neither of us have had anything to eat since breakfast. And you didn't have breakfast."

"Okay. Dinner in town it is."

That seemed easy enough. Too easy?

I had a shower with J.X.'s help, and then J.X. had a shower. I was shaving, watching his reflection—a dark, lean blur—moving behind the patterned glass of the shower door.

I turned off my razor, said over the beat of water against tiles and his tuneless humming, "Listen, J.X., I can't leave. But it's okay if you want to go home. I understand."

His voice echoed from inside the shower. There wasn't even

a pause. "You don't understand anything if you think I'm leaving you here."

I was sort of touched and sort of irked. "You know, I've been taking care of myself quite effectively for...a number of years. I'm the one who *didn't* get poisoned last night."

He turned off the shower taps. Popped opened the shower door. Water made shining rivulets in the sable etchings of his body hair. His hair was black and glossy as a raven's wing.

"Kit, she told you to go home. There isn't any point sticking around."

"You know why she said that. She's feeling guilty."

"She said it because that's exactly what she wants. She wants you to go home."

I said slowly, "You really *don't* like Anna, do you?"

"No. I don't. For one thing, I don't like the way she talks to you."

I saw my bruised, half-shaved, startled expression in the remaining circle of mirror before the steam from the shower swallowed it.

"She doesn't mean anything by that. It's just her way."

"She's a bitch."

It was so succinct and matter-of-fact I couldn't seem to come up with an answer.

"You don't see it," J.X. said. "You're fond of her and you feel like you owe her something. Maybe you do, but my impression of Anna is that she doesn't do anything she doesn't want to do. And I'll tell you something else, I'm tired of those digs she makes at you."

"What digs...?" My voice dropped out. I realized I didn't— did *not*—want to hear this. "Never mind."

"Like last night at dinner. Those little jabs about Miss

Butterwith. And you having writer's block."

"I *said* never mind. I don't have writer's block. Anyway, it's pretty ironic hearing you objecting to someone giving me a hard time over my writing."

He was busily toweling himself off, pastel plush towel mopping shining, brown skin. He spared me a look. "Look, in case I've failed to make it clear, I think you're a fine writer. I think you're wasting your time and talent on the Butterwith books, but if they make you happy, fine. Anna talks to you like—"

"Okay." I cut him off. "Enough. That's not true. You two got off to a bad start. Don't drag me into it."

He continued to briskly saw the towel against his shoulder blades. His expression was closed.

"And I'm staying on for a couple of days," I added. "Just to make sure she's really all right."

His mouth curled up derisively. He refrained from comment.

For once.

Chapter Nineteen

I'd conveniently forgotten that driving into Nitchfield for dinner entailed getting into a car again.

It was stupid to be nervous—especially since I had so little actual memory of the accident—and yet as we walked out to J.X.'s rental car, I could feel my palms dampening, my heart starting to race.

"Would it be easier if you drove?" J.X. asked suddenly over the crunch of our boots in the snow.

"What?" I threw him a quick look.

"You're still edgy about riding in a car. Would you prefer to drive?"

How the hell could he know that? Was it a cop thing or was it because he was paying me the kind of attention Miss Butterwith generally reserved for the rare *cypripedium calceolus* orchid? "I don't know. What I do know is this is ridiculous. I need to get over it."

"It's not ridiculous. I saw that car."

I would have swallowed, but my mouth was so dry there wasn't enough saliva. "Yeah, but I can't even remember the crash. Not really."

"Maybe if you're driving, you'll feel more in control."

I hesitated. I did much prefer to drive, but I needed to

consider his welfare as much as my own comfort. "I don't think it's a good idea with my shoulder."

"Okay." He accepted the logic of that immediately, so I knew it had been the right choice. "If it helps, I'm a very good driver."

"I know."

"And on top of that I've had police driver training."

"I know."

We reached the silver sedan. He unlocked the passenger side and I slid in. The interior smelled of artificial new car scent and, very faintly, hospital antiseptic. My stomach gave a queasy roll.

To distract myself I pulled out my glasses and unfolded the list of names Victoria had given us of those who had taken part in the Santa Pal gift exchange.

J.X. came around to his side, climbed in, started the engine. The windows began to slowly defrost. We could see the lights of the mansion twinkling through the ice-limned trees.

I said, "So here's the info on these two gift exchanges of Victoria's...one was for the Nitchfield Book Club. The other was for the Woolsey Olivier Library."

"She works part-time at the library."

Nice to know he'd taken his responsibility seriously when I'd asked him to check out Poppy's car. At this point he probably knew more about Victoria and the other members of the Asquith Circle than I did.

I continued to study the list as he slowly pulled away from the side of the road. "Hey. Both Nella and Rowland Bride were part of this book-group gift exchange. And Poppy too. Something she conveniently forgot to mention."

"Poppy and Victoria are obviously good friends. They

probably know who had whom for a Secret Santa."

"Maybe." I scrutinized the list more closely in the waning light. "We need to talk to Rowland. Maybe it had something to do with this book group they all belonged to."

"Such as?"

"Who knows. Maybe someone snapped after being forced to read *Life of Pi* for the hundredth time."

"Why don't we leave it to the cops, Kit?"

"You really think the cops are going to look into this whole Secret Santa thing?"

"Yes. I do. If it's connected to the poisoning. Of course."

"I think it's a lot more likely they're going to notice Luke's criminal record and stop there."

There was an edge to J.X.'s voice as he said, "That's not how cops operate."

"It's how some of them operate. I read the news. I watch TV."

He refrained from comment, but I could tell he was annoyed. Well, maybe with good reason. One thing I've noticed in my research, even if I do write about an elderly botanist sleuth, is that being a cop is not like being an office worker. Cops have that band-of-brothers mentality like soldiers or firemen or other action heroes. Okay, in fairness maybe some office workers have that too. The minions at the DMV certainly seem to believe it's them against the rest of us.

"I don't mean you, obviously. I know you'd have been as conscientious as the rap sheets are long."

He grunted. Not entirely assuaged, but mollified. He glanced over at me and his mouth twitched into a reluctant smile.

"What?" I realized what and put up a self-conscious hand

to straighten my specs. "Hey, I've always worn reading glasses. This is not an age thing."

"I know that. I remember you wore them to your panel at the conference where we first met. You looked very intellectual—and sexy as hell. I like 'em. They're cute."

Cute? My three-hundred-dollar Armani tortoiseshell glasses were *cute*? They were supposed to make me look erudite and distinguished.

He added with breathtaking honesty, "I want to fuck you in those glasses."

"Uhhhh..." I made a sound generally only heard when police officers ask what you were doing three Friday nights ago at eight o'clock—and can anyone verify your alibi.

J.X. laughed, a low rasp of sound like warm, soft sand on bare skin. I tried to swallow whatever had lodged in my throat. "You know something else?"

"Er, no." I sounded faint to my own ears.

"You have to stop with the age thing, Kit. You're only five years older than me. We could have gone to school together."

"Only if one of us jumped a year. Which, considering your sexual appetite, is only too possible."

He laughed, but was serious when he said, "You're using those five years to try and distance yourself from me."

"I don't think I am. It *is* a difference."

"Kit, you're forty. You look thirty. You act...well, never mind. You're carrying on like you think you're seventy."

Was I? I guess it was no secret I'd been unpleasantly startled to find myself suddenly hitting the big 4-0. You'd have thought the previous thirty-nine years were sufficient warning. I glanced at his profile. "Okay. Maybe I'm a little hung up on the age thing. You have to admit gay culture is youth-oriented."

"Oh hell. *American* culture is youth-oriented. No kidding. I've probably seen and done a hell of a lot more in my lifetime."

"Well rub it in," I said, offended.

"That didn't come out right. I only meant I think we're a good match in experiences and education. I don't think about your age. There's nothing to think about. Five years is nothing."

"It's the difference between being eligible for social security and not. It's the difference between getting into porn flicks without your mother and not. It's the difference between—"

"Okay, smart ass. You know what I mean."

"Yeah." I did. I thought it over. "You might have a point."

"Age really is a state of mind."

I groaned. "Please. Spare me the Quote.com pep talk. I agree that I might be preoccupied with my age. And..."

"And?"

Was I really going to share this? It appeared I was. "I guess that stems from the stuff going on in my career and from what happened with David."

"That asshole." He growled it with heartwarming promptness. "We lost enough time thanks to him. Don't let him cost us even another day."

"Thanks. I'll try not to obsess."

"Good luck with *that*."

I opened my mouth to retaliate when I realized we had passed the scene of the accident a few fleeting seconds before.

It was an unexpected relief. As a matter of fact, bickering companionably with J.X. had taken my mind completely off my anxiety about being in a car. I glanced at his profile. His mouth was curved in a faint smile. I suspected that he'd deliberately been distracting me.

Rowland was trying to close for the night by the time we found Blackbird Books.

It was a small brick shop with ornate scripted windows and an old-fashioned hanging sign. Blackbird Books was located in the heart of Nitchfield. On one side of the shop was a bakery and on the other was a paint supply store—both closed for the evening.

J.X. parked in the tiny empty alley behind the bookshop and we went around to the front. We hadn't exactly argued over talking to Rowland, but J.X. was not in favor of it, and as per ever, not afraid to say so.

"This will only take a couple of minutes," I assured him. Even if Rowland hadn't been on Victoria's list for the gift exchange, I felt it would be worth chatting with him. He'd lived in Nitchfield all his life and he'd known Anna longer than anyone else in the Asquith Circle.

J.X. glanced past me, nodded and committed himself to nothing as he held the front door open for me.

It was warm and bright inside, smelling of books and hardwood floors and the bakery next door. Bookmark mobiles hung from the ceiling. Cute banners in primary colors urged people to READ.

I spotted Rowland immediately. He stood openly perspiring behind the counter as he tried to assist a distracted-looking woman with a pyramid of books she was apparently returning. On the floor near her feet, two small children were busily pulling all the books out of lower shelves and stacking them in crooked towers.

"Don't do that, Patsy," the woman said automatically. "This man will have to put them all away."

This was Patsy's invitation to create more mayhem. She

209

smiled sweetly and shoved over one of the towers. Her curly-haired partner in crime took note and joined in, chubby hands closing on paperback spines with glee.

Rowland winced at the sound of falling books, wearily turning our way as the birdsong doorbell trilled. His face was puffy and pallid, his eyes red. He was either ill or midway through his metamorphosis into undead.

Our eyes met. I saw the confusion as he tried to place me. Recognition dawned. His expression turned stricken.

"Twelve forty-eight," he said tonelessly to the woman.

She passed over her plastic, he ran her card, and then handed the receipt and a much smaller bag of books to her. She went out calling to the two devil moppets who left a couple of cases worth of books scattered across the polished floor.

"Chris," Rowland said as the door swung shut again. That was all. I could see the memories swamp him. He had to stop talking or embarrass himself. It was that fresh, that painful.

"We were on our way to dinner when we passed by. I wanted to say goodbye before I left Nitchfield."

He made a visible effort. "That's nice of you. Kind." He wiped his forehead and offered his damp hand.

I shook his hand, guiltily aware that it wasn't kindness prompting my visit. Rowland spared a curious glance for J.X. who stood at my shoulder. J.X. nodded politely and vouchsafed nothing.

"This is my...friend J.X. Moriarity." My voice dipped on friend. I've never been good at—or comfortable with—expressing emotion in public. Not that admitting J.X. was my boyfriend was exactly blubbering my feelings, and yet it felt...too personal to share. At least for now.

"You look good. I mean, apart from the black eye and..."

Rowland gestured to the sling. "How are you? I meant to stop by the hospital, but..." His voice cut out again and he visibly struggled for control.

I said awkwardly, "I'm okay. Grateful to..." Well, that was more awkward still.

J.X. said, "Great little bookshop you've got here. Nice selection of titles. Do you hold many signings?"

"Sometimes." Rowland turned to him gratefully. "Not as many as we used to. For awhile every author out there was touring and doing signings. I think readers started taking them for granted." I saw the penny drop, saw recognition dawn, and I sighed inwardly. "J.X. Moriarity. *The* J.X. Moriarity?"

J.X. made self-deprecating noises.

I nearly said, *No, the other one,* but caught myself in time. I felt a real wave of self-contempt. Was I that insecure, that jealous? Because that was the kiss of death to any budding relationship right there.

Instead I pointed to the glossy black and red covers on the bestseller rack next to the counter and said, "Yep, that's the guy."

"Oh *wow,*" Rowland said. It was so genuine, so heartfelt—and so was J.X.'s half-pleased, half-self-conscious smile—that I couldn't resent it. In fact, I managed a self-mocking grin when J.X. threw me an apologetic look.

"Why don't you sign stock while you're here?" I suggested.

"Yes!" Rowland said. "God, yes. That would be fantastic."

J.X. said all the appropriately modest, gracious things and Rowland scooped up the pile of returned books and scurried away. He was back in seconds with stacks of books for J.X. to sign. They seemed to be carrying his entire backlist. I was thrilled for him. Really.

"I think we have a couple of your books too in the mystery section," Rowland offered in afterthought as J.X., borrowed pen in hand, patiently started through the high-rise of literary real estate. "Would you—?"

"Sure. Of course."

Rowland fetched the three hardcover copies of the latest Miss Butterwith, and I signed them quickly. He peeled the star-shaped gold labels indicating a signed copy off a long sheet and stuck them firmly on the covers right over Miss B's beaming face.

"I heard what happened at the house last night. Everyone's talking about it. About Sara dying. It's unbelievable."

"Yes."

"They're saying it's murder. That the wine at dinner was poisoned."

That was the only logical conclusion. No way did corncockle seeds accidentally wind up in a bottle of Sutter Home or whatever that wine had been.

I asked, "What else are people saying?"

"That the poison was meant for Anna."

"I guess that makes sense. I know Sara wasn't Miss Congeniality, but I can't imagine anyone disliking her enough to poison her."

"Not at the risk of killing everyone else," Rowland agreed.

It seemed an interesting comment. I glanced at J.X. He appeared to be entirely focused on dashing off that distinctive signature of his.

I said, "The interesting thing is apparently that bottle was a gift from Victoria."

"Victoria?" Rowland sounded stunned.

"Something she'd got in a Santa exchange program."

J.X. looked up at that. "Secret Santa."

Rowland's expression of confusion cleared. "You're kidding. You mean Victoria is a suspect?"

He seemed to have missed the significance of Victoria having received poisoned wine—or maybe I hadn't made it clear enough. But then it wasn't clear in my mind either. As hard as it was to believe, I kept coming back to the conviction that if Victoria wasn't the killer, she had to be the true intended victim.

"Can you think of any reason Victoria might have a grudge against Anna?"

"No. None. It's crazy to even suggest such a thing."

I found it curious that he was so adamant. "I don't know. She kind of reminds me of the main character in your story. What was her name? Gretchen? The mousy woman who—"

"Victoria isn't mousy. Victoria is *nothing* like Gretchen." Maybe Victoria was nothing like Gretchen, but I didn't see how he could argue that she was mousy. Then again, maybe I was being swayed by outward appearances. I had to assume these people knew each other fairly well.

"Still, Anna can be pretty—well, she's Anna. I could see Victoria might—"

"No." Rowland shook his head. His tight black curls bounced with his insistence. "It's not in Victoria's nature. She would never hurt anyone. Besides, she's perfectly happy living in Anna's farmhouse."

"What if Anna wanted her to move?"

"But she doesn't, does she?"

"I'm theorizing."

"*Why?*"

"Good question," J.X. remarked, still doing his impression

213

of a printing press.

I shot him a deadly look, but bullets seemed to bounce right off his manly chest. Or, in this case, manly profile.

"Even if Anna did want Victoria to move from the farmhouse, she wouldn't *kill* her. That's...that's like out of a book."

J.X. made a muffled sound that could have been a cough but was more likely a laugh.

If he'd been closer, I'd have accidentally elbowed him in the ribs. As it was, I had to settle for ignoring him. Pointedly.

"True, but nearly everyone involved in this case *is* a writer. Or involved in publishing somehow."

As I said it, I had a flash of awareness that I'd hit on something. Something significant.

The next instant it was gone.

Rowland was saying, "Maybe so, but if someone in our group was a murderer, it wouldn't be Victoria. I'd look at Poppy. Or Arthur. Or both of them. Yes, both of them."

Arthur Gohring. The biker writer. I'd forgotten all about him.

"Why's that?" J.X. asked, reentering the conversation.

"Because the rumor is Poppy murdered her husband."

Chapter Twenty

"Murdered as in..."

"Murdered," Rowland agreed. "Nothing was ever proven, but—"

"How is she supposed to have killed him?" J.X. asked. He was all business now. He slid the final stack of signed books across the counter and thrust his hands in his pockets. He looked casually, devastatingly tough and capable. Like those hip young television cops—only genuinely smart and competent.

"She supposedly hired someone to do it for her." Rowland's button-black eyes met mine. "Arthur."

"Arthur? The rumor is Poppy hired Arthur to kill her husband?"

"They were friendly for a time and Arthur had a boat. Now they're not friendly—and Arthur sold his boat."

"That's it? That's the extent of the case against Poppy?"

"She and Phil were headed for divorce. That's common knowledge. And he left her a big insurance policy. That's common knowledge too."

I looked at J.X. His upper lip had that quirk that indicated his particular blend of sardonic amusement.

"What would her motive be for wanting to get rid of

Victoria?" I questioned.

"None. Victoria's the only person I know of who can even stand Poppy. But...she probably knows the truth about Poppy having Phil knocked off."

He said it so casually. Like it was fact. It was kind of frightening. In such ways are outlandish rumors started—and accepted as truth.

I said slowly, "Do you think Poppy might have had that car accident deliberately?"

His eyes filled with tears. I was sorry I had asked, but...

After a struggle, Rowland said, "I think Poppy loves Poppy too much to risk killing herself."

No fan of Poppy's, he.

"We should get going," J.X. said. I was grateful for the interruption. I didn't want to see Rowland break down and I couldn't seem to think of anything else to ask him, although I knew I was missing some obvious points. The sleuth thing isn't as easy to do as it is to write.

Rowland had just supplied Poppy with motive for murder, but not Anna's murder.

"Right." I offered my hand to him. "Good luck with everything."

He hung on to my hand. "Are you coming to Nella's funeral?"

"No, I—when is it?"

"Tomorrow."

"Oh. I didn't realize." I looked to J.X. for help.

He hesitated.

"We haven't decided," I said. I gave Rowland's hand a parting squeeze. "If I don't see you again, take care of yourself."

"Yes." He released me, turned away to scrub at his eyes.

As J.X. and I reached the door he said suddenly, urgently, "Chris!"

I turned back. Rowland had followed us up the front aisle. He was staring at me with painful intensity.

"Did she say anything?"

"Who?"

"Nella. Did she...you were one of the last people to talk to her, you were with her when she...I wondered if she...said anything."

I don't know if I've ever witnessed anything quite that excruciatingly naked. He was in such pain I was briefly tempted to make up some conversation between me and Nella where Rowland had somehow heroically figured in.

"I'm sorry. I don't remember much of the afternoon very clearly. Concussion, you know?"

He nodded reluctantly. "If you do remember something, could you—"

"Yes. Sure."

J.X. shoved open the door, hooked his hand around my good arm and towed me out of the bookstore.

The smell of dirty snow and car exhaust was weirdly bracing as we walked around the building.

"That was awful," I said at last. The weight of J.X.'s hand on the middle of my back was reassuring. Not quite a hug, but not far from it.

"Yes."

"He was completely in love with her. With Nella."

"What was she, nineteen?"

"Something like that. Too young for him. At least..."

"Too young for him." J.X. was uncompromising. "She was a kid. That's the difference there."

"I have no idea what she thought of him. If she thought of him at all. She was obsessed with her writing, with her career."

"Sounds familiar."

"Hey, I wasn't always stodgy and middle-aged."

"I know."

"I got around plenty in college."

"I don't doubt it. You'd have been one cute twink."

I sniffed disapprovingly. "I was never a twink."

"No?"

I glanced at him. He was smiling. "And don't think I don't know what you're doing."

"What am I doing?"

"Deliberately distracting me."

He gave me a sideways look. "Is it working?"

"Sort of. I'm not sure I feel like eating, though."

He patted my back. "You'll work through it."

One look at J.X. and it was love at first sight for Ricardo, the slim, blue-eyed and vaguely waifish waiter at Mamma Zini's Ristorante.

"Can I help you reach a decision, gentlemen?" he inquired pointedly, smiling into J.X.'s eyes after we'd been seated and handed menus. "Any questions about the specials?"

J.X. had a couple of questions about the specials which Ricardo interpreted as an invitation to flirt. He did pretty much everything but wave his breadstick in J.X.'s face. J.X. remained stoic and focused on culinary matters throughout the performance. After my initial irritation, I started to find it sort of funny.

"Now *that's* a twink," I said when Ricardo finally departed with our drink order.

J.X. gave me what is commonly referred to as a speaking look.

I grinned, enjoying his discomfiture. "I'm kind of enjoying being with the best-looking man in the room."

"I was thinking the same thing," he retorted.

"That I was enjoying being with the best-looking man in the room?"

"That I'm with the best-looking man in the room."

I snorted.

J.X. fastened a surprisingly bleak and beady eye on me. "There you go again."

"What?"

"One thing I want to get straight between us right now. I don't want to hear the M word out of you anymore."

"Murder?"

He was not amused. "Middle-aged. Let it go, Kit."

I set my menu aside. "Jeez, you young whippersnappers need to learn to lighten up."

His expression grew reminiscent of those generally worn by villains in illustrations of Edgar Allan Poe's more macabre works.

"Okay. Fine. I'm only as young as I feel, which tonight is older than both of us put together, but whatever. When I get back to L.A. I'm going to buy myself a BlackBerry and a slew of French-cuffed shirts. Possibly a nipple ring."

J.X. relaxed. "That I've got to see."

At that point Ricardo reappeared with our drinks. G&T for

me, Jack Daniels for J.X. I had a feeling it was going to be a while before either of us opted for wine again, regardless of the meal.

J.X. was brisk and businesslike about ordering our meals, and I wondered if he really was concerned about my possible insecurities. I'd never really thought of myself as insecure. Even after the personal and professional disasters of last year, I didn't think I was insecure. Necessarily. My career *was* in a slump, I *was* getting older, and my domestic partner *had* dumped me for a younger man. Was I not allowed to mention that stuff for fear of looking insecure?

Ricardo departed, greatly subdued, and J.X. sipped his drink and regarded me in that solemn way that always made me want to check whether my fly was open.

"Aw. Look at him." I nodded after Ricardo. "He's heartbroken. He was all hopeful because he thinks you knock me around." I winked my still-colorful eye at him.

J.X. swallowed the wrong way and started coughing. We nearly had Ricardo rushing back to the rescue, but I waved him off, briskly smacking J.X. between the shoulder blades.

J.X. wheezed protest.

"There now, there now," I said absently, still patting him.

"Bastard," J.X. gulped when he could speak.

I laughed and reached for my glass.

We chatted about absolutely nothing important until the food came. Lasagna with meat sauce for J.X. and linguini in white clam sauce for me. Ricardo brought more drinks and warned J.X. to leave room for scrumptious dessert.

"I feel like I'm missing something." At J.X.'s expression, I clarified, "About Sara's death and the attempts on Anna's life. I keep feeling like there's something obvious and I can't see it because I'm too close to it."

"Of course you're missing something. You're trying to solve a crime without access to almost any of the evidence, either physical or testimonial." He added in the tone of a man who knows his good advice is going to be ignored, "Which is why you should leave this for L.E. to solve."

"I'm afraid your beloved law enforcement is going to settle on the first and obvious solution."

"Which you think is what? That the handyman did it? Are you so sure he didn't?"

I shrugged.

J.X. put his glass down. "Okay, let's recap for the at-home viewers. Luke does have motive. He's in Anna's will, right?"

"According to you, motive is irrelevant."

"I never said it was irrelevant. I said it's not the most important factor. It is *a* factor, obviously. It's hard to know what might be sufficient motive for someone else. One thing's for sure, a substantial inheritance is usually considered solid motive."

"I don't know how substantial Luke's inheritance is, but substantial enough that Anna felt obliged to comment on it."

"So motive and certainly opportunity. He works on the grounds."

"That doesn't automatically give him access to the wine cellar."

"We don't know that Victoria's wine was in the wine cellar. It could have been sitting out on a counter."

"True." I doubted it in a household as well organized as Anna's, but...true.

"He certainly had means. He works in the garden and the wine was laced with poisonous seeds. Those other accidents too—assuming they weren't accidents—falling on ice, a falling flowerpot, faulty brakes...that's all stuff he could probably contrive. Motive, opportunity and means. He looks good for it, Kit."

"It's too pat. Here he is, right on the scene. An ex-con with motive, means, opportunity."

J.X. said with aggravating patience, "That's usually the way it works."

"It's too easy."

"Why is he in Anna's will, by the way?"

"I don't know. Everyone seems to be in it one way or the other. You're probably in it now."

"Probably not."

Perhaps he was right. Anna hadn't seemed to cotton to J.X. much more than he'd cottoned to her.

"The ladies hinted that Luke and Anna had some kind of romantic relationship, but I didn't get that vibe from Anna. Although she's pretty good at hiding her feelings." I stopped, remembering the day I'd arrived and Anna's comment about having someone in her life again. I hadn't really considered the implications of that. Who was this person? If it wasn't Luke, it wasn't someone I'd met. The thing with Rudolph had been over for awhile, so that couldn't have been what she meant— although Anna had been a bit defensive when I'd asked her about Rudolph. Her housekeeper had assumed it was Rudolph calling from Anna's bedroom. But, again, that could simply have been because Rudolph was the man most likely to take charge in the event of an emergency.

"Interesting," J.X. remarked. "Kind of a Lady Chatterley thing going on with the groundskeeper?"

"Maybe. Anna's been married twice and in between the

wedded bliss she and Rudolph have had this unofficial thing forever. She's still...active sexually. I could see her taking a young, virile lover. Why not?"

"Could her lover be female? Could there have been something between her and Sara?"

The idea startled me, though it shouldn't have. "She's always been strictly heterosexual. At least as far as I know."

Sara and Anna? No way. I hadn't picked up that vibe at all. But what about the fact that Rudolph and Sara had apparently been lovers? Sure, that was partly speculation, but...there had been something between them. Something they had taken pains to keep under the radar.

"Let's leave Luke for now," J.X. said. "He's at the top of my list, but I could be biased given my former day job."

"*You*? No way."

I think it hurt his feelings. "You know, you have your biases too, Kit."

"I know. Sorry." I sipped my gin and tonic. "The irony is both Anna and I were thinking Sara might be behind the attempts on her life."

His brows drew together. "You were?"

"Well, I was. Anna wouldn't admit it, but I could tell she was leaning that way. Sara's story submission to the Asquith Circle was a manuscript she'd apparently only ever let Anna see. Anna tried to persuade her to publish it, but she never would."

"What was the story about?"

"About a woman who got away with murdering her sister when they were children. Apparently Sara's own sister died under some possibly mysterious circumstances."

J.X.'s brows drew together. "You think Sara showed the

manuscript to Anna and then regretted it and tried to kill her?"

"When you put it like that...Sara chose to show the manuscript to the entire group, so that doesn't quite make sense. Then again she was in Anna's will too. And I *think* she may have had designs on Rudolph."

J.X. looked taken aback.

"Yeah, he was a little old for her," I agreed.

"Yeah, and it was a hell of a lot more than five years."

I let that go. "Which gives Sara motive, opportunity *and* means."

"Except she's dead."

"Oh yeah. *That.*" It wasn't funny, of course, just a touch of gallows humor. "That could have been an accident. The hand of fate stepping in. Or poking in. Whatever hands do."

Following this without trouble, J.X. said, "I see. So Sara poisoned the wine, but Sara had a weak heart or something and ended up killing herself?"

"Sure. Works for me."

"You no longer suspect Poppy or Victoria?"

"You're humoring me," I said sourly.

He smiled into my eyes, his own shining in the candlelight. "A little. I figure it's better if we talk it all out now so we can focus on other things tonight."

My cock found itself in unexpectedly cramped quarters, and—much more disconcerting—my ass seemed to itch with unseemly anticipation. What on earth was that about? Surely I wasn't wanting *that* again? I was still tender from the afternoon.

I reached for my glass, drained it. "Poppy," I said briskly, ignoring the desire crawling through my guts. "Although I can't see what her motive would be. If Poppy is behind this, then I think Victoria must have been her target, not Anna, and certainly not Sara."

J.X. shifted in his chair, cleared his throat and said, "Um, right. Poppy. So Poppy wants Victoria dead because Victoria knows the truth about what happened to Poppy's husband?"

"Right."

"Poppy gives Victoria a bottle of poisoned wine which is accidentally handed off to Anna. And Poppy deliberately crashes her car in an attempt to kill Victoria—but misses Victoria and kills Nella. Not to mention nearly killing you and herself."

"Right. The problem is—" I broke off as the door to the restaurant opened and two newcomers bundled against the cold stepped inside the crowded dining room. They were laughing and pushing back parka hoods from damp hair.

"The problem is what?"

"Look who just walked in."

I had to give J.X. credit. He raised his eyebrows but didn't turn. "Who?"

"Bachelor Number Four. Little Ricky is here with a chick who looks like she's auditioning for the last of the gold diggers."

Chapter Twenty-One

Ricky stopped by our table, leaning over and planting one hand on J.X.'s shoulder and one hand on mine. I winced. There was a faint whiff of bourbon as he said, "Great minds think alike. I guess you couldn't take the mausoleum either."

J.X. gave him a look that ordinarily would have sent Ricky bouncing back from the force field. But we were all running low on dilithium crystals that evening.

"How are you feeling?" I inquired. The last time I'd seen Ricky he'd been crawling along the upstairs hallway, sicker than a dog, but the horrors of the night before seemed strangely long ago.

"As you see." Ricky offered a big smile. "Ter-rif-ic."

The bravado was clearly for the sake of the bimbo, who gazed smiling and glassy-eyed from one of us to the other. It still felt sort of inappropriate given the circumstances.

I said, "I guess you didn't know Sara very well."

"Frosty bitch." He heard that and made a face. "Sorry. Not exactly politically correct, I know."

I wasn't sure what the political implications were of Sara's death, but tactless, callous, oh yeah. He got it goin' on.

"She meant a lot to your mother."

"Anna's not my mother." The affable mask slipped and for a

moment his face was hard and much older.

"Right. I only meant—"

"I know what you meant. I may be a lot of things, but I'm not a hypocrite. Sara never had the time of day for me, and I can't say I'm broken up she's dead. I didn't kill her, though. As I told the fuzz."

J.X. raised his head and said coolly, "Sara wasn't the target. Anna was."

The effect on Ricky was instantaneous. He dropped the buddy-buddy act and straightened up. "Says who? Anna?" There was no faking the scorn there.

"You don't believe Anna was the intended victim?"

Ricky laughed, a short, harsh sound. "I think all of us were poisoned last night—except you, Chris—and yet Anna leaps instantly to the conclusion that *she* was the intended victim. That's just Anna all over. She's always got to be the center of attention."

"You have a different theory?" I asked.

"I'm not a mystery writer. No. I don't have a theory. All I know is I could have died last night like Sara. I'm not going back to that house. No way."

"Gosh!" the blonde said. She looked from Ricky to J.X. to me. "*Gosh.*"

Ricky gave her a squeeze. "Don't worry about it, babe. It's all over."

Nice to be so sure. I said, "Do you have any idea of who might want to kill Anna?"

"Take a number. Not everyone loves Anna as much as she believes."

I shrugged. "I'll buy that. But who dislikes her enough to want her dead?"

"I'm going to guess *a lot* of people. You'll never meet a more controlling manipulative bit—broad than my stepmother."

That was apparently his last word on the subject. He gave his blonde a little pat on her parka-ed behind and followed her to their table.

We watched their retreat. "I don't know why the hell Anna is so bound and determined to protect him. He sure doesn't reciprocate."

"No. He doesn't. Kind of interesting, don't you think?"

"Aren't stepmothers universally hated?" I had the only original matched set of parents in my entire social circle, so I couldn't speak from personal experience.

"It might be that. Anna *is* controlling. And manipulative."

I said irritably, "You've known her all of two days."

"You disagree?"

It would be hard to disagree with that. I acknowledged with a face. "She can be controlling."

"Sometimes the solution to the crime lies within the character of the victim. Or in this case, the intended victim."

"That gets back to motive."

He nodded in concession.

Ricardo appeared with the check. "Anything else I can do for you, gentlemen?" he asked J.X. "Dessert perhaps?" I don't know for a fact that he wiggled his eyebrows, but it was in his tone.

J.X. looked at me. I shook my head.

Ricardo sighed regretfully, set the check down at the midway point on the table and sashayed away.

J.X. started to reach for the check.

"I've got it."

He withdrew his hand immediately, and it was like I could see right into his brain. See what a delicate balancing act it was for him. He'd reached for the check to dispel the idea that I, as the older partner, would automatically—in a parental role—be the one picking up the tab, but my response had reminded him that I might be equally or more touchy about the fact that he was the more successful and affluent of the two of us. And that was absolutely right. That had been my instinctive reaction: *I don't need you paying my way.*

God almighty. We had a learning curve ahead of us—and winding roads always made me carsick.

I said gruffly, "The next one's yours."

He offered a quick half-smile.

The heater gusted warmly over our legs, the music—Jack Johnson again—played softly in the background, the breezy, beachy sounds of "Better Together" reminding me of home as J.X. and I started the drive back to the Asquith Estate.

"Warm enough?" he asked.

I smiled though I knew he couldn't see it in the dark of the car interior. "Yes. I'm fine."

I was too. Barely a qualm as we hit the open road. I don't know if it was proof that I really did trust J.X.—certainly his driving skills—or if I was just past the initial unease of being in a car again. As the tires hissed soothingly on the wet road it occurred to me that if we could work things out, this moonlit drive might be typical of many nights and many drives...that perhaps, just perhaps, J.X. and I were heading for a future together.

Maybe.

That was what J.X. wanted—thought he wanted, anyway—

and it was what I thought I wanted.

I said, "Anyway, getting back to Poppy. The problem is that while it's conceivable Poppy might have access to the house and grounds, it would be a lot harder for her to arrange those other accidents. Plus...there's something sort of guileless about Poppy, don't you think? This kind of murder plot doesn't seem like her style. Even her story. You should have read what she submitted to the group. It's horrible for a lot of reasons, but it's very straightforward. The heroine—I use the term loosely—finds her ex-husband at her mercy and she cuts his genitals off."

"Nice."

"Yeah. It's pretty unpleasant. What it isn't, is convoluted or clever. And that's really the problem I have with the idea of Poppy as Lucrezia Borgia. Poppy doesn't seem like someone who would go to this much trouble to get rid of an enemy. Nor does Victoria make a very convincing enemy because if anything she seems to go out of her way to keep Poppy from saying things that might land her in hot water."

"That could be because she believes Poppy is innocent of all wrongdoing. It might change if she knew Poppy really *had* offed her spouse."

"Fair enough. But Victoria strikes me as closemouthed. Someone who would view minding her own business in the light of a personal philosophy. No, I can more easily see Poppy trying to hire someone—probably a cop, given her luck—to kill her enemies for her."

"Agreed. But that's one theory, right? She hired this guy Arthur to kill her soon-to-be ex?"

"Yeah." I thought that over. The real problem I had with that particular theory was the unlikelihood of Arthur going along with any scheme of Poppy's. Granted, we're not always what we write, but our storytelling does reveal things about the way our brain works. Arthur's writing was smart, blunt and violent. Whereas, if her storytelling was an indication, any scheme Poppy cooked up was going to be convoluted and rely heavily on the cooperation of the victim.

I said, "Poppy's reaction when she heard the news about Sara wasn't in keeping with the reaction you'd expect if she was behind poisoning the wine. For one thing, I don't think she'd have kept pushing Victoria to reveal where she got the wine. She seemed genuinely and totally floored."

"Victoria on the other hand—"

"Seemed guilty as hell."

"Apparently with good reason."

J.X. was nodding. "It's natural she'd feel that way. She knew she was the one who'd delivered the wine."

"It would be pretty dumb to poison a bottle of wine you were giving someone as a gift. It would bound to be traced right back."

"But then she has the cover story of receiving it as an anonymous gift."

"Yes. True. But in that case she wouldn't first try to pretend she'd bought the wine, would she? Besides, unless she's an idiot she has to know she'd *have* to hand over these two Secret Santa lists to the police and they'd track down each and every person and then do some crosschecking and figure out who gave what gift to whom. She'd *have* to know that eventually it would all point back to her."

"Yep. That's the way it works."

I watched the white moon over the tops of the trees lighting the whole night sky in a platinum haze.

I said, "With Victoria we have means and opportunity. She's in walking distance of the house and apparently visits frequently. She admits to being there when Anna fell down the stairs. What we don't have is motive."

"She's in Anna's will?"

"Yes, but...I don't know. I know we only have part of the facts here, but what would the hurry be in getting rid of Anna? Victoria seems to have a perfectly comfortable setup living in that farmhouse. I didn't get the impression that Anna planned on changing things anytime soon. Victoria doesn't strike me as much of a material girl. She seems...comfortable, relaxed with her life, with who she is. The only hint I got of anything unsettled was my impression that she cares for Rowland."

"Rowland? Blackbird Bookstore Rowland?"

"Him. Yeah. The chick magnet. So maybe there was some remote reason for Victoria wanting Nella out of the way, but I can't see how she would have brought about that car accident— and she'd be risking killing herself, which really doesn't make sense if the motive is to ultimately win Rowland's hand in marriage."

J.X. commented, "She brought the wine to the house before Nella was killed."

"That's true. Maybe Nella had some health issues that might have made her more susceptible than the rest of us. Something Victoria knew about? Nella was a big girl. That puts a strain on the heart right there. But again, what would be the rush? It's not like Rowland and Nella were planning to run away together. Nella had one thing on her mind and that was making it as a writer."

Once again I had that inkling that I was missing something obvious.

J.X. said, "She's an interesting type."

"Who? Victoria? What do you mean?"

"Well, you commented on how relaxed and comfortable she seems, but I've known a couple of murderers who displayed the same personality traits. One was a serial killer."

"Oh."

"We really don't know much about Victoria at all."

I said in my best seductive tone, "Ah, but you could change all that with a word in the right ear."

He laughed. "Maybe."

I made my voice deeper still. "I could make it worth your while."

J.X. spared me a glance. "Look at you, Mata Holmsi. Keep talking. I'm three-quarters convinced now."

The house was deathly quiet when the bathrobed housekeeper let us inside. She assured us that everyone was in bed, wished us a good night, and departed for the nether regions, turning off lights as she went.

J.X. and I crept quietly up the stairs past the snooty portraits, painted faces looking even more dour after the events of the past days.

Reaching the sanctuary of our bedroom, J.X. locked the door and turned to face me.

"Alone at last." I used my good hand to unbuckle my belt. I had no doubt we were going to fuck, and right there showed a change in our status. If we'd reached the stage of taking sex for granted, we were well on our way to becoming a couple.

J.X.'s face was flushed and a little self-conscious, his eyes, hungry and admiring. "It was practically all I could think about at dinner. Having you again."

My heart gave a little jerk. Just what the old ego needed, but still a little overwhelming. I said feebly, "Maybe we should...try it the other way."

"That would be nice too. I'd like that." J.X. was practically purring as he put his arms around me. "But right now, Kit, I want to bury myself up to my balls in your body and fuck you." He drew the words out. "Fuck you slow and sweet."

Playfully, he humped against me. I could feel the hard outline of his cock through the soft denim of my jeans and his own. My buttocks clenched tight at the idea, clenched in instinctive rejection. And yet at the same instant that tight opening to my body burned to be touched. Burned for that illicit finger on the entrance buzzer of that most private of all private clubs. My heart was jumping around my rib cage like a frightened bird.

"Oh God." I shivered helplessly. "I want it too."

J.X. pulled his sweater over his head and tossed it in the general direction of the chair. His T-shirt followed. I've seen fireman drills that took longer than it took him to strip. Naked, he was beautiful to behold. Flushed, aroused, golden. Part of that beauty, though, was the longing in his eyes. No one had ever looked at me like that. As though I mattered more than anything else. It was salve to my wounded ego, but it was a weight on my heart too. How did anyone live up to that?

Eventually J.X. was going to see that I was just...me. And that everything he disliked about me was still there no matter how good the sex was.

Naturally I was smart enough not to endanger getting laid by expressing any of those thoughts as he helped me undress—which, incidentally took a lot longer than his disrobing because J.X. found it necessary to touch and taste as we went along. He nipped my earlobe, blew on the back of my neck, scratched my nipples, and it was all I could do to keep on my feet beneath that tender onslaught. My legs were shaking by the time we fell into bed.

J.X. bent over me and I stared past his shoulder at the wildly twining grapevine and folds of green velvet. The globe lamp on the dresser threw half his face in shadow, gilded the other half. I gasped as he eased a slick finger into me.

"You're tensing up," he said softly, watching my face.

I bit my lip. He worked his finger deeper, touching the sweet spot, making me writhe. He gave me a couple of seconds' respite then pressed again and again. I jumped as though I'd received an electric shock. It was pleasure, but it was so intense it was alarming. Partly it was sheer physical response, but partly it was the emotional and psychological reaction to letting him in. Literally letting him in—with all that the action seemed to represent.

Some of it must have shown on my face.

"Do you think being older and wiser you shouldn't like this?" I could hear his curiosity, but I could hear his gentleness too.

"I don't like it. I mean, I never have before."

"You do now." I could hear the smile in his voice. "Jesus. Your face is wonderful to watch. It's intense, isn't it?"

I nodded helplessly, closing my eyes, biting my lip as those clever, clever fingers twisted again.

J.X. said in that rough velvet voice, "It's like this massive turn-on because it's *you* and you're letting me do this to you, and you like it so much—even though you think you shouldn't."

I moaned. He had the dynamic down cold, his and mine both. And the funniest thing was for all David and I had wrestled with the power dynamics of sex, for the first time in my life I was willingly and completely submitting—and discovering it had little to do with my body and everything to do with my mind.

Jesus. It felt fucking unbelievable to just accept unquestioningly what J.X. was doing, to simply respond when asked, and to allow myself to feel. Really *feel*.

He withdrew his fingers with a final caress and replaced them slowly, slowly with the silky push of his cock. Jesus, he was *big*.

"Don't tighten up. You can take me, Kit. Just keep breathing."

I keened again and forced my muscles to relax. J.X. continued to shove his way in, slower than molasses and just as sweet in a dark, peculiar way.

"Oh *God*," he groaned, a shuddery groan. "Oh God..." His hands, warm and caressing, guided me into position, and then he began to move in those slow, deep strokes. "Okay...?"

I nodded urgently, pushing back to meet him, wanting it now, wanting to feel him deeper, to feel him pulsing right there under my heart.

A hoarse voice begged, "Harder," and it was *me*. Me shoving my ass into the cradle of his hips, trying to impale myself on that thick, rigid burn, needing more and more.

"You're wonderful, Kit. *Jesus*."

I felt him tremble, transfixed, and there it was. White heat running through the network of nerves and muscles, flooding my bloodstream. I threw my head back as though in a high fever, arching up from the blankets and sheets in a kind of convulsion of pleasure at the wet, hot burst of life pouring into me, spilling through the cracks and filling up the empty places.

Chapter Twenty-Two

I woke to one of those rare moments of perfect mental clarity. I've no idea what I dreamed. In fact, I'd slept so deeply, I'm not sure I dreamed at all, but as I lay blinking at the first pearly flush of light filtering through the velvet draperies, my relaxed mind drifted over the events of the last days and it dawned on me why I kept feeling like I was missing something obvious. Everything that had happened since Anna had first phoned to tell me of her plight had been exactly like something out of a mystery novel.

A classic, twisty mystery novel—the kind of thing Anna wrote.

And it was unlikely that was a coincidence.

Was that because someone hated Anna so much he had deliberately devised a plot to mimic one of her own stories?

That would have to be someone who knew Anna's work very well—and hated her very much.

There was only one person who I could think of who knew Anna's work that well—mystery novels in general that well—and whose brain might work in the same serpentine fashion. But the idea was preposterous.

At no time had I considered Rudolph a suspect in the attempts on Anna's life. Violence seemed utterly and absolutely out of character.

Besides, what would his motive be?

Ah, but there it was again. Anna's will. Anna had left Rudolph her entire literary estate. A literary estate worth millions.

But Rudolph was a wealthy, successful man in his own right. It was hard to picture him dispatching Anna for all her worldly goods.

And the cruelty of such a plan as this? Pantomiming her work. Killing the people she loved. I couldn't see that avarice let alone that kind of cruelty in Rudolph.

Granted, there was the matter of that on-again, off-again romantic relationship of theirs. The relationship that was now over because Anna had said she had someone new in her life.

I didn't know Rudolph well enough to determine whether he was the jealous type. I was guessing he would be a good loser, a good sport, but there were signs that he'd also found a new romance—with Sara.

Although Sara was now dead.

Conveniently dead?

J.X. stirred, his arm tightening around my waist. I absently kissed his forehead.

My new theory—it wasn't even really a theory, more like unbridled speculation—meant that beneath Rudolph's kindly, courtly exterior beat the heart of a cold-blooded killer. That was just...really hard to believe.

I remembered Ricky saying how controlling and manipulative Anna was, but somehow I never got the feeling she was controlling or manipulating Rudolph. Rudolph was no pushover for all his quiet, gentlemanly way. Of course there could be some pressing motive for Rudolph to want to get rid of Anna, but I hadn't seen any hint of it during my visit. They seemed as friendly and relaxed together as they ever had so it was unlikely she was contemplating taking this new book to a new house or demanding a new editor. In fact...

In fact, Rudolph hadn't even known Anna had completed a new book.

And she *had* completed it because I'd seen Sara carrying galleys upstairs.

Wait. No. I had seen a parcel that looked familiar, that *looked* like galleys. I didn't know for a fact they had been galleys. And really, that would be pretty dubious because if Anna had completed a manuscript, and that manuscript had reached the stage of galleys, Rudolph would *have* to be aware of it.

Unless she was publishing the book somewhere else.

Which Sara would certainly know.

But why would Anna take a manuscript elsewhere?

I scowled at the ornate bronze grapevines twisting through the green velvet draperies. They seemed very symbolic at the moment.

The other possibility I hadn't really considered was that Anna could have made up this entire murder plot in an attempt to...an attempt to *what*? Gain attention for this new book? A marketing ploy was the very thing Anna had said she dreaded being suspected of.

But you couldn't believe everything people said. Me being a case in point. What if Anna *had* faked those original attempts and then someone had used them as the perfect cover to make a genuine attack on Anna's life? Someone like Sara.

If I recalled correctly, Anna had used something very similar in one of her novels. It wasn't exactly an original. I'd used it myself in *Miss Butterwith's £ of Prevention*.

Which might just bring us back to Sara. Sara would be ideally situated to see through such a ruse of Anna's and take advantage of it for her own ends. Only then to be hoist in her own petard? It wasn't impossible, right?

J.X. gave a soft, sudden snort. His eyelids fluttered, he rubbed his nose, yawned, opened his eyes.

He smiled.

Smiled right into my eyes with such unguarded warmth and affection that I felt winded. I couldn't remember the last time anyone had looked at me like that—anyone who wasn't J.X.

"Oh, it's you," I said, as though I'd only now noticed him curled around me.

"Morning," J.X. mumbled. "How'd you sleep?"

Fair question. At our previous slumber parties, I'd been unable to sleep. At all. But my insomnia hadn't troubled me once this weekend. In fact, I'd slept, as they say, like the dead.

Granted, I'd been doped up a lot of the time, and last night I'd had a pretty good workout before... My face warmed remembering.

How the hell much did I drink last night?

J.X. was still smiling. He kissed my shoulder. "God. You were wonderful last night, Kit. Just...wonderful."

I smiled back weakly.

"You've never been so uninhibited. No. *Wild.*"

I cleared my throat.

His brows drew together as my discomfort registered. "Are you...you're not sorry about what we did, are you?"

That deserved a quick and honest answer. "No. I'm...off balance."

He tilted his head, his eyes intent. "Because it turns out you like to be fucked?"

Because right now it feels like a need. *Because I don't just like it, I* love *it.* But I didn't say that. Couldn't. Not even to J.X. Not even to my lover. Why? I didn't want to believe that it was something so ridiculous as being caught up in some antiquated heterosexual concept of sexual roles. No, I had a feeling it had more to do with my fear of needing anything. Or, more exactly, any*one.*

Okay, and maybe, *maybe* a tiny fear that there was something wrong with me because I'd ostensibly, out of the blue, developed a taste for, well, sexual submission. It had never been my nature, it *wasn't* my nature, but there was no denying I wanted it—yearned for it—now. Wanted the freedom of totally letting go, of letting someone else—someone I trusted—be in charge of...everything, including my body. What in the hell was *that* about? Midlife crisis? Was I going to need a dog collar to go with those French-cuffed shirts and the BlackBerry?

I said vaguely, "I just think we should do it the other way next time."

He placed a knowing hand on my groin and my cock jumped in response. Nuzzling me beneath my ear, J.X. nipped my earlobe and said throatily, breath warm, "If that's what you want, honey. We're going to do anything and everything you want."

My body was instantly flushed with desire, my cock rigid, my heart starting to thud in time to the heavy femoral pulse. Holy hell. It was like being seventeen again. It was *crazy.*

"Satin and steel," J.X. murmured. His hand closed around my cock, slid leisurely up the length. Slid down.

Up.

Down.

Lazy and slow.

"Thinking of crossing over to romance?" I managed, closing my eyes against the intensity of my reaction to that caress.

I spread my legs and his other hand moved to my balls, squeezing gently. I swallowed hard as my cock rose up into his palm.

"Roll over, Kit." J.X.'s voice was slightly unsteady.

My heart thundered into overdrive. My eyes snapped open. "Actually...we need to get going. I mean, moving. In a southwesterly direction. We're losing the morning." I sat up—no small feat given how badly I wanted to give in to what my body was clamoring for—and threw back the covers, letting in the chilly morning air.

"It really does bother you," J.X. said after a moment.

He looked beautiful and wanton, sprawled between the sheets, his thick cock nested in silky dark hair. He looked like a porn model. Except no porn model ever wore that meditative expression.

I was tying my robe closed—or trying to—and I spared him a look. "Maybe. But not for the reasons you think."

"Are you sure *you* know the real reason?"

"Hey." I halted my flight to the bathroom. "I already told you. I'm way out of my comfort zone. But I'm hanging in here. I'm trying to be honest with you. Fair with you."

"I know." J.X.'s grimace was rueful. "And I know I'm pushing too hard. I just...I've been waiting a long time for you."

I resisted the urge to yield, return to the warm fug of our bed and his strong arms. "Yeah, I know. Remind me again how you whiled away those long, lonely years waiting for me to come to my senses?"

"I didn't say I joined the priesthood."

"That would be one interesting holy order."

He sighed. Patted the mattress. "You sure you wouldn't like to—?"

"I wonder if Nero Wolfe had this kind of trouble with Archie Goodwin?"

He laughed and sat up. "All right. You win." He rolled out of bed, landing on his feet. It occurred to me that was one of the things I liked about J.X. He was good-natured even when he didn't get his way. I really hadn't had a lot of that in my life.

"So what's the plan?" J.X. leaned toward the mirror in the bathroom, carefully trimming his beard. "Am I changing our plane tickets again?"

I reached for a towel. Wiped my face. "Let's leave it for now."

"Kit." He lowered the clippers.

"Wait. Hear me out." I lowered the towel. "I've heard everything you said, and I heard what Ricky said last night. I've known Anna a long time, but I realize that I don't *know* her, if you follow. I'm fond of her. That doesn't mean I'm blind to her faults."

He was too polite to say what he was thinking. "You think you owe her, but I can guarantee—based on the short time I've known Anna—she doesn't do anything unless there's something in it for Anna."

"Whether Anna is manipulative or controlling is beside the point. You can't kill people for being selfish or self-absorbed. Or I'd be on the endangered-species list too."

"There's no comparison."

"You wouldn't have agreed three months ago." I dropped

243

my shaver back in my kit bag. "Look, Anna asked for my help. Aside from the novelty of anyone needing my help, I told her I would. I'm not going to go back on that—unless she tells me to go and really means it."

"I think she really meant it."

I shook my head.

He shook his head right back at me—and then reached over and pinched my butt.

I jumped. "Hey!"

His smiling eyes met mine in the mirror as he edged around me and headed for the door. "By the way, Nero Wolfe never had a sweet little ass like yours."

I laughed. It sounded nervous to my ears. Unsurprising, I guess. It was fun but also disconcerting to be treated like...well, like J.X. treated me. It was a long time since I'd thought of myself as young or sexy.

We dressed and headed off to breakfast. Downstairs we could see the household staff bustling around, dusting and vacuuming. Unlike the day before there was no immediate sign of the police.

"Do you think the cops have finished processing the crime scene?"

"No." Meeting my gaze, J.X. said, "They're done with the preliminary investigation, sure. But Sara's room is still sealed off."

"How do you know?"

"I had a look around while you were in the shower."

"Is anyone guarding Sara's door?"

"No. The room is taped off, though. The only reason the entire house isn't locked down is because Anna is Anna. Anybody else in this burg would be spending the week with friends."

I considered the possibilities as we started down the grand staircase.

"What about Nella's funeral?" I asked. "Are we going to pay our final respects?"

"I don't want to go to the funeral. And the only reason you want to go to the funeral is to play amateur sleuth."

"I didn't say I wanted to go. I *don't* want to go. I hate funerals."

"Good. Then we're in agreement."

"Besides, I can look around Sara's quarters more easily if everyone's out of the house at this funeral."

He nearly missed a step. "You better be kidding me. That room is sealed off. That room is a crime scene."

"Of course I'm kidding."

J.X. gave me a long, suspicious look and nearly missed another step.

This time I grabbed for his arm. "Hold the railing like a big boy."

"I'll big boy you," he growled.

"Okay, but after breakfast. I have to keep my strength up."

Rudolph was the only person in the dining room. He sat at the long, polished table, a lonely figure in the empty elegant room as he ate his hardboiled egg out of a china egg cup.

An egg cup. That was something you didn't see much—outside of old movies. But it seemed par for the course this weekend.

It was the first time I'd seen him since the terrible night he'd dragged me to Sara's room. He looked like he'd aged a decade, though he was still immaculate, still dignified in his solitariness.

"Good morning." He twitched a pallid smile.

"Morning." J.X. and I echoed each other as we headed for the sideboard.

"How are you doing?" J.X. asked Rudolph while I piled my plate with everything remotely edible. There was enough food in the chafing dishes for the original conference attendees. Maybe no one was communicating with the household staff now that Sara was gone.

"I'm all right." Coming from Rudolph that weary admission was revealing.

"Have you seen Anna this morning?"

"No." That was it. My conversational offering fell flat on its hopeful face.

The silence in the room reminded me of a funeral home. But that wasn't far wrong. This was a house of mourning. Everything about Rudolph bespoke bereavement.

I had to revise at least one of my theories.

Besides, face to face with Rudolph, the idea that he was capable of murder was ludicrous. It was like suspecting Jimmy Stewart. Hell, it was like suspecting Harvey the invisible rabbit.

J.X. carried his modestly filled plate to the table, sat down across from Rudolph. "*Are* you all right?"

I had to admire the directness of that. The question seemed motivated by nothing more than kindness. For all I knew kindness *was* all that was motivating it. J.X. had already made it clear how strongly in favor he was of letting local law enforcement do their thing.

Rudolph's face worked. He got control and said, "Truthfully? No."

His feelings were so exposed it seemed natural to say, "I didn't realize until the other night that you and Sara were close."

"Yes." He put down his spoon and gave up all pretence of eating. "We...it was one of those things that takes you unaware. I think we both fought it, but..." He gave a funny, strained smile. "I thought I was too old to feel that way again."

Was there an echo in here?

Perhaps seeing our surprise, he said, "Sara wasn't at all like she appeared on the outside. She was a wonderful girl. That reserve was a defense mechanism. Underneath it, she was very sensitive and a bit shy. Very warmhearted, very generous, very...loving."

I'll take your word for it was my first cynical thought, but I recanted immediately. No one was in better position than I to know how easily shyness gets misread for arrogance or coldness or indifference.

"You kept your relationship secret from Anna?" That was J.X., as usual getting right to the point.

Rudolph looked uncomfortable. "It was an awkward situation. Sara worked for Anna."

Yeah, that was one awkward thing. The other awkward thing was Rudolph had once been Anna's lover.

"So Anna never knew?" I don't know what made me ask, but something flickered across Rudolph's face, an emotion that disquieted me.

"Not until—" He couldn't finish it.

"I'm sorry, Rudolph. Really sorry."

He nodded, reached into a pocket and withdrew a pristine silk handkerchief. He didn't do anything so plebian as to blow his nose, but he did efficiently whisk away all traces of grief.

We gave him a couple of seconds to compose himself. I asked, "Did Anna tell you she was afraid someone was trying to kill her?"

"Not until last night." There it was again. That tightness in his face when he referred to Anna. Something had happened between them. What?

Rudolph added, "I told her she was a fool for not going immediately to the police. I told her that Sara might still be alive if she had."

Oh. Well, maybe that explained what had happened between them.

"Do you have any idea who might have—?"

He fixed me with a stern look. "Christopher, I know you're trying to help. I realize that Anna roped you into this—and I'm aware of how difficult it can be to say no to Anna—but you should have told her no when she tried to involve you in this— this catastrophe."

I glanced at J.X. Ignoring my silent cry for help, the bastard cut off a corner of French toast and chewed contemplatively while gazing out the grand picture window at the snowy day. I turned back to Rudolph.

He said, "Anna told me last night your theory that Sara was behind these accidents merely because she'd let Anna read *Death and Her Sisters.*"

"It wasn't exactly a theory. More an…idea."

"Anna has always been a little paranoid, but the idea that Sara would harm her is lunacy. It's complete fantasy. First of all, Anna isn't the only person Sara showed the manuscript to. I saw it months ago and on my recommendation Sara sent the book to Wheaton & Woodhouse. They're publishing it this spring."

"They're *publishing* it?"

"Yes. The idea that Sara would try to kill Anna because Anna knew some terrible truth is not merely ridiculous, it's offensive. That book is complete fiction. Sara's twin sister died in an auto accident when they were eleven. There's no mystery about it, let alone anything sinister. Sara took the pain of losing her sister and translated it into fiction. A wonderful piece of fiction."

"Why didn't *you* choose to publish the book?"

His mouth quivered. "I'd have loved to publish the book but I was aware that Anna might not be thrilled given the fact that she's been suffering writer's block for several years, and Anna is a dear friend. Also, I didn't want there to be any suggestion that nepotism was responsible for getting Sara's book published."

"Nepotism?" J.X. rejoined the conversation.

"Sara and I plan—" He stopped. Steadied his voice. "Planned to be married in the summer. Which is another thing—the insulting notion that Sara would want Anna out of the way to rid herself of a romantic rival."

"I never said that. I never suggested such a thing."

"Anna suggested it last night when she accused Sara of murder."

"She..." My eyes met J.X.'s. Apparently we'd missed one hell of a party the night before. I said carefully, "Anna came right out and accused Sara of trying to kill her?"

"Yes. She said she'd had time to think it through and she was convinced Sara was behind it all, and that Sara was the victim of her own machinations."

"Rudolph, I admit I did wonder whether Sara's manuscript could have been based on her own life, but the rest of it, no. I had no idea. And Sara was just one...possible suspect."

He struggled to control his anger. *"One possible suspect. You treated it like a game, like a puzzle, and now Sara and Nella are both dead."*

"No," J.X. intervened. "Kit was trying to help Anna. Don't put this on him. Anna should have gone to the police at the beginning. All Kit did was respect her wishes. The responsibility lies with Anna."

"The responsibility lies with whoever killed Sara and is trying to kill Anna," I said.

Abruptly we were out of things to talk about.

Chapter Twenty-Three

I'm not sure what transpired between Anna and Rudolph later that morning, but apparently they made up their quarrel of the night before because when I finally spoke to Anna they were about to leave for Nella's funeral together. She didn't invite me or J.X. along, for which I was grateful.

She stopped by to speak to us again a few minutes later. We were in the library. J.X. was on the phone to the Nitchfield PD—mostly to humor me, I think—when we both jumped at the sound of her crisp, "Christopher, darling."

J.X.'s eyes messaged me in warning. I crossed the parquet floor to head Anna off as she entered the room on her crutches. She was dressed in a severely elegant black suit. Her auburn hair was coiled in soigné fashion on her head.

"Hey there. I thought you'd left," I said brightly. Talk about sounding guilty.

Anna didn't seem to notice. "We're on our way out. I wanted to find out your travel plans."

I hesitated. "Anna, are you sure you want us to go?"

She smiled warmly. "Yes, darling. I can't thank you enough for all you tried to do, but it's in the hands of the police now—where it should have been from the beginning."

I resisted the temptation to look at J.X. He had turned

away from us and was speaking very quietly into the phone. I said, "Have there been any developments since yesterday?"

"Our local police aren't very forthcoming, but the impression I got yesterday was they were taking our theory about Sara very seriously."

"Oh. Right." Our theory. I knew I sounded tentative as I said, "We had breakfast with Rudolph. He was pretty upset at the idea that Sara was behind those attempts on your life."

"I know." Her green gaze was rueful. "My poor Rudolph. I didn't handle it at all well last night. She took him in completely—as she did me." Anna made an engaging moue. For all the stress and the strain of the past few days, she seemed much less tense, less worn. The relief of believing the threat to her life was gone? "He was furious with both of us."

I was pretty sure she didn't mean her and Sara.

"Well, he was relatively calm at breakfast, but he doesn't believe Sara was guilty, and he's got some good points."

She gave a short, slightly exasperated laugh. "Don't you start. It's bad enough with Rudolph defending her. The terrible truth is that Sara was a clever and talented sociopath. She took us all in."

It was odd how broken up Anna had been over Nella, and yet she seemed almost indifferent to Sara's fate. Granted, she was convinced Sara had been trying to kill her. That betrayal was bound to affect her feelings. I remembered what Dicky's betrayal had done to me—let alone David's.

But Anna didn't seem hurt. She seemed... "How long did Sara work for you again?" I inquired.

"Nearly five years. But...as you know, we never really know anyone."

You could say that again.

I said, "Did you know *Death and Her Sisters* is being published by Wheaton & Woodhouse?"

She blinked at me a couple of times as though she was thinking of something else. "Sorry?"

"Sara's manuscript. Did you know she'd submitted it and it had been accepted?"

"No. Who told you that?"

So even last night when they'd been arguing about Sara, Rudolph had refrained from giving Anna that piece of information. Why? Sensitivity to Anna's writer's block? But Anna's writer's block was over. She'd told us all at the fatal dinner party.

The memory of Sara's face at that announcement flashed into my memory. Anna's news had come as a complete surprise to her. And how could that be? She worked with Anna every day.

So Anna's writer's block had *not* come to an end?

Or Anna had kept it secret from Sara?

I said, "What's the name of this new project of yours again?"

Anna stared at me and then gave her head a tiny shake as though a bug had flown into her ear. "What?" Her tone was sharp.

"You said you were writing again. That you had a new project. I was wondering what the title was?"

"It's untitled, darling." Her gaze flicked to J.X. who was still on the phone.

"Is it completed?"

"Yes. No. The rough draft is complete, but it is *very* rough." Her laugh was devoid of humor. "So no. It's not completed. It's not ready for submission. Why the fascination? You haven't

253

shown this much interest in my work since you were taking my writing course."

J.X. hung up the phone and came to join us. He slipped a casual arm around my waist. "We've got plane reservations for tomorrow morning."

Through the police department? I opened my mouth, met his dark, meaningful gaze, and swallowed what I'd been about to say.

"Excellent. Well, I'm certainly going to miss you two." Some of Anna's tension had drained away at J.X.'s words. "We'll have a lovely farewell dinner tonight." She shifted her crutch and smiled at me. "I'm truly grateful for all you tried to do, Christopher. I know this hasn't been easy for you. You've been a dear, loyal friend to me in my hour of need."

I'm not sure what I said in response. I felt numb in the wake of appalling realization.

Anna checked her diamond-studded wristwatch. "I have to go. Rudolph is waiting. We'll see you in a few hours."

I couldn't think of anything to say. I nodded.

J.X. nodded too. He was smiling but his eyes looked like chips of obsidian.

Anna turned, maneuvering her crutches with the speed and agility of a much younger woman.

Neither J.X. nor I spoke till the *thump, thump* of her receding footsteps died.

I turned to J.X. "You didn't change our reservations did you?"

"Not yet, but we're not having dinner here tonight. I'll tell you that much now."

"Tell me the rest of it too."

"Nitchfield PD got the coroner's report on Sara Mason. She

died of a massive dose of *Agrostemma githago*."

"Corncockle."

"Bull's-eye."

"When you say massive dose...?"

"Try ten times as much as was found in the wine we all drank at dinner."

My knees gave out and I sat down on the boulder-sized leather-covered ottoman. He squeezed my shoulder comfortingly.

"Sara was the target all along."

"We don't know that for sure." He said it automatically. When I raised my head to look at him he didn't bother to defend it.

I said dully, "I think Anna killed her."

"Kit—"

"And I think I helped her."

I could see he wanted to reassure me, give me some comfort, but he was too honest. He said, "You did the best you could with the information you had."

"She used me."

"Yes." It was unwilling.

"Does Nitchfield PD know?"

"Know what?"

"That Anna was behind it all? That the attempts on her life were all bullshit and that she was plotting to murder Sara all along?"

"No. And neither do you. Not for a fact."

I gave him a bitter look.

"You have a theory. You don't have any proof, Kit. There's no evidence—"

I stood. "Then we'll get the evidence."

Sara's room was still sealed, and J.X. and I nearly came to blows over my determination to get inside.

"If they haven't figured out who killed Sara, they're sure as hell not going to figure out who broke into her room."

J.X. was staring at me with horror—and remaining firmly planted in my path.

"Remember that little thing called forensic evidence? Hell, remember circumstantial evidence? Or how about standing here red-handed? Nitchfield PD is on their way right now."

"I'm not asking you to break the law, just let me do what I need to do."

"What is it you think you need to do?" The question had to be rhetorical because it was clear he wasn't letting me in that room while he was capable of preventing it.

"I need to find something. Some...proof."

"Like what?" He glanced automatically down the hallway, and I saw a maid carrying a stack of linens on her way to Anna's room. The maid politely ignored us though we couldn't have been easy to overlook whispering and arguing in front of the clearly marked door to a crime scene.

What *did* I think I might find inside? Evidence of other projects, works in progress. No one got to be as good a writer as Sara without a lot of practice. Her rough drafts and first efforts might easily provide the basis for new work from Anna. Not that I believed Anna had killed Sara for her works in progress. There was the morbid fantasy of an aspiring writer, for sure. No, I had a feeling Anna's motive for turning on Sara was more complex than ending her own case of writer's block. The lure of a new manuscript had perhaps been the final incentive, but I didn't think that was the first, let alone only reason.

"How should I know?" I groaned. "*I* fed the cops that whole line of Anna's bullshit about those attempts on her life. Anna faked it all. No wonder it all sounded like a figment of her imagination. It was."

J.X.'s eyes were sympathetic, but his tone was brusque. "You don't know that for sure."

"The hell I don't."

He caught my arm, forcing me to pay attention. "You *don't* know any of this for a fact."

"Do you think I'm right?" It really did matter to me.

"Yes." He said it without hesitation.

"Then?"

"It's beside the point. I think you're right because I know you. And I know Anna. I know her enough, anyway. These cops *don't* know you. Anna is a big fucking deal in this town, and no one is going to accuse her of killing her secretary without substantial proof."

I yanked my arm away. "Then let's *find* some goddamned proof."

"Like what? A note from Anna saying she did it? Because that's about what it would take at this point."

There was something else he wasn't telling me. I could read it in his eyes. What? Something he didn't want me to know.

"I'm willing to bet money that this new as-yet-untitled project of Anna's is one of Sara's first efforts. Or maybe an earlier draft of *Death and Her Sisters*. Anna looked ready to faint when I said the book was going to be published."

"Okay, but Sara's laptop has already been confiscated by the police."

"She had to have back-up files. Someone as methodical as

Sara? No way did she trust it to a cyber-data backup and recovery site and let it go at that. She'll have made copies, maybe even disks."

"She probably used an external hard drive, which the cops will have."

A brilliant idea struck me. "We could search Anna's office. We might find what we need there."

J.X. was not impressed. "And what do you think is going to happen if you're found searching Anna's office or trying to break into her computer? The cops aren't going to understand what you're doing and they aren't going to have any sympathy with it."

"It doesn't matter."

"It's going to matter when they arrest you."

I turned on him in exasperation. "So we should just leave it alone? We should just let her get away with it? Let her get away with murder? Is that what you're saying?"

"I'm saying you do *not* want to get caught trying to make off with evidence from this crime scene. Kit, will you please listen to me? It's already on record that you came here to play amateur sleuth. Yes? That's not an endorsement of your overall credibility—or stability. I'll tell you flat out there is a perception that you're a flaky-writer type. Wandering around the hospital half-naked and crocked on pain meds didn't help your image."

I felt myself turn scarlet with recollection. But it was just for an instant. "Oh screw them all," I snarled. "Screw their small-town minds and mores. Their lack of imagination isn't my problem."

J.X. ignored that. "You're on record saying you thought there was a plot against Anna. Now you want to go on record saying you think Anna is the plot mastermind, that she killed her PA. Think about how that's going to sound."

"I don't care how it's going to sound."

"I do. I care for your sake how it's going to sound because if this gets into the papers and there isn't any proof against Anna, you're going to sink your career for nothing."

I stood still.

He said quietly, "*Think*. I know you're upset, but stop and really look at this objectively."

I felt my resistance start to crumble in the face of his unshakable and calm certainty. As angry and betrayed as I was, I wasn't ready to destroy what was left of my career, especially knowing that Anna would remain unscathed and unassailable.

"She used our friendship. She used me. She used me to commit murder."

He pulled me into his arms. "I know." He kissed my temple. Kissed the bridge of my nose. The warmth was real and tangible. I felt an unfamiliar and alarming desire to howl my anger and hurt and guilt onto his broad and capable shoulder. It was almost liberating to know that I could have a moment of weakness and it would be met by sympathy and that J.X. wouldn't think anything the worse of me for breaking down.

I didn't break down although I closed my eyes. Let myself be comforted for a few seconds. "God knows how long she planned it. Weeks. Maybe months."

"I know." He nuzzled my ear.

"I fell right into it."

He was nibbling my earlobe.

"Your timing is off." I pushed him away.

J.X. sighed and raked a hand through his hair. "I know. Speaking of timing, we need to get out of here."

I nodded reluctantly. "And speaking of getting out of here, see if you can get us on a plane tonight. I don't think I can face

Anna again and not do something you'll regret."

He scanned my face. Nodded grimly.

The police were still searching the house for the mysterious source of Sara's poisoning when Rudolph and Anna returned from the funeral.

I was in the library listening to J.X. schmooze our way onto a new flight when I saw the long black car pulling up the drive.

Rising, I went to the window and stared out. First Rudolph got out of the car and then he helped Anna, who was slower and clumsy on her crutches. I watched them walking across the courtyard and was forced to admit that they made a strikingly handsome older couple in their black, fur-trimmed coats.

I was perfectly positioned to see their faces. Anna had been crying, but she was smiling now and gazing up at Rudolph with unselfconscious affection. It was a completely unguarded moment and I could see the love she felt for him. My stomach knotted. That's the problem with real-life villains. Rarely are they black and white.

As for Rudolph, he was smiling indulgently down at her, a protective arm wrapped around her as they moved slowly up the front steps to the house.

The receiver rattled into its cradle behind me. J.X. said, "Okay. If we move fast we can make this flight out of Bradley International. If we miss it, they'll put us on standby. Either way, we're getting out of here tonight."

I blew my nose a final time.

Silence. He came up behind me.

"Are you okay, Kit?"

"Oh hell yeah."

He put his arms around me. "Is there anything I can do?"

"I think you're doing it." I sniffed, gently freed myself. "Let's do this."

Detective Eames was in the main hallway when Rudolph and Anna entered and we were in time to hear him break it to Anna about Sara's body being loaded with poison.

"How is that possible?" Anna said, and she sounded truly shocked, truly horrified.

Not as shocked and horrified as Rudolph, who was literally struck silent. His face was haggard with pain. He and Anna clung together in the wake of it.

"Could it have been suicide? Is that what you think?" Anna asked at last.

Detective Eames was unable to vouchsafe comment on what he thought. He said the police were still searching for the source of the poison, but it appeared as though Sara Mason had eaten cereal shortly before her death.

"Cereal?" Rudolph repeated numbly.

"Oh fucking hell," Anna murmured—shocking Eames, I think. "Yes. Yes, that's true. She used to have a bowl of some god-awful granola or something like that every night. She was very health conscious. Fanatical, really."

"That's what your kitchen staff said. They said you'd given orders for Ms. Mason's groceries to be tossed out."

Anna's jaw dropped. She looked around bewilderedly. "That's not true. Cook was asking me what to do about some spoiled soy milk, and I...well, I suppose I did say to dispose of it. The *milk*. I'm afraid I had assumed your people had already gone through the food."

"We did. This cereal was evidently overlooked. At the time we were under the impression we were looking for a liquid."

"Miscommunication all around then. Oh, but this is

fucking *ghastly.* I'll never forgive myself if—" She broke off as her gaze fell on J.X. and I standing in the library doorway on the periphery of this gathering. I had the impression that she wasn't thrilled to see us, although she summoned a weary smile. "Had a nice afternoon, darlings?"

"As a matter of fact we've got to leave now or we'll miss our flight," J.X. said.

"Oh?" Anna looked startled. "You're leaving *now?*" Her eyes sought mine.

"Yes." I couldn't manage more than that one single flat word.

"But is that all right?" Anna asked Eames.

Eames nodded. "We've already discussed Mr. Moriarity and Mr. Holmes's traveling plans. They're good to go."

"I don't quite know what to say." Anna stood motionless.

Not as motionless as Rudolph. He looked like he'd turned to stone. He hadn't said a word since Eames had mentioned the poisoned cereal.

Chapter Twenty-Four

It took us less than fifteen minutes to pack. When we carried our bags down to the front hall it was empty. No sign of anyone. Even the police seemed to have scattered to the far winds.

"I'll bring the car around." J.X. set his suitcase down next to mine.

"I'll be right back," I told him, turning back to the staircase.

"Wait. Where are you going?"

"I want to say goodbye."

"Kit." He started after me, stopping after a step or two when I put my hand up.

"It's all right. I'm not going to do anything crazy. Just...don't leave without me."

His expression was fierce. "I'm not going anywhere without you."

I took the stairs fast and reached the second level out of breath, but that was more about anger than exertion. I retraced the steps to Anna's room, remembering walking this way with Sara that first afternoon.

Anna was in her room staring out the window at the frozen lake.

"Didn't we already say goodbye?" she asked without

turning.

"*Why*?" I demanded. "Why the *hell* did you have to drag me into it?"

She did turn then, her expression one of polite inquiry. "I don't know what you're talking about, darling."

"Do me the courtesy of sparing me the bullshit. You faked a bunch of tries on your life to make Sara's murder look like a backfired attempt to kill you. You framed Sara for her own murder."

Anna smiled, the smile I remembered from classrooms long ago, when a student, against the odds, had managed to get something correct. "If you'll recall, that was your theory. I'd gone to some pains to spread the clues around. I tried to make sure no particular person looked guilty. But then you popped up with the theory that Sara was trying to kill me to conceal the murder of her sister."

"There was no murder of her sister."

"True. But you didn't know that. Sara never spoke about her sister. Never spoke about anything personal, in fact. She was a very private person." She added, "Not particularly imaginative, which is surprising in a writer. And devoid of any sense of humor."

I had a sudden, shocking urge to shove her out that lovely picture window. It took a second or two before I could ask, "Did you do it for Rudolph or was it for *Death and Her Sisters*?"

Anna's face changed again. "I can't believe the little bitch submitted that manuscript without talking to me first. After everything I did for her."

"You mean like killing her?"

"Keep your voice down, Christopher," she said softly. "Fair warning. I could ruin you if I wanted to. You're hanging on by your fingernails now. One word to your editor at Millbrook House and you and Miss Butterwitch will be a footnote in the next edition of *Murderess Ink*."

"You go right ahead. You're a fucking lunatic, Anna. What I still don't get is why you dragged me across the country to be a part of this?"

Her eyes darkened with emotion. "If anyone should understand, it's you."

"What should I have understood?"

"What it's like to be a has-been," she cried, and now she seemed to be appealing to me. "What it's like to know your career is over. To lose your lover to someone younger and stronger. To lose *everything.*"

I felt the poison arrows hit, but the pain barely registered. "You can't get it back by killing your...your rival."

Unnervingly, she laughed. "I might have agreed with you once, but you're wrong about that. The only reason Rudolph and I weren't still together was Sara, and ironically her death is serving to bring us back to where we were before she interfered."

Even if I'd tried, I couldn't have hid my feelings—and I didn't try. Anna snapped, "You know nothing about it. Right now you feel magnanimous toward David because of J.X. but J.X. won't stay with you. Why would he? He'll be gone to greener pastures as soon as the novelty wears off, as soon as it becomes clear to him that your careers—your lives—are going in two different directions."

"Even if that's true, it wouldn't justify—it wouldn't change anything."

She said with utter certainty, "Oh, it's true. And it will change *everything.*"

It took effort to drag the focus of the conversation back to where it needed to be. "What about Nella? Did you do something to Poppy's car?"

She recoiled, staring as though I were the crazy one. "I *loved* that child. How could you accuse me of something like that?" She seemed honestly horrified. "Even if it had been physically possible, I'd never have done anything to hurt her. I would never do anything to hurt anyone...who wasn't trying to destroy me."

I didn't think I misread the warning.

"So this was all about getting Rudolph back? And now everything is supposed to be back to normal?"

She raised her chin. "He never really left me. Sara was merely a distraction. It hadn't gone far between them and now it never will."

"Yeah right. So you and Rudolph are going to live happily ever after and he's going to publish Sara's stories under your name? Maybe Sara showed him her other stories too."

"What do you mean *too*?" Her eyes narrowed.

I started to tell her that Rudolph had advised Sara to submit to Wheaton & Woodhouse—that they were engaged in fact—and not only had he seen *Death and Her Sisters* long before the Asquith Circle, he was probably familiar with most of her work. But a baleful little notion whispered in my mind and silenced me.

Why warn her? Why give her time to prepare lies and excuses. I'd seen Rudolph's face in the hall when the police were talking. He wasn't stupid. Not by any means. No one knew Anna and the way her brain worked better than Rudolph. He was kind and civilized and he would try not to see it for as long as possible, but the sick knowledge was already taking root in his brain.

No. The last thing I wanted to do was give Anna a heads up. Let her stumble right into her own trap the way she'd made it look like Sara had done.

I answered, "You thought she wouldn't show *Death and Her Sisters* to the writing group, but she did."

"She won't have shown any of the others. She didn't think they were any good." Anna's smile was wry, and I saw where Sara had got the impression her work wasn't any good.

The righteous anger that had been driving me drained away. I felt tired and empty. I made myself ask, "How long were you planning this?"

She understood. "It's not what you think. I didn't have designs on her work. I don't deny that in my frustration I said things to discourage her. She was only writing for herself and she was so goddamned good without ever trying. It wasn't fair. It wasn't right."

"But you're trying to steal her work now."

"What does it matter? How does it help anyone to lose those stories? No, I didn't do it for the work. The plan came to me a month ago when Rudolph was visiting and I saw the way she tried to monopolize his attention. The only thing I had left and she was trying to take that too."

"Kit!" J.X. yelled from down the hall.

Both Anna and I froze.

She said quickly, softly, "There's no evidence, no proof left. I was very careful. I'm a *very* good mystery writer. It's your word against mine, and you're not foolish enough to jeopardize what you have left of a career."

"Kit." J.X. had reached the doorway. He sounded angry. "We've got to go *now*."

From the hostile blaze in his eyes as his gaze found Anna, I understood that the urgency wasn't only about missing a plane flight. He feared for me in the Wicked Queen's chamber. I was touched.

I nodded.

"Take care, Christopher," Anna said as I turned away, and it was a warning, not good wishes.

"You too, darling," I replied in the same spirit.

"What were you doing?" J.X. asked as the elegant, gaily lit house grew smaller and smaller in the side mirrors.

"You know what I was doing."

"Kit." I could hear the frustration though he was trying to bank it down.

"She admitted it."

He didn't expect that. He risked a quick look my way. "You're serious? She admitted it? All of it?"

I nodded.

J.X. was thinking rapidly. "But there's still no proof. It would be your word against hers."

"I know."

He chewed his lip, considering. "Did she tell you why she dragged you into it?"

I gave a short laugh. "Because she's a freaking psycho? I don't know. I asked her."

"You asked her that?"

I nodded.

Another quick look my way. "I'm sorry, Kit. This is total hell for you, I know. But even if she did admit it, you can't safely pursue this. You've just got to trust that...justice will out."

I snorted. What was there to say? He was right.

I thought about the things Anna had told me. About my career being over. About the fact that J.X. would not stay with me.

Both seemed to carry the ring of irrefutable truth. Was that fear or instinct? I glanced in the side mirror once more. The house had vanished into the white distance. There was only the swish of the windshield wipers and the shush of the tires on the slushy highway.

For a few miles I was lost in the whiteout of my own bleak thoughts. Finally I remembered that I wasn't alone. I glanced over at J.X.

"Are you flying straight back to Frisco?"

His honey-colored skin turned a darker shade. "Uh, no. I'm flying to L.A. with you." I didn't say anything and he said cautiously, "Is that all right?"

"Sure."

"I mean, we've got some things to talk over. We might as well do it while we're both in the same room."

"Right."

"Like..." His voice cracked.

I stared at him. "What's wrong?"

"Nothing."

"Something's wrong. You're beet red and your voice—"

He interrupted, "I know this isn't the time for this discussion, but we're going to pursue this, right? We agreed."

"I—right."

He relaxed. Gave me a quick, happy smile. A big white smile.

I wondered what the hell I'd agreed to.

My final conversation with Anna cost us making our flight on time. We spent part of the evening in the airport lounge on standby and caught the redeye to Los Angeles.

It was a mild and smoggy February morning when we landed. We grabbed a taxi at LAX and headed straight for Chatsworth, for home.

The driver kept the radio blasting news as we wove in and out of cars on the 101.

J.X. was slumped against my shoulder, head back at an uncomfortable angle, mouth open as he snored melodiously into my ear when the radio announcer said in his cheerful deep voice, "Mystery fans worldwide will be saddened by the death of Anna Hitchcock, often referred to as the American Agatha Christie."

I sat up, listening tensely as the shining cars and palm trees flashed by.

"Hitchcock was found dead of what appears to be an overdose of sleeping tablets, in her Connecticut mansion earlier this morning. Her body was discovered by her long-time lover and editor Rudolph Dunst. Dunst told reporters that the sixty-eight-year-old author had been despondent over an ongoing inability to write coupled with the recent death of two of her closest friends. Police are investigating the possibility of suicide."

The taxi driver's brown eyes met mine in the rearview mirror. "You like mysteries?" he asked over the wintery howl through the cab's rattling windows.

I gazed out at the smoggy gray morning.

"I used to," I said.

About the Author

A distinct voice in GLBT fiction, multi-award winning author Josh Lanyon has written numerous novels, novellas and short stories. He is the author of the critically praised Adrien English mystery series as well as the new Holmes and Moriarity series. Josh is an Eppie Award winner and a three-time Lambda Literary Award finalist.

To learn more about Josh, please visit www.joshlanyon.com or join his mailing list at groups.yahoo.com/group/JoshLanyon.

CPSIA information can be obtained at www.ICGtesting.com
Printed in the USA
BVOW070847111011

273363BV00002B/1/P